"I don't want you here."

"Too bad, I'm staying." J.T.'s own anger faded as quickly as it flared. Wow, she was something. All fire and ice.

Had he really thought she was cool and dispassionate? Beneath that calm surface was spirit enough for any man. More than most could handle. He stared into her turbulent gray eyes and felt raw desire rip through him.

He wanted this woman more than he'd ever wanted any woman in his life.

Consumed with need, he couldn't think for a moment. His gaze zeroed in on that lush mouth, trembling now with the force of her emotions, and heat speared through him. He leaned closer, his gaze fixed on her mouth as his head began a slow descent.

"Kate, you're not throwing me out."

Dear Reader,

Welcome back to Special Edition, where a month of spellbinding reading awaits you with a wonderful lineup of sophisticated, compelling August romances!

In bestselling author Jodi O'Donnell's memorable THAT'S MY BABY! story, *When Baby Was Born,* a pregnant woman with amnesia meets a cowboy she'll never forget! Beloved author Ginna Gray sweeps us away with another installment of her miniseries, A FAMILY BOND. In her emotional book *In Search of Dreams,* a woman with a scandalous past tries to say no to the man who vows to be in her future. Do you think a reunion that takes seventeen years to happen is worth waiting for? We're sure you'll say yes when you read *When Love Walks In,* Suzanne Carey's poignant story about a long-ago teenage passion that is rekindled—then a secret is exposed. When the hero of Carole Halston's *Because of the Twins...* needs help caring for his instant brood, the last thing he expects is a woman who turns his thoughts to matrimonial matters, too! Also this month is Jean Brashear's *Texas Royalty,* in which a tough, once-burned P.I. seeks revenge on the society girl who had betrayed him—until she manages to rekindle his desires *again!* And finally, Patricia McLinn kicks off her compelling new miniseries, A PLACE CALLED HOME, with *Lost-And-Found Groom,* about a treacherous hurricane that brings two people together for one passionate live-or-die night—then that remembered passion threatens to storm their emotional fortresses once and for all....

We hope you enjoy this book and the other unforgettable stories Special Edition is happy to bring you this month and all year long during Silhouette's 20th Anniversary celebration!

All the best,

Karen Taylor Richman
Senior Editor

Please address questions and book requests to:
Silhouette Reader Service
U.S.: 3010 Walden Ave., P.O. Box 1325, Buffalo, NY 14269
Canadian: P.O. Box 609, Fort Erie, Ont. L2A 5X3

GINNA GRAY
IN SEARCH OF DREAMS

Silhouette®

SPECIAL EDITION®

Published by Silhouette Books

America's Publisher of Contemporary Romance

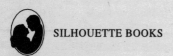 SILHOUETTE BOOKS

ISBN 0-373-24340-5

IN SEARCH OF DREAMS

Visit Silhouette at www.eHarlequin.com

Printed in U.S.A.

Books by Ginna Gray

GINNA GRAY

A native Houstonian, Ginna Gray admits that, since childhood, she has been a compulsive reader as well as a head-in-the-clouds dreamer. Long accustomed to expressing her creativity in tangible ways—Ginna also enjoys painting and needlework—she finally decided to try putting her fantasies and wild imaginations down on paper. The result? The mother of two now spends eight hours a day as a full-time writer.

IT'S OUR 20th ANNIVERSARY!
We'll be celebrating all year,
Continuing with these fabulous titles,
On sale in August 2000.

Intimate Moments

#1021 A Game of Chance
Linda Howard

#1022 Undercover Bride
Kylie Brant

#1023 Blade's Lady
Fiona Brand

#1024 Gabriel's Honor
Barbara McCauley

#1025 The Lawman and the Lady
Pat Warren

#1026 Shotgun Bride
Leann Harris

Special Edition

#1339 When Baby Was Born
Jodi O'Donnell

#1340 In Search of Dreams
Ginna Gray

#1341 When Love Walks In
Suzanne Carey

#1342 Because of the Twins...
Carole Halston

#1343 Texas Royalty
Jean Brashear

#1344 Lost-and-Found Groom
Patricia McLinn

Desire

#1309 The Return of Adams Cade
BJ James

#1310 Tallchief: The Homecoming
Cait London

#1311 Bride of Fortune
Leanne Banks

#1312 The Last Santini Virgin
Maureen Child

#1313 In Name Only
Peggy Moreland

#1314 One Snowbound Weekend...
Christy Lockhart

Romance

#1462 Those Matchmaking Babies
Marie Ferrarella

#1463 Cherish the Boss
Judy Christenberry

#1464 First Time, Forever
Cara Colter

#1465 The Prince's Bride-To-Be
Valerie Parv

#1466 In Want of a Wife
Arlene James

#1467 His, Hers...Ours?
Natalie Patrick

Chapter One

"Quit! Whadda you mean? You can't quit!" Charlie Van Horn bellowed.

The bellicose editor-in-chief of the *Houston Herald* stuck out his chin and glared at his top reporter across the cluttered surface of his desk. The beady-eyed look and pugnacious set of his jaw would have reduced any other person on his staff to a stammering wreck.

J. T. Conway grinned.

"Sure I can, Charlie. This is a newspaper, not a prison." Sitting slouched on his spine with his long legs stretched out and crossed at the ankles, J.T. gazed back at his boss with a devilish twinkle in his blue eyes, the picture of unruffled male confidence.

The veins in Charlie's neck bulged, and his face turned an alarming shade of purple. Pressing all ten fingertips to the desktop, he levered his stocky body out of the chair and leaned forward. The threatening stance merely widened J.T.'s grin.

"Now you listen to me, Conway, I don't know what kind of game you're playing, but I don't have time for it. Now get back to work. I've got a paper to run."

"This is no game, Charlie." J.T. withdrew an envelope from the inside pocket of his suitcoat, leaned forward and tossed it onto Charlie's desk. "That's my formal resignation. It's effective in two weeks."

Without bothering to open the envelope, Charlie tore it in two and tossed the halves over his shoulder in the general direction of the overflowing wastebasket.

"Nice shot," J.T. drawled as the pieces hit the top of the pile and slid to the floor. "But I still quit."

Charlie spat out a string of curses that turned the air blue. When that failed to faze J.T., he plopped back down into his chair, plucked a half-chewed cigar from the ashtray and stuck it in his mouth. "All right. What's this about?" he growled. "Is this a bluff to get more money? Hell, man, you're already the highest-paid reporter in Houston. Not to mention your generous expense account."

"This isn't about money."

Leaning back in his chair, Charlie laced his ink-stained fingers together over his belly and rolled the foul-smelling stogie from one side of his mouth to the other. He never lit the disgusting things anymore. At his wife's insistence, he'd quit smoking a year ago. She would skin him alive if he started again.

However, whenever Clarice wasn't around he always had an unlit cigar stuck in his mouth like a nasty, brown pacifier.

"Then what is it you want? More vacation? A bigger picture with your column? A fancier car? A bigger desk? What?" Before J.T. could answer, an arrested look came over Charlie's face. "Aw, hell, don't tell me this is another push to get your own office. How many times do I have to tell you, the other reporters would set up a howl if I okayed that. No. No way. Forget it, Conway. It ain't gonna happen."

"Charlie, you aren't listening. I'm not putting the squeeze on you for anything. I'm resigning. Period. That's it."

Charlie stared at him. Slowly his anger faded into shock. His flabbergasted expression was so comical J.T.'s grin returned.

"You're really serious," the older man said in an incredulous voice, sagging back in his chair as though he'd just had the wind knocked out of him.

"I'm serious."

"Have you lost your mind? Dammit, man, you've been with this paper for twelve years. You've built a name for yourself in this town. Why in God's name would you throw away a successful career? Are you having a midlife crisis or something?"

"Maybe." J.T. hesitated, not sure he wanted to explain his reasons. However, from his boss's expression it was apparent that he wasn't going to accept the resignation until he did.

"I want to write a novel. That's what I've always wanted to do with my life, not be a reporter. When I took this job it was supposed to be temporary, but I got caught in a rut. Anyway, I have enough money put away to live comfortably for a few years, so I decided to give it a shot."

"Oh, good night, nurse. Not another one," Charlie muttered, rolling his eyes. "I've never met a reporter who didn't think he had the next great American novel in him. I thought you were different. Shoulda known better."

"Looks like it," J.T. replied with his usual nonchalance,

but his smile didn't reach his eyes. Normally he was slow to anger, but Charlie's derision touched off an uncharacteristic spurt of fury that he barely managed to hold in check.

Charlie slammed his hand down on his desk. "Do you know what the odds are of getting a book published? Particularly a novel? You're living in a dream world."

"Actually…I have an in. An old friend of mine is a vice president at Hubbard and Rhodes Publishing. He wants to see my manuscript when it's finished. But that's not the only reason I'm leaving. I also want to devote time to finding the rest of my family if I can."

"Why, for Pete's sake? I'd think after learning that that hard-nosed cop was your brother the last thing you'd want would be to go looking for another one. Hell, this one may turn out to be even more annoying."

"Matt's not so bad. Anyway, my missing sibling may be a sister."

"Humph. That could be worse. I've got four of them. Take it from me, sisters are a real pain in the arse. They're either driving you nuts with all their chatter and giggling and all that feminine clutter, or worrying you to death making eyes at boys. I spent half my twenties checking out the losers that came sniffing around my sisters."

J.T. grinned, his good humor restored. He had a mental picture of Charlie protecting his sisters like a junkyard dog. They'd probably wanted to kill him for his efforts. "You may be right, but I have to try. If I don't I'll always wonder."

For most of his life J.T. had known that he was adopted, but it hadn't been until six weeks ago that he had made the startling discovery that he was one of a set of triplets, and that his old nemesis, Matthew Dolan, was actually his brother.

Until recently Matt had been a detective with the Houston Police Department. He and J.T. had been butting heads for the past twelve years whenever J.T. showed up at a crime scene to get the story.

Discovering that they were brothers had been a shock to both of them. At first neither he nor Matt had been ready to initiate a search for their missing triplet. Recently, however, J.T. had grown curious.

"How the devil do you expect to find this person, with nothing to go on except that he or she presumably has the missing third piece of a medallion and was adopted at age two? Talk about your needle in a haystack. It's a waste of time."

"Not necessarily. As a matter of fact, I already have a lead to check out."

"Humph. So you're determined to do this, are you?"

"Yep. I've put it off too long already."

Charlie rolled his eyes and muttered another curse. "All right, fine. Do what you gotta do. But there's no need for you to quit. Take a leave of absence."

"I don't—"

Charlie held up his hands. "Just hear me out. You take all the time you need. Go write your novel. Look for your other sibling. When you're done and you find out you're not Hemingway, then you come back here. Your job will be waiting."

"Charlie—"

"No, I don't want to hear it. I'm not going to let you throw away your career on a whim. Just go get all this nonsense out of your system once and for all, then come back here where you belong."

J.T. was torn between exasperation and gratitude. It touched him that the cantankerous old coot thought enough of him to hold his job open, and it irritated the living hell out of him that he ridiculed his dream.

He held the older man's gaze for several moments. What if Charlie was right? What if his talent didn't go any deeper than knocking out sensationalized accounts of the news? It was a depressing thought—one he refused to accept.

J.T. wasn't in any mood to argue, though, and he could see by Charlie's bulldog expression that he wasn't going to back down. Hell, why fight it? He could always resign later.

"Okay. You've got a deal," J.T. finally said.

"There is just one condition."

"Uh-oh, here it comes."

"Aw, don't get your shorts in a wad. I just want your promise that if you come across a good story you'll call it in, that's all."

J.T. thought it over. Where he was heading, probably the most exciting thing that ever happened was an elk wandering into town now and then. "Sure. Why not?"

"Good. That's settled. Now tell me, where're you going?"

"Oh, no. Forget it. I know you, Charlie. If I tell you, you'll be on the phone to me every day with an assignment, or wanting to know when I'm coming back."

"So? What if I need you? What if an international crisis happens? What if World War III breaks out? How the hell am I supposed to get in touch with you?"

"You aren't. Look, if it'll make you feel better, I'll check in now and then, but that's it. Take it or leave it. Either way, in two weeks, I'm outta here."

Cleaning out his desk and parting from his colleagues and friends was difficult, but for J.T. the hardest part of leaving was saying goodbye to Matt and Maude Ann and the kids.

Which was why he put off doing so until the last minute. When his belongings were in storage, all the last-minute details were handled and his laptop and the clothes he would need were loaded in the back of his Jeep Grand Cherokee, he drove north out of Houston to Lake Livingston.

J.T. knew that putting distance between himself and Matt at this point sure as hell wasn't going to do much for their relationship. But then, he wondered if anything could.

Though they were brothers, a wall of reserve existed between him and Matt that neither of them seemed capable of breaching.

Perhaps it would always be there, J.T. mused. Maybe they had been separated too long to ever come together as brothers. They'd led different lives, had different upbringings, different outlooks. It saddened him to think so, but it was beginning to look as though it was too late for him and Matt to form any close fraternal ties. Certainly they had not gotten closer during the six weeks since they'd learned about their kinship.

It was a different story with his sister-in-law. He and Maude Ann had hit it off as friends from the moment they met, long before her marriage to Matt three weeks ago. He could talk to Maude Ann, laugh with her, tease her, tell her his hopes and dreams.

Of course, being a psychiatrist, she was trained to be a good listener and she had a sharp understanding of human nature, but there was more to it than that. He and Maudie were kindred souls. He was going to miss her like the devil. And he was going to miss the kids.

As he anticipated, Maude Ann was far more upset by his news than his brother. "You're leaving? But why?" she asked in a stricken voice.

"I finally realized that I was feeling guilty about the

compromises I'd made. So now I'm doing something about it.''

"Oh, J.T., don't misunderstand me. I think it's great that you're finally going to do what you've always wanted. Really. And I'm positive you'll be a success. You're a wonderful writer. I just don't understand why you have to leave.''

"There are too many distractions in Houston. It would be too easy to get sidetracked with other things. I need to find someplace quiet where no one knows me so I can concentrate on my writing.''

"You don't have to leave the state, for heaven's sake. You could come here.''

J.T. raised his eyebrows. "Here? Live at the Haven? With you and Matt and the kids?''

Henley Haven was a foster home for abused and neglected children that Maude Ann had started several years ago. The structure was a former fishing lodge on the northern shore of Lake Livingston that belonged to Lieutenant John Werner, Maude Ann's godfather and Matt's former boss at the HPD.

In the past year Matt had been shot twice in the line of duty, and the wounds had left him with a limp, ending his career as a police officer. Now he and Maude Ann ran the Haven together.

"Look, Maudie, I appre—''

The front door opened to the sound of pitiful wailing. An instant later ten-year-old Yolanda Garcia appeared in the doorway with a bawling Timothy on her hip. "He fell and hurt his elbow,'' the girl announced shyly.

Matt rose and limped to where the children stood. "Hey, buddy, let's have a look.''

Even from where he sat J.T. could see that the injury wasn't serious. The skin was red but unbroken, with only a few white scrape marks marring the surface. From Timothy's wails you would have thought he'd received a mortal wound.

Chin quivering pathetically, the four-year-old looked up at Matt with tear-drenched eyes and stuck out his elbow. "It *huuurts* real bad, Matt."

"I'll bet it does," Matt replied gravely.

Instantly, responding to the gruff empathy, the little boy sniffed and quieted.

Matt examined the scrape with the same seriousness he would have given a bone-deep cut and moved the arm back and forth to test its mobility. "It doesn't look too bad. Yolanda, why don't you take him in the bathroom and clean his elbow."

"Sí, Señor Dolan."

"A little antibacterial spray and a Band-Aid and you'll be fine, buddy." Placing a kiss on the scrape, Matt ruffled the boy's hair, winked at Yolanda and sent them on their way.

J.T. smiled and shook his head. It still amazed him that his stern brother had settled so easily into marriage and parenthood.

Matt had been a confirmed bachelor and a dedicated police officer, whose whole life and identity had been wrapped up in his job. Yet, not only had he accepted the loss of his career with surprising grace, at his insistence, he and Maude Ann had begun proceedings to adopt all five of the kids currently assigned to her care immediately after they were married.

The instant the children disappeared toward the back of the lodge, Maude Ann turned her attention back to their discussion. "Why not stay here? We're out in the country, but it's only a two-hour drive to Houston if you did need to go back. We have the woods and the lake and we're miles from our nearest neighbor. And this lodge has plenty of bedrooms. It's perfect.''

''No offense, Maudie, but with all these kids, this place is anything but peaceful.''

''There are only five children here at the moment,'' she said with a huff. ''Matt and I aren't taking in any more until we learn if the adoptions are going through. Besides, I thought you liked the children?''

''I do. They're great kids and I love them all, but you have to admit, they're anything but quiet.''

As though to prove his point, at that moment the front door banged open again. This time seven-year-old Tyrone burst into the foyer with Jennifer and Debbie hot on his heels. The last one inside slammed the door shut on the run, and the trio pounded up the stairs with the girls shrieking dire threats at Tyrone if he didn't give ''it'' back and the boy laughing his head off.

J.T. gave his sister-in-law a dry look. ''I rest my case.''

''I know they can get a bit rambunctious, but if it's quiet you need we can—''

''Sweetheart, leave the man alone,'' Matt said, speaking up for the first time. ''If J.T. wants to get away, that's his business. This is his decision to make, not ours.''

A wry smile tugged at J.T.'s mouth. He should have known that Matt wouldn't raise any objections. The prickly animosity between them had mellowed somewhat since they'd discovered their kinship, but they were hardly bosom buddies. J.T. suspected that Matt was probably relieved he was leaving.

''But we're his family. He belongs here with us.''

''Maudie,'' Matt said in a warning voice.

''Oh, all right.'' Maude Ann sighed, and her shoulders slumped. ''I know. I'm being selfish.'' She took both of

J.T.'s hands and squeezed them. "But I hate for you to go. I'm going to miss you."

"I'm going to miss you, too. All of you." They gazed at each other in silence, each aware of what neither wanted to voice. If the adoption of the children failed to go through, all five of them would probably be moved to another foster home before he returned and they would never see them again.

"Hey, don't worry," J.T. said gently when Maude Ann's eyes grew suspiciously moist. "I'll keep in touch. I promise."

"You'd better," she warned. "Because if you don't I'll come get you and haul you back."

"So, when are you leaving?" Matt asked.

"Actually, I'm on my way now. I just stopped by to let you know I'm going. And, uh…there is one other thing you should know. I've decided to take a stab at looking for our missing sibling."

Matt frowned, and J.T. waited for him to object. From the beginning Matt had not been gung-ho about locating their other triplet. Though he was more flexible since Maude Ann had come into his life, he still resisted change and detested any sort of upheaval in his personal life. A legacy, J.T. suspected, from their birth mother deserting them when they were toddlers.

"If you want to search, that's your decision. But I think you're setting yourself an impossible task. With so few clues and sealed adoption records, where do you even start?"

"Actually…I already have." J.T. reached inside his shirt and pulled out the jagged piece of a medallion that he wore on a chain around his neck. Matt wore a similar one that fit perfectly with J.T.'s, forming two thirds of a silver disk. The medallion pieces had been given to them by their birth mother. "A few weeks back I posted a notice on an Internet missing-persons bulletin board, asking if anyone knew, or knew of, someone who owned a medallion piece like the ones we have. I also included a drawing of the missing section.

"I've already received quite a few responses. Some of them were bogus and most of the rest turned out to be nothing, but one seems promising. Here, take a look at this." J.T. pulled a square of paper from his wallet and handed it to Matt. "I downloaded this about three weeks ago."

Matt unfolded the paper and began to read aloud.

"The man you are looking for is Zach Mahoney. Your best chance of locating him will be through his sister, Kate Mahoney, who operates a bed-and-breakfast in Gold Fever, Colorado. Zach is a drifter, but he shows up now and then at the B&B.

"I advise you not to reveal that you're looking for him. The Mahoneys, particularly Zach, are suspects in a criminal case. Kate is protective of her brother, and if either of them suspects someone is looking for Zach, he will go to ground."

Frowning, Matt looked up from the paper and shot J.T. a hard look. "This isn't very encouraging."

"I know."

"It appears that at best the man's a bum. At worst, a crook. Are you sure you want to locate him?"

J.T. sighed. "To tell you the truth, no. But I don't have a choice. I don't think either of us has. Until we find him, we're always going to wonder. Face it, Matt, the three of us share a bond, like it or not."

Matt's mouth firmed into a grim line, and J.T. saw his jaw tighten. "I guess you're right. I just hope we're not buying ourselves a load of trouble."

"You two do realize that this could just be someone with a grudge against this Zach Mahoney person, don't you?" Maude Ann said. "Whoever posted this anonymous reply could just be trying to stir up trouble for him. It could even be that he's not your brother at all."

"Yeah, I know. Either way, though, I have to find out."

"So, what are you going to do now?" Matt asked.

"Now? Now I'm going to do just what I told you. I'm going to go find a nice, peaceful place and write." His gaze swept back and forth between Matt and Maude Ann. "From what I could learn about it, Gold Fever, Colorado, sounds as though it will suit just fine."

Chapter Two

Kate Mahoney pushed her shopping cart through the aisles of Hendricks Grocery with single-minded purpose: to get her shopping done as quickly as possible and make her escape.

Luckily, today the only other customers in the store were Gert Krueger and Jonell Abbott; although, that was bad enough.

If Gert had her way, Kate and her brother would be rotting behind bars. Jonell wasn't quite so obvious, or so vocal, but her animosity was just as strong. Both women shot her withering glares whenever she passed them in the aisles.

Otto Hendricks's mouth thinned when Kate pushed her cart up to the checkout stand and started unloading her groceries. Neither he nor his wife, Shirley, spoke, nor did Kate. Keeping her expression blank, she transferred her purchases onto the counter while Otto rang them up on the ornate, old cash register. Like everything else in Gold Fever, the machine was a relic.

Shirley bagged Kate's groceries, her face pinched up like a prune. When her husband finished ringing up the items he curtly announced the total, and without a word Kate counted out the required amount in cash and loaded the sacks into her cart.

Neither Otto nor Shirley offered to help, nor did they wish her goodbye when she turned to leave. As Kate opened the door and pushed her cart out onto the sidewalk, she heard an indignant huff and Gert's querulous, "I swear, I don't know how that woman has the nerve to show her face in this town."

"I know," Shirley agreed. "It makes my blood boil to have to wait on her. You ask me—"

The door swung shut, cutting off the venomous tirade. Kate paused to draw in a deep breath of cool mountain air, then zipped up her windbreaker and turned toward home.

She walked purposefully with her head high and her gaze focused straight ahead, pretending not to notice the stares that followed her or how people she had known most of her life stepped aside to avoid any sort of physical contact with her. A few doors down the street, Donny Bowman stepped from his family's bakery and headed in her direction. He had given Kate her first kiss, had taken her to the senior prom and afterward had declared his undying love for her, but when he looked up and spotted her, his face hardened. Kate's chin came up another notch, and she met his cold stare with unapologetic directness. It was Donny who finally broke eye contact and looked away.

The corners of Kate's mouth curved ever so slightly. Good. Let him glare and grumble, she thought. He won't see me cringe or hang my head and slink away like a whipped dog.

Thankfully, Gold Fever was a small place, only about eight blocks square. Main Avenue was a spur off Highway 550, about a half mile away, and the only paved street in town. The others were dirt and gravel.

In minutes Kate reached the north end of town where the paving ended. With a sigh of relief, she started up the sloping dirt road. The grocery cart bumped and rattled over rocks and potholes as she pulled it along behind her.

Kate hated going into town, and put off doing so until she had no choice. Even during the height of tourist season she kept to herself as much as possible, venturing down into town merely to buy supplies and pick up her mail at the post office.

The cart was heavy, and soon her arm began to ache. She could have made it easy on herself and driven the SUV into town, but she enjoyed walking and getting out in the fresh air. Winter was just around the corner, and once it arrived she wouldn't be able to walk to town.

Climbing the gentle slope, she looked around at the soaring peaks and smiled. How she loved it here. As a six-year-old, the first time she and her family had driven over the last pass and started down the winding road into this high mountain valley, she had been enchanted. In twenty-three years that feeling had never left her.

A gust of wind sent a chill through Kate and tugged a blond curl loose from her French braid. She shivered and pushed the dancing tendril away from her face and tucked it behind her ear. During the past couple of weeks, storms had powdered the tops of the mountains with fresh snow. Even in summer, snow capped the jagged peaks, but now the white mantle was growing longer, sagging unevenly like a cheap petticoat, edging downward a little more with each weather front that came through. Soon the town would be buried under a blanket of snow and ice, and Gold Fever's few souls would hunker down before their fires for the long winter, venturing out only when absolutely necessary.

Kate's gaze followed the switchback path of the road upward to the house sitting majestically about five hundred feet up the base slope of Smithson Mountain, overlooking the town. She picked up her pace, impatient suddenly to get back inside the protection of its walls. The huge rose-granite house was now known as the Alpine Rose Bed-and-Breakfast, but to Kate it would always be her place of refuge, her home.

The last guests had checked out yesterday, and though most of the tourists who rented rooms from her were nice people, Kate had been happy to see them go. She was looking forward to the respite from the seven-day-a-week work schedule of running a bed-and-breakfast, as well as to her annual period of solitude.

Besides, she needed time to get the place winterized before the snows came in earnest. She had already begun spreading a thick layer of compost and mulch around the bases of the rose bushes that surrounded the house. There were also storm windows to hang, outdoor faucets to insulate, porch furniture to store in the garage.

When she was done with those chores she had to lay in a larger supply of food and art supplies and stock up on books and needlework projects and jigsaw puzzles—things to keep her occupied during the next five months.

Kate rattled around all alone in the big house in the winter, but she didn't mind. Though she had not been born an introvert, out of necessity she had developed into one over the past four years. Now she had become accustomed to the winter solitude and looked forward to sleeping late and having only herself to please. Most of all, she looked forward to having her home to herself once again.

Kate had barely reached the house and put away her groceries and was passing through the foyer when she heard a vehicle coming up the road. She stepped outside onto the porch and shaded her eyes with her hand, wondering who it could possibly be. Other than Zach, who was in Arizona, and an occasional delivery or repair person, the only people who came to her door were tourists, and the season was over.

Probably just someone who was lost, she thought as the green Jeep Cherokee climbed toward her. Often a motorist got confused and took the spur road instead of following the highway north. Most quickly realized their mistake and backtracked, but a few ended up on the dirt road from town that led to her doorstep.

Kate crossed the porch to wait at the top of the steps. The Jeep came to a halt at the end of the walkway and a tall, dark-haired man climbed out.

"May I help you?" she inquired politely.

"I sure hope so." He grinned at her over the top of the vehicle. Taking his time, he paused by the Jeep, hands planted on his hips, and drank in the spectacular panorama of snow-capped mountains all around and the picturesque Victorian town nestled in the valley below. When he'd looked his fill, he skirted the vehicle and started up the brick walkway, shaking his head. "Man, that's some view."

"Yes, isn't it."

Watching the man approach, Kate experienced an odd flutter in the pit of her stomach. With his dark good looks and lean build, the man exuded a potent masculine aura that was palpable even from a distance.

That sexy, loose-limbed saunter alone was enough to raise the coldest woman's blood pressure. Oh, yes, he was a good-looking devil, she thought as he came to a halt at the foot of the porch steps. His features were strong and beautifully formed, chiseled just enough to save him from being pretty. No doubt he left a trail of palpitating female hearts in his wake wherever he went.

Judging from the way her own was thumping, Kate realized ruefully that she was no more immune than the rest of her sisters. Either that, or she'd been alone far too long.

The man placed one foot on the bottom step, and the faded denim jeans stretched taut over well-defined muscles. Bracing his hand on his thigh, he flashed her a disarming smile. "This is the Alpine Rose Bed-and-Breakfast, I hope?"

"Yes, it is. May I help you with something?"

"I need a place to stay."

"I'm sorry, but I'm afraid as of yesterday, the Alpine Rose is closed for the winter."

"You're kidding. I had no idea you weren't open year-round."

"There wouldn't be much point. Tourists love this area during the other seasons, but since we don't have a ski resort nearby, our harsh winters tend to keep them away."

The man sighed and looked out over the town again. Then he turned back to her with a persuasive smile. It was pure practiced charm, Kate knew, but that didn't stop her heart from giving a little kick when he turned those vivid blue eyes on her.

"Could I perhaps persuade you to make an exception for me?"

"I'm sorry—"

"No, wait. Before you say no, hear me out. I'm not looking for a room for just a night or two. I'd like to book a stay for at least six months."

"Six *months?* Oh, I'm sorry, Mr...."

"Conway. J. T. Conway."

"Mr. Conway, I'm not running a boarding house. This is a first-class bed and breakfast. The people who stay here usually do so for only a few days."

"I know, but what's my alternative? The Miners' Lodge? I stopped in there and had a look before coming here. No, thanks."

Kate stared at him. He had her there. She wouldn't wish that place on anyone. The Miners' Lodge had been a brothel in the nineteenth century, and other than to change the sheets, she doubted the current owners had done anything to improve the cubbyhole rooms. They ran a pool hall and restaurant and bar in the downstairs. Occasionally they rented out one of the upstairs rooms—mostly to the young crowd who typically stayed in youth hostels. Those who sought elegance, comfort and good food came to the Alpine Rose.

"Mr. Conway, I'm doing you a favor by refusing. The elevation of the town is just over nine thousand feet. Our winters are brutal. We get snowed in for days at a time. Trust me, you would hate it."

He pursed his lips thoughtfully and glanced down at the town. "Does anyone live in Gold Fever during the winter months?"

"Yes. There are about three hundred year-round residents.

"Do you stay through the winter?"

"Yes."

"Then I'm sure I can manage."

"Mr. Con—"

"You don't understand, Miss, uh…?"

"Kate Mahoney. I own the Alpine Rose."

"Well, Miss Mahoney, solitude is exactly what I'm looking for. It won't bother me a bit to be snowed in. You see, I'm writing a novel set in this area during the gold rush, and I really need to stay here to conduct my research and get the feel of the place.''

''I see. Nevertheless—''

''If you're worried that I'll be a lot of trouble, don't. Most of the time I'll be in my room writing, or down in town doing research and interviewing the old-timers around here. This is a big house. You won't even know I'm here. I promise.''

Oh, she'd know he was there, all right, Kate thought. No woman under the age of ninety could fail to be aware of the presence of a man like J.T. Conway under her roof. Her feminine radar would pick him up even if she put him on the third floor in the old servants' quarters.

Instinct told her that the smart thing would be to refuse his request. The man unsettled her, although she wasn't sure why. It was more than merely his looks; she'd had good-looking men stay in her home before. But there was something about J. T. Conway...

She had every right to refuse. She needed a rest from looking after guests, and she was looking forward to a period of solitude and self-indulgence. When she had the house to herself she could take long bubble baths and sleep late and run around in sweats and socks and never put on makeup. Shoot, she could run around bare-beamed and buck naked, if she wanted to.

Still, she could use the money. A house as old as this one was constantly in need of repair. And, as he said, it was a big place. How much trouble could one man be?

Sensing that she was weakening, he quickly took advantage. ''Look, we can agree on a monthly rate and I'll pay you the six months rent in advance. It's yours regardless of whether or not I stay the full six months. How does that sound?''

Six months rent up-front? Kate made a quick calculation

in her head, and temptation tugged at her. A few of the rooms could use fresh paint and wallpaper. By next spring the carriage house would need repainting and there were several other repairs she needed to tackle to keep the place in top condition.

She bit her lower lip. "I don't know," she said uncertainly.

"And of course I'll pay extra for the additional meals."

He named a generous figure, and Kate flashed him an annoyed look. Darn it. He wasn't playing fair.

"Oh, and if you have any concern about being alone in the house with me for months, you really don't have to worry. Not that I don't find you attractive, mind you," he added with a flirtatious wink. "I do. But I assure you I've never forced my attentions on a woman."

I'll bet, Kate thought. Men like J. T. Conway didn't have to. Just the opposite. He probably had to beat women off with a club.

Actually, she hadn't given a thought to that aspect until he mentioned it. Kate was accustomed to having strangers in her home. However, never anyone for a long period of time.

Kate wasn't concerned for her safety. She had no illusions about her looks. She knew that she had a delicate sort of beauty that some found appealing, but she was hardly the type to drive a man wild with lust. Of course, some of the men who had stayed at the B&B had made passes at her, but she put a stop to that soon enough. With the married ones, a threat to tell their wives usually did the trick.

What bothered Kate was the gossip J.T. was sure to hear in town. Most of her guests didn't stay long enough to learn about the scandal or hear the accusations against her and her brother. But if Mr. Conway was going to be around for months, talking to the locals and digging through the town's old newspaper files, he was certain to find out about the crime.

How would he react? she wondered. With scorn? Or avarice? It was usually one of the two.

J. T. Conway's opinion of her didn't matter one way or the other, but she didn't care for the idea of being cooped up all winter with someone who thought she was a criminal.

"I can give you references if you'd like," J.T. pressed when she continued to hesitate. "My pastor back in Houston, a retired police detective and former girlfriends. You can call them, ask them anything you want."

Kate arched one eyebrow. "Former girlfriends? Are you sure you want to risk that?"

His devilish grin flashed again. "I'm on friendly terms with all my ex's. If you want to call them I'll be happy to turn over my little black book to you."

"That won't be necessary." Kate gave him a level look. "I have a sturdy lock on my door, Mr. Conway. I also have a pistol, and I'm an excellent markswoman."

The last statement was a blatant lie. Not only did she not own a hand gun, she'd never touched one in her life. The only weapon she'd ever fired was her father's old shotgun.

That he remained on friendly terms with his ex-lovers said a lot about his character, but it didn't hurt for him to believe she could and would defend herself if the need arose.

J.T. did not seem in the least intimidated. He tried to put on a serious face, but laughter twinkled in his eyes, and his mouth twitched suspiciously. "I'll keep that in mind. So, Miss Mahoney, does this mean you'll let me stay?"

Kate met his pleading gaze for several seconds. Finally she sighed. "Very well. You can stay."

Yes! J.T. thought, fighting down the urge to let out a whoop. He was in! First step accomplished.

"Great. You won't regret it."

Her dry look told him she wasn't convinced of that, but she merely turned back to the door. "If you'd like to get your things we'll go in."

"Sure thing." He hurried out to his Jeep and returned moments later carrying a large bag over his shoulder and a case containing his laptop and followed her inside.

"Very nice," he said, looking around at the impressive entry hall.

"Thank you. The house was built by Elijah Smithson between 1880 and 1883. He was the first prospector in the valley to find gold. As it turned out, his claim was not only the first, it was the richest strike ever made here. Throughout the town's history, the Shamrock Mine was the largest and most profitable in the valley. Two-thirds of the local miners worked there."

Amusement tugged at J.T.'s mouth. She sounded like a tour guide. No doubt the spiel was one she gave to all her paying guests. Kate Mahoney was the epitome of the cool, efficient innkeeper—polite and informative, but business-like. He had a hunch it was a persona she assumed to keep a distance between herself and her guests.

Nice try, honey, he thought with a cynical twist to his mouth. But it's not going to work with me. Before the winter is over you and I are going to become well acquainted.

"I'm surprised he stayed in such a remote place after striking it rich," he said to Kate. "Especially if Gold Fever was like most rough-and-ready mining towns of that era."

"Oh, Mr. Smithson built a mansion in Denver, too, like the other gold tycoons, but he liked to keep a close watch on the mine operation. Personally, I think he also enjoyed being a big fish in a small pond. This house served as a constant reminder to all the locals of his status."

"Mmm, you're probably right," J.T. agreed, arching his neck back to look at the enormous, domed, etched-glass skylight that spilled prisms of light into the foyer. "Why else would he build a place like this and perch it up here where he could look down on everyone else?"

"Yes, I agree. Now if you'll come with me, I'll give you a quick tour of the downstairs so you'll know your way around."

She led the way down the wide central hallway toward the back of the house. An appreciative smile curved J.T.'s mouth as he watched her thick braid swing against her back and the enticing sway of her gently rounded hips.

As they passed them, Kate gestured toward the two sets of double doors on either side of the hall. "On the left is the guest parlor, on the right the family parlor. Next on the left is the dining room, and across the hall from it is the library. Feel free to use them anytime you like.

"You may even find some valuable research material for your novel in the library. My father was a mining engineer and the superintendent of the Shamrock Mine for years. He was also something of a history buff. All I ask is that you return any books that you use when you're done."

"Fair enough. And, thanks. I'll take you up on that offer."

A little past the center of the house the hallway came to a T at the base of the massive stairway. Kate gestured to the short hallway on the left. "This leads to the butler's pantry, downstairs powder room and the servants' back stairs, but I would prefer that you not use those as they're narrow and steep. I rather not risk a guest taking a fall."

"Old Elijah didn't waste money on niceties for the hired help, huh?" J.T. said with a crooked smile.

"No. Although, I don't suppose he was any worse than any other wealthy person of that era. In those days there were definite distinctions between the classes. Now, if you'll follow me, Mr. Conway, we'll go to my office and get you checked in.''

''The first door is the entrance to the kitchen,'' she said in her brisk, tour guide voice as they made their way down the right hallway. ''That door at the end of the hall opens to the porte cochere. When it's snowing you may want to pull your vehicle under there and enter through that way. Here we are.'' She opened the last door on the left and led the way inside a comfortable-size room. ''This used to be the housekeeper's room, but I use it as my office now. Please, have a seat, Mr. Conway.''

The formality of registering and paying six months rent in advance took only a few minutes. When they were done, Kate led the way back down the hall to the stairs.

''There is an elevator. It was put in years ago, and it's pokey, but if you'd prefer to use it we can.''

''That's okay. I don't mind the stairs.''

At the base, the stairway was at least ten feet wide, with massive, hand-carved newel posts and spindles. Six steps up, at a wide landing, the stairs split and turned at ninety-degree angles, one flight going right, the other left.

Kate took the flight of stairs to the right, continuing her spiel as they climbed, but J.T. listened with only half an ear. He was too busy studying the stained-glass mural that made up the outer wall of the next landing.

It depicted a woman in eighteenth-century dress strolling through a garden, carrying a basket full of freshly cut flowers. J.T. darted a quick look over his shoulder and spotted a companion stained-glass mural on the opposite landing of a gentleman astride a white horse. Light streamed in through both windows, bathing the entire stairwell in shafts of rainbow hues that created an almost surreal atmosphere.

To have the enormous pieces commissioned, then hauled

up to this remote mountain town by horse and wagon must have cost old Elijah a mint, J.T. mused in awe, craning his neck for one last look as he followed Kate up the next section of stairs.

"Excluding the servants' quarters on the third floor, the house has ten bedrooms. I rent eight of them to guests."

Which leaves one available for your brother whenever he decides to drop in, J.T. thought.

"Originally there were fourteen bedrooms on this floor, but four had to be sacrificed when the house was remodeled around 1910 to add bathrooms."

"Fourteen bedrooms, huh. That's a lot, even for a millionaire."

"Not really. The Smithsons had a large family. There were already three children when the house was built and eight more were born after they moved in."

Kate stopped outside a door at the end of the hall. "Since you're the only guest, you may have your choice of rooms, but I think this one will best suit your needs." Opening the door, she led the way inside.

"As you can see, being a corner room, it is quite large, and there's a desk in the alcove that you may use. There's also a private bathroom right through that door. The fixtures are antique but you'll find the plumbing is sound."

"I'm sure it'll do fine."

Kate stayed just inside the door as J.T. strolled to the center of the room. He looked around, impressed with the room's size and immaculate condition. Even though heavy emerald-green velvet draped the four tall windows on the two outer walls, plenty of light streamed in through the lace panels that covered the panes.

The cabbage-rose wallpaper and the rose-patterned rug covering most of the oak floor were not to J.T.'s taste, but they were in keeping with the Victorian structure. So was the massive antique furniture. It was all right, he supposed, but not something he'd choose for himself.

Then the bed caught his eye, and he instantly revised his opinion. The thing was magnificent. The mahogany headboard stood at least eight feet tall and the footboard three and a half or four. Both were intricately carved. The mattress looked bigger than the king-size bed he'd just put into storage and was almost as high as his waist. For someone Kate's size the small set of wooden steps beside the bed would be a necessity.

"Wow. Now that's what I call a bed."

"It belonged to Mr. Smithson," Kate explained. "He was a big man. I believe he had it custom-made. It does have a new mattress, though. I'm sure you'll find it comfortable."

"No wonder he had eleven children." J.T. sent Kate a flirtatious glance and winked. "A bed like that would inspire any man."

To his amusement, the talk of beds seemed to make her uncomfortable. Color bloomed in her cheeks, though she held her head high and pretended to be unaffected.

"The closet is small, I'm afraid. They were added at the same time as the bathrooms, but between it and the armoire, I think you'll have adequate space for your clothes."

"I'm sure they'll do fine." He watched her fidget and struggle to cover her discomfort. Well, well, well. So Ms. Kate Mahoney was uncomfortable with the subject of sex, was she? Now that was a puzzle worth looking into.

He judged her to be in her late twenties. Most women her age were experienced and worldly and would have barely noticed the mild innuendo.

"Good. Then I'll leave you to get settled." She started to leave, then turned back. "Oh, by the way, Mr. Conway—"

"Please, call me J.T. We're going to be sharing this house for the next six months, so I think we can dispense with formality, don't you?" he said, giving her a coaxing smile.

An appalled look flashed over her face before she could control it. Obviously, the lady would prefer to keep a safe distance between them. The question was, why?

J.T. watched her frantically grope for a reason to refuse the suggestion and saw the instant when she realized there was nothing she could say without sounding like a stiff-necked prig. "Very well. If you insist."

"As I was about to say, meals are served in the dining room. Breakfast is at eight, lunch at one and dinner at seven."

"Okay. But if I don't show up, go ahead without me. When I'm working and it's going well, I don't stop for anything."

"But, you have to eat...."

"Don't worry about me. Just stick whatever you've prepared in the fridge and I'll zap it in the microwave later."

Kate looked horrified by the suggestion. He watched her struggle with the idea, but finally she nodded. "Very well," she said, making no attempt to hide her disapproval. "If that's what you wish."

She turned again to leave, but he stopped her.

"Actually, I don't like to be disturbed at anytime when I'm working. So if the sign is out," he said, pointing to the small needlepoint Do Not Disturb sign hanging from the inside doorknob, "I'd appreciate it if you wouldn't knock on my door except in case of an emergency."

"I clean the room every morning. How am I supposed to do that if I can't get inside?"

"Don't worry about it. I sure won't. You can muck out when I come up for air."

"Mr. Con—" One of J.T.'s eyebrows shot skyward, and she grimaced. "That is...J.T., the Alpine Rose has built a reputation on excellent service, good food and spotless accommodations. Guests don't "zap" their own food nor are rooms allowed to get into a state where they require 'mucking out.'"

"Don't worry, your reputation is safe. I won't tell anyone if you don't."

She didn't look pleased, but after a moment she sighed. "Very well, if you insist. Now if you'll excuse me, I have work to do."

When she had gone, J.T. stared at the closed door, his expression thoughtful. Kate Mahoney was not at all what he had expected.

His mouth twisted ruefully the instant the thought ran through his mind. He wasn't supposed to "expect" anything. He was a reporter. He was supposed to approach an investigative assignment unbiased, with no preconceived ideas or opinions. True, he wasn't there to get a story, but he wanted to apply the same fairness.

The trouble was he was finding it wasn't quite so easy to hold to that ethical standard when the matter was personal.

J.T. sighed and raked his hand through his hair. No matter how hard he'd tried to keep an open mind, the implication in that Internet message kept eating at him. Just the idea that a brother of his might be involved in something illegal colored his thinking—not only about Zach Mahoney, but Zach's adopted sister, as well.

Because of that message, J.T. had been prepared to meet someone more hard edged and worldly, not a soft, fragile-looking beauty like Kate.

She wasn't his type, of course. He preferred feisty, vibrant women with vivacious personalities—women like his new sister-in-law, Maude Ann. Looking into Kate Mahoney's calm gray eyes was like gazing into the cool depths of a mountain lake. With her blond hair and pale coloring, she reminded him of the delicate angel his mother used to put on top of their Christmas tree every year—exquisite to look at, but untouchable.

Yet there was something about her that played havoc with his libido. The instant he'd gotten a good look at her, he'd felt as though he'd received a sharp blow to the gut.

Strangely, her quiet reserve intrigued him. She didn't appear to be shy, exactly. She hadn't seemed in the least timorous or skittish. A wry smile twitched his mouth. That is, not until he'd made that crack about the bed. She'd been calm and businesslike, her gaze direct and unflinching. No, he had a feeling her reserve had more to do with wariness than timidity.

The question was, what was the cause? Guilt? An innately suspicious nature? Or past mistreatment?

J.T. gazed at the bed once again. He pictured Kate lying there, those solemn gray eyes glowing with warmth, that tender mouth parted in a temptress's smile, her long hair an unbound tangle around her face.

The tidy French braid that hung down her back was as thick as his wrist and the color of ripe wheat. The whole time he'd talked to her his fingers had itched to unwind that plait, run his fingers through the silky strands, see that glorious mane spread out on his pillow like liquid gold.

He shook his head. "Don't be a fool, Conway," he cautioned himself. "The lady may look like an angel, but for all you know she could be a crook, so don't go getting any amorous ideas."

J.T. wandered over to one of the windows and pulled back a lace panel. The sun had already dropped behind the mountains, casting long purple shadows over the town below. Here and there lights were beginning to flicker on.

Gold Fever, with its false-front buildings and fancy Victorian architecture, looked quaint and picturesque, like a scene on a Christmas card—idyllic, peaceful, free from troubles and the normal human failings and vices.

But J.T. had learned that things were seldom as they seemed, that people—even the best of them—harbored dark secrets. He also knew that, human nature being what it was, there was always someone anxious to talk about them.

Chapter Three

The telephone started ringing as Kate reached the bottom of the stairs. Taking the shortcut through the butler's pantry, she darted into the kitchen and snatched the receiver from the wall phone. "Alpine Rose Bed-and-Breakfast. How may I help you?"

"Well? How does it feel to be a lady of leisure?"

"Zach! It's so good to hear from you. And I was feeling really great while it lasted, but as of about a half hour ago, I have a guest who is staying through the winter." Briefly she filled him in on how J. T. Conway had talked her into letting him stay, but when she was done, Zach was not pleased.

"Dammit, Sis, I don't think it's a good idea to let a strange man stay there with you all winter long."

"Zach, strange men stay here all the time," she chided.

"It's one thing to have single men staying there during tourist season when there are other guests around. It's something else to be all alone with one for months. You could get snowed in with this guy. What if he turns out to be a rapists or pervert or a serial killer?''

"Zach, I'll be fine. Mr. Conway is a nice man. I'm sure he's harmless,'' she said with long-suffering patience. She wasn't about to admit to Zach that on some basic man-woman level J.T. made her antsy. She adored her brother, but he had a tendency to be overprotective where she was concerned.

While she didn't believe for a moment that J.T. posed a threat to her safety, Kate knew perfectly well that men like J. T. Conway exuded a sexual magnetism that played havoc with a woman's heart and common sense—even a practical woman like herself—but she resolutely pushed that unsettling thought aside. She could not afford to give in to Zach on this. The man would wrap her in cotton wool if she didn't stand up to him.

"How old is this guy?''

"Well I wasn't so rude as to ask him such a personal question, but he appears to be about your age.''

"*My* age! Trust me. He's not harmless.''

Kate laughed. "And what, dear brother, does that say about you? Hmm?''

"That I'm a normal, red-blooded male. And unless this Conway guy is a total nerd or a freak, so is he. Which is why I want you to give him his money back and send him on his way.''

J. T. Conway? A nerd? Or a freak? Hardly. Laughing, Kate refused, and they argued for a few minutes more. She insisted that all she had to do was keep her distance and treat J.T. as she would any other guest, and she'd be fine. "Besides,'' she added, "In a year or two the house will need a new roof. The Alpine Rose is doing all right, financially, but a major capital expenditure like that will stretch the budget thinner than I'd like. Now the extra money has been dropped into my lap like a gift. It would be stupid to turn it down.''

Zach cursed and raged, but in the end he had no choice but to accept her decision.

When they said goodbye, Kate headed out the back door, grabbing a battered pea jacket that belonged to Zach from the rack on the service porch. The sun had already dropped behind the mountains, but twilight lingered a long time in the high country. It would be an hour or so before full darkness descended, and she had too much to do to waste time.

She marched up the incline to the old carriage house that was now a combination garage and toolshed. Ten minutes later, wearing a pair of work gloves and the oversize coat with the collar turned up against the biting wind, she loaded compost into a wheelbarrow and pushed the unwieldy thing around to the front of the house.

Kate had spread most of the load onto the beds when J.T. came out the door to retrieve more items from his vehicle.

He smiled when he spotted her and called, ''That looks like hard work. Need some help?''

It had been so long since anyone other than Zach had offered to help Kate in any way that she was taken aback. For a second she could only stare at him. Then she gave herself a mental shake and scooped up another shovelful of compost from the wheelbarrow. ''Thank you, no. I can manage.''

Nice as it would be to have help, she couldn't possibly accept. He was a guest, after all, not a friend or a hired hand. One, furthermore, from whom she intended to keep her distance. She couldn't very well do that and accept favors from the man.

Besides, as she'd told him, she could manage. She'd run this place with no help from anyone for four years, hadn't she?

"You sure? I don't mind. I've been driving for days. Physical activity is just what I need to work out the kinks."

"Thank you, but no."

J.T. shrugged. "Okay. Suit yourself."

Out of the corner of her eye, Kate watched him lope down the steps and stride out to his Jeep. When he lifted the rear cargo door and bent over to pull out two cases, her gaze was drawn to his backside. Helplessly she noted how the faded jeans molded that firm flesh, and experienced an odd pressure in her chest.

She forced her gaze upward, but that was no help. Beneath the dark pullover, the muscles in his back and broad shoulders bunched and rippled as he easily hefted the cases out and headed back up the walk.

"If you'd like, you can park your car under the porte cochere," she called to him as he climbed the front steps. "It's more convenient than the garage in bad weather. That's a distance beyond the house and I keep it locked all the time, but if you prefer to garage your Jeep I'll get you a key."

"The porte cochere will do fine. Thanks."

J.T. made several more trips to the car and back. Each time Kate tried not to look at him, but she couldn't seem to stop herself. There was something about that devilish smile and chiseled good looks and that drew the eyes like steel shavings to a magnet. That killer body and easy, hip-rolling saunter didn't hurt any, either, she admitted ruefully.

Feeling foolish, Kate attacked her work with renewed vigor when he drove the Jeep around to the side under the porte cochere and disappeared inside for the last time. "If you don't get a grip, my girl, it's going to be a long six months,'' she muttered, stabbing the blade of the shovel into the pile of compost.

Full darkness had fallen, and she was working by the dim glow of the front porch light by the time she finished. Already the temperature had dropped to a bone-chilling level. Exertion had kept Kate warm while she worked, but when she paused to rest a moment and arch her back, the cold seeped in, and a hard shiver rippled through her. With an exhausted sigh, she trundled the empty wheelbarrow and shovel around the house and back up the incline to the garage. When they were stored, she padlocked the garage and hurried to the house.

An hour later, showered and dressed in a navy turtleneck sweater and gray wool slacks, Kate stepped out of her room and headed for the stairs.

Her room was on the same side of the house as J.T.'s, but at the opposite end of the long hall, overlooking the back terrace and outbuildings.

At the head of the stairs Kate paused and glanced toward J.T.'s room. Wall sconces cast dim pools of light at intervals along the corridor, but there were no signs of life from that end, no sounds, no light coming from under his door.

Had he fallen asleep? she wondered. Or had he gone out?

The last thought brought an uneasy tightness to her chest, but she ignored it and continued down the stairs.

Reaching the first floor, Kate noticed light spilling from the library and heard the soft rustle of paper. She found J.T. sitting at her father's desk, poring over a book and scribbling notes on a yellow legal pad.

The desk lamp cast his strong features in planes of light and shadows. The sleeves of his pullover were pushed up, exposing muscular forearms covered with a dusting of short, dark hair. Around his neck he wore a silver chain, but it disappeared beneath his sweater to nestle in the dark thatch that peeked out of the V neck of the garment. His shoulders were broad and his brown hair slightly mussed where he'd unconsciously winnowed his fingers through it as he read.

He was utterly masculine and appealing. More than any man had a right to be, Kate decided.

J.T. was so engrossed in the book he didn't notice her standing in the doorway. She debated whether or not to say something or clear her throat to get his attention, but in the end she left him to his work and went to the kitchen to finish preparing dinner.

Half an hour later, steaming biscuits and the stew that had been simmering all day in the slow cooker sat on a warming tray on the buffet and a place had been set for J.T. at the dining table. Kate lingered in the dining room to make sure he had everything he needed before returning to the kitchen, but when he hadn't shown up by ten after seven she went back to the library.

"I'm sorry to interrupt, but dinner is ready," she said quietly from the doorway.

He looked up and blinked at her, like someone coming out of a daze. "What?"

"Dinner. It's on the buffet in the dining room. You can help yourself."

"Oh, yeah, right. Dinner. Be right there," he said in a distracted voice, but even before the words were out of his mouth his attention reverted to the book.

Kate waited, watching him, but he made no effort to move. She doubted he even realized that she was still there. Finally she shook her head and left.

Minutes later he looked up, startled, when she returned and placed a tray on the desk beside his elbow. "What's this?"

"Your dinner. Normally I only serve meals in the dining

room, but since you obviously can't tear yourself away from whatever you're reading, I'm making an exception this once."

He grinned as she poured iced tea from a small pitcher and adjusted the dishes and silverware just so on the lacy placemat. "Thanks, but you didn't have to go to so much trouble."

"It's no trouble. Well, not much, anyway." Kate moved the tiny individual salt and pepper shakers closer to his bowl, and stepped back, then darted forward again to smooth out a fold in the napkin. "I couldn't very well let you go hungry."

He seemed to find her nervous perfectionism amusing. The corners of his mouth twitched, and his eyes twinkled at her. "I appreciate that."

"Yes, well, you'd better eat before it gets cold."

Obediently he took a bite of stew, and his eyes widened. "Oh, man, this is delicious. I think I'm in love."

Before she realized his intent, he grabbed her hand and pressed it to his cheek. His skin was warm and his five-o'clock shadow prickled against her palm. A wave of heat raced up her arm, making the fine hairs there stand on end.

"Now that I've tasted your cooking, you have to marry me, Katy," he declared solemnly, rubbing his bristly cheek against her palm. "I'll die of starvation if you don't. You've ruined me for ordinary food."

Flustered, but determined to maintain her dignity, Kate pulled her hand free and eyed him coolly. "I doubt that. It's just a simple stew."

"Not to a bachelor who's used to eating TV dinners or restaurant food. The only thing that would make this meal better is a little company. Why don't you pull up a chair and join me?"

"I'm sorry, but I've already eaten," she lied, backing

away. "Besides, I wouldn't want to interrupt your research. If you'll excuse me, I'm going to clean the kitchen and call it a day. Please feel free to work in here as long as you like. All I ask is that you put your dishes in the sink and turn out the lights when you're done." Not quite able to meet those laughing eyes, she bade him good-night and turned to leave.

"Night, Katy."

Kate ground her teeth. She had intended to make a quick exit, but at the door she turned and fixed him with a stern look. "My name is Kate. Not Katy. I *hate* to be called Katy."

J.T. threw back his head and laughed, a rich, robust sound that sent a tingle down her spine. "I'll remember that."

The next morning J.T. was halfway down the stairs when he caught a whiff of fresh-brewed coffee. In desperate need of a jolt of caffeine, he picked up speed and followed the aroma trail like a bloodhound.

His nose led him to the dining room. A warming tray on the sideboard held several covered dishes, but it was the coffeepot that caught his eye the instant he stepped through the doorway.

"Bless you, Kate," he murmured, making a beeline for the sideboard. On the first sip he groaned and closed his eyes. Whatever else she was, the woman made one helluva cup of coffee.

He was still savoring the brew when he turned around and focused on the table for the first time. It was an exquisite piece, made of solid cherry and long enough to seat twenty people. Currently, though, only one place was set for breakfast.

J.T. frowned. What the devil was this?

Following faint sounds, he pushed through the swinging door at the back of the dining room and found himself in the butler's pantry. He walked through the narrow, cabinet-lined room to another swinging door at the other end. Using one finger, he pushed it open a crack.

Kate sat at the kitchen table, muttering something and writing on a tablet while she ate breakfast. Alone.

J.T.'s eyes narrowed. Oh, no you don't, sweetheart. Not on your life. You're not keeping me at arm's length that easily.

"Call Lewis Goodman and insist that he deliver firewood," Kate murmured to herself, adding the note to her list of chores for the day. "Make a pie. Polish banisters. Finish composting." Trying to think of what else she needed to do, she paused to take a sip of coffee, then jumped and nearly choked when J.T. pushed through the pantry door with a cheery, "Morning, Kate."

"Mr. Conway!" She shot to her feet, dabbing at her mouth with a napkin. The last thing she'd expected was for him to come barging into her kitchen. "Uh...do you need something?"

"Yeah. Some company."

Only then did she notice that he carried a plate loaded with scrambled eggs, sausage and biscuits in one hand and in the other a cup of coffee and utensils. Before she could react, he placed everything on the kitchen table and pulled out a chair.

"Wh-what are you doing?"

"Joining you for breakfast. You don't mind, do you?" he asked with an ingenious smile.

"Uh, actually guests eat in the dining room."

"Ah, but I like this better," he said, casting an admiring glance around. "Not that your dining room isn't nice, mind you. It is. This is just more cozy. But we can eat in the dining room, if that's what you prefer.''

"We? Oh, no. You don't understand. I meant just you. The dining room is for guests."

"Ah, c'mon, Kate, it's just plain silly for me to have my meals alone at that banquet table like some aristocrat, while you eat alone in here."

His chiding tone brought her chin up. "I'm sorry that you don't agree with my policy, but—"

"Oh, I'll admit it's probably a good policy when it comes to overnighters. I can see where you might not want to get too chummy with people who are just passing through, but in this case it's just not practical. Kate, we're going to be sharing this house for the next six months. It'll be a lot more comfortable for both of us if we don't stand on ceremony."

Maybe for him, but she wasn't at all sure she could ever feel comfortable around him. Just having him in her kitchen had her nerves jumping.

J.T. flashed a grin. "Oh, sweetheart, you really are price-less. Surely you didn't think that for six months we would just exchange polite hellos when we passed on the stairs now and then?"

That was exactly what she'd thought, and she could see by his amused expression that he had read as much in her eyes.

"Kate. Kate. And I suppose in the evenings you expect me to use the formal parlor while you sit across the hall in the family parlor." He shook his head. "No way, sweet-heart. Trust me. It just ain't gonna happen."

His eyes twinkled as he leaned closer and touched her cheek. Kate started, but he merely smiled. His forefinger trailed over her skin, leaving a prickly line of fire in its wake, but all she could do was stare at him.

His voice dropped to a coaxing murmur. "So why don't you just forget about your rules and relax, hmm? Don't think of me as a guest. Think of me as a roommate. A pal. We'll keep each other company over the winter and get to know each other. I promise you won't be sorry. I'm a really likable guy. Cross my heart," he vowed with comical sincerity, drawing an X on his chest with his other hand.

Kate had no doubt that he was. That was a big part of the problem. She considered herself a sensible woman, but she also knew that she was lonely, and therefore vulnerable. J.T. was the kind of man who could blithely traipse through her life and steal her heart without even trying. Probably without being aware of doing so.

It was a demoralizing thought, and she nearly groaned. Nevertheless it was true.

Other than his flirtatious manner, which Kate suspected was merely part of his personality, he had not given any indication that he was interested in more than friendship. Yet just beneath the surface, a strong current of awareness sizzled between them. Kate felt it whenever they were together, and she knew that J.T. did, as well.

On the surface his offer of companionship seemed innocent enough, even a positive thing, but she wondered how much exposure to J.T.'s charm and blatant sexiness she could survive and still remain heart-whole.

One thing was certain, she wasn't interested in finding out the hard way.

As much as she yearned to love and be loved, to have someone who would always be there for her, no matter what, she had been burned too badly once before. She wasn't ready yet to risk another serious romance, or even a casual love affair. Even if she were, she'd be a fool to consider J.T. as a candidate. Come spring, he would go on his merry way, and she'd be left with a broken heart. Again.

As solitary and lonely as her life was, it was preferable to that sort of pain.

However, keeping J.T. at a distance did not seem to be an option. It appeared that her only other defense was to become a casual friend and hope she could keep things light between them.

J.T.'s gaze dropped to his caressing finger as it touched the corner of her mouth and lingered there.

Kate's breath caught. The tiny reaction did not escape him. His smile deepened, and for an instant she thought she saw something flare in his eyes. However, when his gaze lifted to hers once again they twinkled with good humor. "So what do you say? Deal?"

Tipping her head back, Kate broke contact with that tormenting finger and gave him an arch look. "Do I have a choice?"

"Not really," he replied with such cheerful cockiness that she had to fight back a smile of her own. "And now that we have that settled, whadda ya say we eat? I'm starving."

Grinning, he held her chair for her. Left with little choice, Kate reluctantly resumed her seat.

She kept her gaze on her plate and tried not to fidget. She wasn't used to having someone in her kitchen, or to sharing mealtime with anyone.

For several minutes neither spoke as they applied themselves to the meal. Or at least, J.T. did. Kate was too tense to eat another bite. She merely moved the remains of her breakfast around on the plate and wondered how she had lost control of the situation so quickly.

J.T. was one of those men who thoroughly enjoyed dining and savored every bite. For all his slender build, he consumed an amazing amount of food. Like most women who enjoyed cooking, Kate liked to see a man with a hearty appetite, and despite her skittering nerves, when he complimented her on the meal, she experienced a rush of pleasure.

"Thank you," she replied stiffly. "My mother taught me. She was an excellent cook."

Pausing to take a sip of coffee, J.T. looked around. "This really is a magnificent home." He leaned back, sipping his coffee and took another, longer look, taking in the brick floors and massive beams that spanned the ceiling, the tall walnut cabinets and copper pots hanging above granite-topped counters and, finally, the cheery fire dancing in the kitchen fireplace. "How long have you owned it?"

"Actually, my brother and I own the house jointly. We inherited it four years ago when our mother passed away."

"Really? Excuse me for saying so, but I didn't realize mining engineers made that kind of money. A place like this had to have cost a fortune."

"When my family came here twenty-three years ago, the house had been sitting vacant for over thirty years. They bought it for a song."

"You're kidding. A gorgeous place like this?"

"Yes, well, the real estate market in Gold Fever has never been great. None of the Smithson heirs wanted it, no local could afford the place, and until my parents came along, no outsiders were interested in putting money into a hundred-plus-year-old mansion in a tiny mountain town miles from nowhere."

"After being vacant so long, it must have needed a lot of work."

"Yes, but mostly cosmetic. Structurally the house was sound. It was built out of granite during a time when craftsmanship and quality were the norm.

"My parents did most of the work themselves. It took them almost thirteen years to complete the job." She smiled fondly, remembering. "I've lived here since I was six years old, and the whole time I was growing up we stepped over paint cans and drop cloths and dodged saw horses and ladders. There was always some part of the house being restored. I have fond memories of Mom and Dad working together, sanding the banisters and the wainscoting in the library, stripping musty wallpaper and refinishing floors and woodwork and furniture."

"They did a great job. But it's kind of a big house for a family of four, isn't it?"

"Yes, but from the start, the plan was to turn it into a bed-and-breakfast after Dad retired and Zach and I were grown and gone."

Kate's nostalgic mood faded. "The trouble was, he was killed in a mining accident before he had a chance to retire. He was just fifty-nine at the time."

"I'm sorry. That must have been rough."

"Yes. It was. Dad didn't have much life insurance, and the mining company that owned the Shamrock at that time declared bankruptcy before a settlement could be made, so what had been a retirement dream became a necessity for Mom. A few months after Dad died, she turned the house into a B&B."

"I see. Your guests must love this place. I'll bet a lot of them come back year after year."

"Yes, many do."

J.T. looked around the room once more and mused, "A house this size must be a constant financial drain, though. Utilities alone must be staggering. It doesn't seem like it would be cost effective. Especially since you're not open year-round."

Kate's spine stiffened. She fixed him with a narrow-eyed stare. "Is there some reason you're interested in my finances, Mr. Conway?"

"Uh-oh, we're back to Mr. Conway, are we? Sorry, I didn't mean to be nosy. Just a writer's natural curiosity. It's an occupational hazard, I'm afraid."

"I see." She scrutinized him for several moments, but after a while she gradually relaxed. "I suppose that's understandable. Actually, operating expenses are not as much as you might think, thanks to an ingenious builder and my Dad's innovations. A hot spring supplies water and radiant heat throughout. Dad had the foresight to install solar panels all along the back side of the roof and there are three wind generators behind the barn. Between the two I have plenty of electricity, but there is also a backup generator for those few times when the stored energy runs low. The summers here are comfortably cool so there is no need for air-conditioning and little for heat, but the fireplaces in every room handle what there is. In the winter I am here alone, so I close off the empty bedrooms and heat just the parts of the house that I use."

"Mmm. Interesting." He was quiet for a moment, then said casually, "You mentioned a brother. Does he help you run the place?"

Kate tensed again and shot him a sharp look, but J.T.'s expression was innocent enough. Apparently once again his question had been prompted by nothing more than idle curiosity.

"No. Zach hasn't lived in Gold Fever for years." Not since their mother married the Reverend Bob Sweet, and changed all their lives, Kate thought sadly. "He takes care of repairs and whatever needs doing when he's here, but as I said, he has his own life."

Time to back off, J.T. told himself, reading the suspicion in her eyes. You're going to have to take it slow with this one, Conway. The lady is as wary as a gazelle in lion territory.

J.T. finished off his eggs and drained his coffee cup, and cocked an eyebrow at Kate. "Speaking of chores, can I give you a hand with anything today before I get started on my book outline? I'll be glad to help you finish the composting, or whatever else needs doing."

"No, thank you. I have everything under control."

"You sure? I don't mind lending a hand."

"I'm quite sure, thank you."

Chapter Four

Just over a month later Kate felt foolish for having worried at all. She rarely saw J.T.

Apparently the muse had him firmly in its grip. Every day, all day and late into the night, he was either in the library with his nose buried in a book or holed up in his room, tapping furiously on his laptop keyboard. Thanksgiving came and went, but J.T. hadn't seemed to notice.

He showed up for meals only occasionally, and though it pained her to do so, she put his food in the refrigerator as he'd requested. Sometimes he got around to eating it and sometimes he didn't.

Kate tried to tell herself it was none of her concern. If the man wanted to starve himself, it didn't matter to her.

But it did. Like it or not, she was a born nurturer. A mother hen, her father and Zach used to call her, just like her mother. Which was why they had both taken so well to running a B&B, Kate supposed.

Taking care of people, seeing to their needs and comforts was a pleasure to her, and it came as naturally as breathing. Try as she might, she simply could not go about her business without worrying that J.T. wasn't eating right.

In mid-December, when he failed to show up for dinner the third evening in a row, she could take it no longer. It simply wasn't healthy to skip meals, she told herself as she marched up the stairs. For all she knew, he could be passed out on the floor from hunger at that very moment.

Pausing outside his door, Kate listened, but there was no click of the laptop keyboard from the other side, only silence.

Could he be asleep at seven in the evening? Oh, Lord, what if he really had passed out? Or was ill?

She raised her hand to knock, then hesitated. Shifting from one foot to the other, she chewed her bottom lip. Maybe she should leave him alone. After all, he had been emphatic about not wanting to be disturbed. But then, the Do Not Disturb sign wasn't hanging on the doorknob.

Taking a deep breath, she tapped lightly on the door. When nothing happened she knocked again, louder this time. She waited for what seemed like minutes, but still the only response was silence.

Concern began to bubble up inside her, filling her chest. Kate looked around, as though help would appear out of nowhere. Should she go in? He could be ill. Or hurt.

"J.T.? J.T., are you in there?" She knocked again, then pressed her ear to the panel and listened.

Nothing.

Panicked now, she pounded the door with the side of her fists. Her hand was poised to deliver another round of thumps when J.T. snatched the door open and barked, *"What?"*

"I...I—"

He didn't look anything like the cheerful man who had invaded her kitchen only six weeks ago. J.T.'s face was thunderous, and his eyes had a wild look, as though he'd just been jerked awake from a dream or a trance. Exhaustion had smudged dark circles under his red-rimmed eyes. His rumpled clothes looked as though he'd slept in them, his hair hadn't been touched by a comb in Lord knew when, and at least three days worth of beard stubble shadowed his jaw. He looked untamed and fierce.

And dangerous.

"I, uh…I came to tell you that dinner is ready."

"Dinner?" He stared at her. A low sound started deep in his throat and rumbled up. When it reached a crescendo he clapped a hand against his forehead and dragged it slowly down over his face. Against his palm, his beard stubble made a scratchy sound like course sandpaper.

He opened his eyes again, and they fixed on her like twin blue laser beams. "You interrupted me to tell me that *dinner* is ready? Dammit, woman, I'm *working* in here!" he roared. "I specifically told you not to disturb me when I was working except for an emergency. And by that I mean there'd better be fire or a helluva lot of blood involved. Got it?"

Kate's first instinct was to take a step back. Instead she raised her chin and pointed to the intricate copper doorknob. "You said not to disturb you when the sign was out. It's not. I thought perhaps you'd fallen asleep."

He bent toward her until they were almost nose to nose and snarled through clenched teeth, "If I had been and you woke me I wouldn't be any happier than I am now, I promise you."

Any trepidation she felt evaporated in the face of his obnoxious attitude. Kate's spine stiffened and her voice turned as frosty as Wisconsin in winter. "I was simply concerned. Breakfast was hours ago, and you didn't show up for lunch. I thought you would be hungry by now.''

''If I was I'd have come down to dinner, now, wouldn't I? What I am is busy. Just stick the food in the fridge like I asked. I'll eat it later if I get hungry. Now good night.''

He stepped back and slammed the door before she could reply. Astonished, Kate stared at the wooden panel just inches from her face. Before she could moved or even re-act, the door jerked opened again partway.

A beady eye glared at her through the crack. J.T.'s hand shot out, hooked the Do Not Disturb sign over the outside doorknob, withdrew, and the door snapped shut again.

The sound was followed by the sharp click of the lock.

Kate stared at the swinging sign with disbelief, her temper coming to a boil. Never in her life had anyone slammed a door in her face!

She was so angry she was tempted to haul off and give the door a hard kick. If she hadn't valued the old paneled walnut—and her toes—she would have.

Teeth clenched, her eyes narrowed into slits, Kate stood there for several seconds, glaring at the intricate grain of the wood and debating with herself about banging on it again and giving him a dressing down that would blister his ears.

Finally, though, she huffed, spun on her heels and stomped back down the stairs. See if she would ever try to be nice to him again. From now on the obnoxious oaf could starve for all she cared.

And to think that she had been worried about falling for him. Ha! Fat chance.

Kate didn't see J.T. again that evening, nor all the next day, but she would not allow herself to worry about him. He could hole up in his room and rot for all she cared. If she'd known he was a Jekyll and Hyde she would never have agreed to let him stay in the first place.

The second morning after their run-in she entered the kitchen to find dirty dishes in the sink. Kate gave the mess a sour look and loaded it all into the dishwasher, determined not to feel relieved that he'd finally eaten something.

After a solitary breakfast, Kate spent the morning finishing the outside winterizing. Though the sun was shining, the wind had a bitter bite, a reminder that the first storm of the season was bearing down on the mountains. As soon as she went back inside she telephoned Lewis Goodman for the third time in as many days, and got into a heated argument with him over the firewood he had been promising to deliver for over a month.

Lewis, like everyone else in Gold Fever, hated doing business with Kate, but not enough to turn down her money. Particularly since she ordered more firewood than anyone else in town. However, he always made the transaction as difficult for her as he could.

"You'll get your firewood when I'm ready to deliver it," he barked.

"Lewis, the weather service is predicting snow by the end of the week. I *need* that firewood. I'm warning you, if you don't deliver it soon, I'm going to call a woodcutter in Durango or Ouray."

He gave a confident snort, and she could almost see his smirk. "You won't do that. It'll cost you three times as much if they have to haul the wood all the way up here."

"It'll be worth it not to have to put up with your rudeness and game playing!" she snapped, and hung up the telephone before he could argue more.

Between her maddening boarder and Lewis, Kate's mood was less than serene. Needing an outlet for the fury churning inside her, she attacked her inside chores with a vengeance.

First she gathered all the laundry and lugged it down to the basement—all, that is, except what was in J.T.'s room. Which was just one more thing that was getting under her skin. She would probably have to muck out his room with a shovel if he didn't surface soon.

When the washing machines were chugging away, she returned to the kitchen, where she cleaned out the refrigerator and scrubbed the oven, stove top and vent hood, but even when the jobs were done she was still simmering.

Hoping to work off the rest of her anger, she spent the entire afternoon cleaning out the kitchen cabinets and putting in new shelf paper. In between chores she made several trips to the basement to transfer washing to the dryers and fold and put away the clean laundry.

Throughout it all there was no sign of J.T. When Kate dragged her weary body upstairs to shower before cooking dinner, she didn't so much as glance in the direction of his room.

Two hours later Kate put the salad she had just made into the refrigerator, then returned to the stove and dropped a pinch of mustard seed into the boiling water, added the pasta and gave it a stir.

"Mmm, something sure smells good in here."

Kate's heart did a little jump, but she quickly composed her features and flicked a glance over her shoulder. J.T.'s head was stuck inside the partially opened door that led in from the hall.

His eyes twinkled at her, and that wicked grin flashed, but Kate merely gave him a dismissive look and turned her attention back to the simmering pots.

"Uh-oh."

Kate still did not respond, and from the corner of her

eye, she saw him push the door open wider and cautiously step into the kitchen. She angled her shoulder to present him with her back and lifted the lid on another pot. Steam rose in a cloud, filling the air with the citrus scent of julienne carrots simmering in orange juice.

"You're still upset with me, aren't you?"

The question came from the vicinity of her right ear a second before a firm hand settled on her other shoulder. The spoon Kate was holding clattered against the side of the pot and her head snapped around. She found herself looking into a pair of vivid blue eyes, mere inches from her own.

She hadn't expected to confront him at such close range, and her heart gave another kick. His fresh-from-the-shower smell mingled with the cooking aromas and went straight to her head and numbed her brain. Kate commanded her feet to move, but the message didn't seem to be getting through.

J.T. smiled sheepishly. "I guess I forgot to tell you that I'm a bear when I'm working, huh?"

"I guess you did," Kate replied in a frosty voice, not giving an inch.

"The rest of the time I'm really easy to get along with. Honest. I am. I swear it. Just ask any of the people who know me. They'll tell you." His smile changed from rueful to coaxing, and his twinkling eyes beguiled. "It's just that when I'm writing I need all my concentration. Interruptions stop the flow and I see red."

At last she managed to sidle away a couple of feet. She felt marginally better with some space between them, but the sidelong look she shot him remained sullen. "That's hardly an excuse. You were insufferably rude."

"You're absolutely right. I shouldn't have yelled at you."

"Or slammed the door."

"Or slammed the door. I'm sorry, Kate. Really. I'd been working for over thirty-six hours without a break and was exhausted. After you left I crashed and slept until noon." He held up his hands when she started to speak. "I know. That's still no excuse, but well…here, I got you these. Maybe they'll help."

He whipped a bouquet from behind his back and held it out to her.

"Oh." Kate's mouth dropped open, and her hand flew to her chest. "Spring flowers? In December? How on earth…? Where did you get them? There's no florist in Gold Fever."

She was unaware of taking the bouquet from him, but suddenly she had her face buried in a cloud of daisies and daffodils. Eyes closed, she inhaled the sweet scent and smiled.

"So I discovered. The nearest one I found was in Durango."

Kate raised her head from the fragrant blossoms and stared at him, overwhelmed. "You went all the way to Durango and back just to get flowers for me? But…when? How? All day I thought you were up in your room working."

"I sneaked out this morning while you were arguing with someone on the telephone. What was that all about, by the way?"

"Oh…nothing. Just a disagreement with a local supplier." There was no way to tell him about her on-going battle with Lewis and other merchants without getting into the reason for their animosity, and she wasn't willing to discuss that.

She gazed at the bouquet and told herself not to be foolish. A bunch of flowers couldn't erase his obnoxious behavior.

It didn't do any good. She was hopelessly touched.

Fingering a satiny yellow petal, she shook her head. "I still can't believe you did this, that you drove all that way for flowers."

"I had to do something to prove that I was sorry." Ducking his head boyishly, J.T. wiggled his eyebrows and gave her a cajoling smile that no woman under the age of ninety could resist. "So? Am I forgiven?"

Kate wanted to cling to her righteous anger a bit longer, but it wasn't to be. Charmed in spite of everything, she shot him an exasperated look and sighed. "Oh, I suppose so."

"Great!"

Taking her unawares, he grasped her shoulders, bent over the bouquet she held cradled against her breast and caught her mouth in a kiss that sent shock waves all the way to her toes and rendered her mindless.

Sizzling heat streaked through Kate, flushing her skin and making her heart pound, her head spin, her stomach flutter. Strange and thrilling sensations bolted through her like a current of high-voltage electricity.

J.T. must have felt it, too. After only a moment he broke off the kiss and raised his head. The flirtatious grin was gone. In its place was a look of mild surprise and unmistakable male interest.

"Well, well," he murmured. Keeping his gaze locked with hers, he released one of her arms and reached to take the bouquet from her, but Kate held firm to the flowers with one hand and placed the other flat against his chest to hold him back.

"No, J.T. No." She shook her head, struggling to shake

off the haze of passion and regain her senses. "We can't...we can't do this."

He chuckled, but this time the sound was husky and sensual, and sent prickles over her skin. With ridiculous ease, he picked up her hand and brought it to his lips and placed a warm kiss against her palm. "Sure we can, sweetheart. I want you, and you want me." His lazy grin widened. "Don't even try to deny it."

"I wasn't going to, but—"

The oven timer erupted with a nerve-shattering buzz, and Kate jumped as though she'd been poked with a cattle prod.

"What! Oh! Let go. I have to take the chicken out of the oven before it's ruined."

"Kate," he began, but she pulled her arm free of his grip, snatched up a pair of oven mitts and whirled away to open the oven door.

When she turned from depositing the pan of Dijon chicken on the range top, she braced for anger and wounded male pride, but J.T. seemed his usual cheerful self.

Perfectly at ease, he leaned back against the counter, his legs crossed at the ankles, arms folded over his chest, and watched her with an amused smile tugging at his lips.

He raised one eyebrow. "You were saying?"

"I was saying no."

"Really? That's funny. That didn't feel like no to me."

"I'm not saying that I'm not attracted to you, J.T. Or that...well...that I don't want...uh..."

"Want to make love with me?" he finished helpfully.

Kate frowned but didn't bother to deny the statement. "It just wouldn't work."

"Oh? And why is that?"

Every cell in her body still hummed like a struck tuning fork, but she struggled to appear calm and firm. "For one thing I barely know you. For another, I'm not in the habit of sleeping with male guests.''

"Roommate," he corrected.

"Roommate, guest, tenant, whatever you want to call it," she said, impatience edging her voice. "The fact is, getting involved with you just wouldn't be a sensible thing to do.''

"I see. And do you always do the sensible thing, Katy?"

"I try my best." This time she refused to acknowledge his use of the hated nickname. He'd only said it, she was sure, to rile her.

"Hmm." Cocking his head, J.T. tugged his bottom lip between his thumb and forefinger, and studied her, considering. Finally he nodded. "Yeah, you're probably right.''

Kate blinked. "You're not angry.''

"Naw. This whole thing was my fault, anyway. That was supposed to be just a quick makeup kiss between friends. I got a little carried away, is all. Don't worry about it.''

Friends? Merciful heavens! If that was the way he kissed friends, she could not begin to imagine how he kissed a lover.

Before she could think of something to say, he straightened away from the counter, sniffed the air appreciatively and rubbed his palms together with relish. "So, when do we eat?"

"Oh!" Kate quickly turned back to the stove. "Have a seat. Dinner will be ready in just a minute," she said over her shoulder, pulling a platter and serving bowl from the cabinet. "Just as soon as I dish everything up and set the table.''

"I can set the table."

"Oh, but—"

"Kate, Kate." Clamping his hand on her shoulder, J.T. shook his head and gave her an admonishing look, then followed it up with one of those devastating smiles that temporarily short-circuited her brain. "I know you've got a lot of stubborn pride, but you have to learn to accept help gracefully. Now take your flowers and put them in water, and while you dish up the food I'll set the table."

Kate opened her mouth to protest, but, shaking his head, J.T. put a finger under her chin and closed it again.

"Ah, ah, ah. No arguing," he commanded, bending close and grinning into her startled eyes.

Surprise and confusion left her speechless for a moment. Finally, deciding she didn't have the emotional energy left to do battle, she accepted defeat. Besides, she could see that he wasn't going to give an inch.

Throughout dinner, J.T. chatted away, displaying not the least hint of embarrassment. That torrid scene they had shared just moments earlier might as well not have happened, for all the notice he gave it.

Kate didn't know whether to be relieved or insulted. Her own system had yet to settle.

He talked about the snags he had encountered in developing his plot, about the invaluable information he'd found in her father's library. Now and then he asked questions about her family, but she chalked them up to the writer's curiosity he'd told her about and put him off with vague answers.

Kate was so disconcerted she didn't pay close attention to what he was saying half the time. Mostly, she merely nodded and smiled her way through the conversation.

When they finished eating she offered to make coffee, but he shook his head.

"No, thanks, I'll pass. I thought I'd go to town tonight. Have a beer or two and nose around a bit."

"Oh. I see." He had her full attention now. She stared

at him, experiencing a quick rush of dread. If he went to town he was sure to get an earful, about her and Zach.

Her first instinct was to try to get him to change his mind and stay in that evening, but she dismissed the foolish idea. What did it matter? Sooner or later he would find out, anyway.

"Very well. As you wish," she said with a polite smile.

Half an hour later Kate sat on the horsehair sofa in the family parlor. The antique settee was the most uncomfortable piece of furniture in the room, but it afforded her a clear view of the foyer. She pretended to read a book, but every few seconds her gaze darted to the wide doorway.

At last she heard a faint sound from the back of the hall, followed by approaching footsteps and a softly whistled tune. Then J.T. sauntered into view, heading for the front door.

"Excuse me, J.T."

"Oh, hi. I didn't see you there." He halted just outside the parlor doorway and flashed a charming smile. "I was just on my way out."

Setting aside her book, Kate rose and reached into her pocket. "Before you go you'd better have these." She crossed to the doorway with her hand outstretched and dropped a key into his palm. "It's the house key."

J.T.'s eyebrows rose. "You lock the house at night? I assumed in a sleepy place like this, no one locked their doors, that crime would be almost nonexistent here."

It was, in the normal sense, but there were a few in town who weren't above harassing her or vandalizing her property, particularly after they had spent an evening at the Miners' Lodge brooding and boozing. She'd run trespassers off more than once.

Kate wasn't about to admit that to J.T., though. Instead she shrugged. "Better safe than sorry."

J.T. looked at her for so long she had to resist the urge to squirm. Then he gave the key a little toss and closed his fingers around it. "Yeah, I guess you're right." A crooked smile tipped up one corner of his mouth. "I'll see you tomorrow. Have a nice evening."

When he had gone, Kate walked to the front window and pulled back the lace curtain. She watched him stroll down the front walk with his hands in his pockets, then climb into his Jeep and start the engine. She followed the red glow of the vehicle's taillights as it headed down the mountain.

How long would he stay after he heard the talk in town? And why, she wondered dismally, did the thought of him leaving depress her?

J.T. heaved a relieved sigh the instant he shut the Jeep door. He had to get out of that house or go quietly mad.

If he'd stayed another minute he wouldn't have been able to keep his hands off Kate. All through dinner her scent had driven him nuts. So had those soft gray eyes. And that mouth, still slightly swollen from his kiss. He could still taste its softness, feel that slight quiver that shook it.

Hell, he'd been tempted to rake all the dishes off onto the floor and take her right there on the kitchen table.

Only that wariness in her eyes had stopped him.

And thank heaven for that. The situation was too delicate to upset it with an affair. Besides, if Zach was his brother, he doubted he would appreciate J.T. putting the moves on his adopted sister.

The kiss had accomplished one thing, at least. For those few moments when she'd melted in his arms he'd breached that wall of reserve and wariness that surrounded her.

"You must be losing your touch, Conway," J.T. muttered to himself as he eased the Jeep around a hairpin curve.

Usually he had no trouble getting people to relax and open up to him. That was why he'd been so successful as an investigative reporter. A little easy banter, a bit of charm, and strangers were spilling their life stories and all their secrets as though they'd been bosom buddies for years. The Irish gift of gab, his father had called it.

Kate Mahoney, however, seemed to be immune. Or maybe she just wasn't the talkative type. J.T. chuckled to himself. Talkative, hell. Sweeping away that wariness and getting her to trust him was going to take some work.

Still, he wasn't entirely displeased with the progress he'd made so far. He'd laid the groundwork. Even pried a bit of information out of her. Soon she would be accustomed to having him around and would let down her guard. But he had to go slowly....

Most of the shops were dark and there wasn't a soul in sight on the streets of Gold Fever when J.T. parked in front of the Miners' Lodge.

His breath puffed out in a white cloud when he climbed out of the SUV. It was only a little before nine, but already the yellow light of the street lamp revealed tiny frost crystals hanging in the frigid air. As he hurried to the door of the bar he blew on his hands to warm them and made a mental note to buy himself some gloves.

A wall of warmth hit him the instant he stepped inside, along with the combined smells of cigarettes and beer and fried food. Clint Black wailed from the jukebox in the far corner, his mellow baritone competing with the clack of billiard balls, the hum of conversation and the low volume of the football game on the TV above the bar.

J.T. paused in the open doorway, stunned. Except for the television, walking into the Miners' Lodge was like stepping back in time. The massive, carved-mahogany bar stretched along one wall of the long room. Hanging over it was a painting of a voluptuous, nude woman. Smaller nudes adorned the other three red-and-gold-wallpapered walls, along with gilt-framed mirrors and fancy sconces that held kerosene lamps. Several belt-driven fans and crystal chandeliers hung from the twenty-foot-high, pressed-tin ceiling. In the far corner a potbellied stove radiated heat.

J.T. shook his head in amazement. He'd wanted eighteenth-century ambience, and he'd sure found it.

Frigid air swooshed in around him, drawing a chorus of barked commands from the other patrons to ''close the damn door.''

''Sorry,'' he said to the room at large, and hastily complied.

Conversation stopped when the customers realized that the newcomer wasn't one of them. Curious eyes watched J.T. shrug out of his coat and hang it on one of the hooks beside the door, then tracked him to the bar where he hiked up onto a stool.

''Man, it's cold out there,'' he remarked to the man sitting to his left. ''The temperature must've dropped forty degrees since the sun went down.''

''What'll ya have, mister?'' the barkeep asked, eyeing him with the same curiosity as his patrons.

''Guiness.''

The man was back in seconds with the drink. The bar's other occupants returned to what they had been doing, but every few seconds someone glanced J.T.'s way, even the pool players.

''You lost, mister? Or just passing through?''

J.T. took a drink before looking at the man on the stool next to his. ''Neither. I'm in town for an extended stay.''

''No kiddin'?'' The man looked surprised. ''We don't get many tourists this time of year.''

"I'm not a tourist. I'm a writer. I'm here to do some research for a novel I plan to set in this area."

"Well, now, you don't say." The man's eyes lit up, and he turned more fully toward J.T. "What kinda story is it you're writing? By the way, the name's Cletus. Cletus Taylor."

"J. T. Conway," he returned, shaking his hand. "And the background for the book is hard-rock mining in the 1880s."

"Well, sir, you sure came to the right place. Mining built this town. Up until just a few years ago every man in Gold Fever worked the mines, one way or another. I was a powder monkey, myself. You know, the guy who sets the blasting charges. It was dangerous work, but the pay was good. 'Course, things are different now. Ever since they closed down the Shamrock Mine, the only thing that's kept this town going is tourism."

Cletus's mouth took on a sour twist. "Now seven or eight months outta the year the town is full of gawkers in Bermuda shorts and sandals. And I swear, every last one of them has at least one camera hanging around his neck. Some have two or three. They snap pictures right and left like this was an alien planet or something. And hardworking miners are waiting tables and selling trinkets in the shops. Them that's workin' at all. It's humiliating, that's what it is." He shot J.T. a morose look and took a long pull on his beer.

"Ah, c'mon, Cletus," the man on the miner's other side chided. "There ain't nothing wrong with shopkeeping. For most of us, it's either that or leave Gold Fever to look for work. I'll be dad-blamed if I do that. My family has lived here since 1870. Anyway, selling trinkets beats the hell out of starving."

The man leaned around Cletus and offered J.T. his work-worn hand. "Name's Otis Brown. Me 'n' my missus own the Mountain Blue Jay, over on Main Street. We specialize in wood carvings and such. I used to work in the mines, too."

The ice broken, several others wandered over to introduce themselves and put in their two cents about the fate of gold mining and the hardships that resulted for the miners.

"So, where're you staying?" Cletus asked. "Not here, surely?"

"Hey!" the barkeep barked. "There's nothing wrong with the rooms I rent out. Me 'n' the missus run a clean place here."

"Hold on, Fred. I didn't say your place wasn't clean. But since the man's gonna be here for several months writing a book he's gonna want more than just a tiny room. He'll need a place that's comfortable where he can spread out. Ain't that right, Mr. Conway."

"Right. And call me J.T."

"Well, now, J.T., I don't rightly know of any place that's available 'round here," Cletus said.

"Might be that you could rent out the old Tuttle place," Otis suggested. "It's been boarded up for years now, ever since May and Leon moved to Leadville."

"Good idea." Cletus's face brightened. "Leon got himself a job working in a zinc and lead mine near there. It ain't gold mining, but a man's gotta take what he can get nowadays. Their old place is empty so you'd have to move some furniture in, but you'd have plenty of room. If you want, I can give them a call and ask if they'd be willing to rent it to you."

"Thanks, Cletus, but that won't be necessary. I'm staying up at the Alpine Rose."

The statement had the impact of a bomb. Instantly a thick silence fell over the group.

Fred, the bartender, kept his gaze on the glass he was drying and Cletus's jaw clenched so tight the muscles in his face stood out. Several others stared at their drinks or the floor and shifted uncomfortably.

"Is that so?" Otis finally said. "I, uh…I thought the Alpine Rose was closed for the season."

J.T. chuckled. "It was. I had a helluva time persuading Ms. Mahoney to make an exception and let me stay through the winter, but I finally talked her into it."

"Humph. I'd sooner sleep in a tent," Cletus grumbled into his beer.

"Really?" J.T. cocked an eyebrow. "Why is that? It seemed to me like a great place to stay."

"If you don't mind the company you keep. Me, I'm more particular."

"Ah, c'mon, give the man a break, Cletus," a man named Joe Dodson said. "He doesn't know anything about what happened four years ago, so you can't blame him for renting from Kate. Anyway, the Smithson mansion is the nicest place in town to stay. Even Fred here will admit that. Won't you, Fred?"

"Yeah, yeah," the bartender replied grudgingly. "If you like that hoity-toity fancy stuff."

A mix of excitement and dread knotted in J.T.'s chest. Just a little push. That's all it would take, and he'd learn what his brother—if Zach Mahoney *was* his brother—was accused of doing.

"I gather Ms. Mahoney isn't a favorite around here."

Cletus spat out an oath. "Damn right she ain't. If she had any decency in her, she'd leave. Nobody in Gold Fever wants her or her brother here."

"Really? Funny, she seems like a nice enough woman to me. What's the problem?"

"Kate Mahoney and that family of hers are nothing but thieves. *That's* the problem."

"Now, Cletus, we don't know for sure that—"

"Don't you 'now Cletus' me, Otis Brown. Maybe the law can't prove anything, but everyone in this town knows that no-good brother of Kate's is to blame for what happened. And she had to have been in on it, too, seein' as how close the two of them always were. Reverend Sweet was a decent, God-fearing man. He woulda never done what he done if he hadn't been lead astray by that no good stepson of his, and you know it."

"For Pete's sake, what did they do?" J.T. demanded, running out of patience.

Cletus turned hard eyes on him. "They ran a scam on the people of this town that stripped every last one of us of our life's savings, that's what."

Chapter Five

She couldn't sleep.

Kate raised up on one elbow and punched her pillow into a different shape, then flopped back down.

It didn't help. Sighing, she stared through the darkness at the shadows on her ceiling, cast by the security lights outside shining through the bare tree branches.

She had gone to bed early, thinking she would be able to sleep, after the exhausting day she'd had, but it wasn't to be. She had been too tense, too sick at heart, imagining what J.T. was being told about her and what his reaction would be.

The luminous hands on the bedside clock read 3:14. J.T. had returned over two hours ago. She had heard him drive up under the port cochere and let himself in through the side door.

Ever since he'd left for the Miners' Lodge, she'd been dreading facing him in the morning—so much so that she had been sorely tempted to put on her robe and go knock on his door just to get it over with, but she hadn't quite had the nerve.

How, she wondered, would he handle the situation? Would he be straightforward and mention what he'd heard about her and Zach? Bring it all out in the open and ask to hear her side before forming an opinion? Or would he pretend he hadn't heard the talk, but watch her with suspicion and distrust when he thought she wasn't looking?

Well, why should she care one way or the other? she thought, disgusted with herself. J.T. was nothing to her. If he thought she was a thief and a con artist, so be it. There was nothing she could do about it, anyway. One thing she'd learned over the past four years was that people would believe what they wanted to believe, and opinions, once formed, were almost impossible to change.

She flounced over onto her side. After a moment she hissed and rose up to punch her pillow again.

That was when she heard them.

Kate sat up and cocked her head. They were merely the faintest of sounds, soft "plops" coming in rhythmic intervals from behind the house, and fainter, irregular thumps farther up the incline. If she hadn't been awake she might never have heard them at all.

Kate eased out of bed and shoved her feet into her slippers. Pulling on her robe as she went, she crept across the room to the back window and inched the lace curtain open a crack. Her eyes widened, then narrowed as they focused on the silhouette of a man just beyond the back terrace, digging in her garden.

The chicken wire and layers of straw that she had worked so hard to put in place lay scattered to one side. He had already made several small craters in her carefully tended and insulated winter bed of endive.

Drawn by a metallic thump, her gaze swept up the incline to the garage, where yet another man was trying to cut the padlock off the doors with what appeared to be a pair of hedge clippers.

Kate saw red. "Why those dirty, no-good…"

All sense of caution vaporized in an atomic blast of temper.

Enraged, she stomped to the closet, threw a coat on over her robe, filled the pockets with shells from a box on the shelf and grabbed her father's old double-barreled shotgun.

"Think you can come sneaking around here, tearing up my property," she grumbled racing out of the room. "We'll just see about that."

Her coat and robe flapped out behind her as she flew down the stairs and out the back through the kitchen. On the service porch she paused just long enough to break open the shotgun's action and thumb a shell into each barrel before shoving the screen door open.

Before it slapped back into place, she cleared the steps in one leap, crossed the terrace, took aim and fired.

The blast jerked J.T. from sleep with a suddenness that jackknifed him straight up in the bed. "What the hell!" He looked around, wild-eyed, his heart pounding, but all he saw through the darkness were the shadowy shapes of the furniture.

He rubbed his hands over his face. Must have been a bad dream, he thought groggily, relaxing his shoulders.

Below his window someone yelled, and he jerked to attention again, the hairs on the back of his neck standing on end.

He glanced at the clock and knew something was wrong.

"Kate!" Throwing back the covers, J.T. snatched up his

jeans, but he had barely stepped into them when another blast ripped through the night.

"Holy—" That was gunfire!

Without bothering to fasten his jeans, J.T. yanked a sweater over his head, stepped into his boots and took off. "Kate! *Kate!* Dammit, Kate, where are you!"

He raced down the hall to her room, but the door was standing wide open. He doubled back to the stairs and leaped down them three at a time. The shots had come from the back of the house, so he headed that way.

In the kitchen he found the back door standing wide open, and his alarm level tripled.

"Kate! Kate!"

When he received no reply, J.T. raced outside, only to come to a stunned halt in the middle of the terrace.

Mouth agape, he watched Kate, in her nightclothes and toting a shotgun, scramble over the three-foot retaining wall that surrounded the terrace to chase after two men in ski masks who were pounding, hell-for-leather, down the driveway and shouting every breath.

"Run! Run for your life! The fool woman's got a gun!"

Kate hit the ground on the other side of the wall and took off, her long nightgown and robe flapping around her ankles beneath the heavy coat, her unbound hair bouncing and swirling out behind her in the breeze like a pale banner.

"Kate! Wait!" J.T. shouted, but she ignored him, and seconds later she rounded the back corner of the house in hot pursuit.

Cursing under his breath, J.T. took off, too.

He cleared the corner just as two more men cut across the front lawn to join the first pair in a foot race down the sloping road. They headed toward the shadowy shape of a pickup truck, parked a hundred yards beyond them at the first hairpin turn.

Relief poured through J.T. when he spotted Kate standing at the end of the driveway. Then he saw her digging into her coat pocket and realized that she had only stopped to reload.

"Ah, jeez!"

Sprinting toward her, J.T. watched, horrified, as she shoved two shells into the gun, snapped the action shut and braced the stock against her right shoulder.

"Kate! Don't!"

The shotgun exploded with a muzzle flash and deafening roar. The men screamed and poured on more speed, nearly knocking one another down in their race to be first to the pickup.

Kate staggered back under the gun's recoil, but the instant she recovered she gamely took aim again.

"Kate, for Pete's sake!" J.T. reached her in time to knock the barrel end of the gun skyward just as she pulled the trigger on the second barrel.

She staggered back two steps, but when she recovered she turned her fury on him. "What did you do *that* for?"

"To keep you from killing somebody!" he yelled right back. "Have you lost your *mind*, woman?"

"Oh, for Pete's sake. Nobody's going to get killed. I'm shooting rock salt. Anyway, they're out of shotgun range. Now get out of my way, city boy."

She moved to step around him, already digging in her coat pocket for more shells, but J.T. hooked his arm around her waist from behind and held her back.

"Whoa! *Whoa!* Where do you think you're going?"

"Lemme *go,* you idiot! Can't you see they're getting away!"

"So let them."

She made a strangled sound and kicked and bucked, but when she couldn't break free she strained against his encircling arm and yelled at the retreating men, "Lily-livered cowards! Vandals! Don't think those ski masks are fooling me, either! Darn your sorry hide, Cletus Taylor! You, too, John! Brian! Ward! You come around here again, destroying my property and I'll fill your backsides with lead! You hear me?"

Cletus? What the devil was Cletus doing sneaking around the Alpine Rose in the middle of the night? J.T. wondered.

If the men heard her they weren't answering. They reached the pickup, and after a bit of pushing and shoving, one scrambled into the back and the others piled inside. An instant later the headlights came on and the engine roared to life. The driver gunned it, and they took off, tires spinning and gravel flying.

The pickup careened down the twisting road at breakneck speed, but J.T. didn't relax his hold on Kate until it reached the bottom of the mountain. She was so angry she was vibrating. He wouldn't have put it past her to run after them all the way to town, taking potshots.

When he finally released Kate she made a sound remarkably like a snarl and glared at the receding taillights of the truck until it disappeared down a side street in Gold Fever. Then she whirled on J.T.

"And as for you!" She jabbed her forefinger into his chest hard enough to make him grunt. "Where do you get off interfering, huh? If you hadn't butted in and held me back, I would have peppered their behinds good. Those clumsy idiots were falling all over each other trying to get away. I could have gotten within range easi—"

An appalled expression came over her face when her gaze flickered past him to the front of the house. "Oh, no!"

Oblivious to J.T. now, she took off across the lawn toward the area where she had flushed out the second pair of men.

"Now what?" J.T. rolled his eyes and started after her.

The security lights that bathed the house in a soft glow all around also revealed what the men had been up to.

"Oh. *Ohhh!* Those neanderthals dug up my rose beds!" Kate cried, staring at the gaping holes. "Just look at my prize Mr. Lincoln rosebush. They cut its roots. It'll probably die!"

"Now, Kate, don't get upset. I'll help you put everything right tomorrow." J.T. tried to soothe her, but either she chose to ignore him or she was too enraged to hear.

Whirling around, she stomped for the rear of the house, muttering every step of the way. "Sorry, no-good, sneaking bums. Come creeping up here in the middle of the night, digging up my flower beds, tearing up things. I'm going to kill that Cletus.

"Oh! And would you just look at *this* mess!" she spat, coming to a halt beside the mutilated garden.

The tubers and bulbs she'd recently planted were uprooted and scattered around, along with the soil that Cletus had dug up out of the holes. The four-foot-deep layer of straw she had used for insulation was scattered everywhere, and the chicken-wire covering lay several feet away, bent and twisted.

Kate surveyed it all with her mouth folded into a tight line, her fury almost palpable.

J.T. came to a halt beside her and frowned at the ruined garden. "What a mess."

She drilled him with a pithy look. "Surely you're not surprised."

"What's that supposed to mean? Hey!" he yelled, but his protest bounced off her back as she stalked toward the house.

By the time he caught up with her, she was pacing the kitchen like a caged lion. The shotgun was propped in the corner by the hall door, and her coat lay over the back of a chair.

"What the devil did you mean by that crack?" he demanded, slamming the back door behind him. "You act like I'm to blame for all this."

Kate reached the other end of the kitchen, swung back and shot him a simmering look. "Well, you're the one who got them stirred up."

"Got who stirred up? I don't know what you're talking about." But he had a strong hunch. It had started forming when she identified Cletus as one of the culprits.

"Oh, please! Do you take me for a fool?"

Pinching the bridge of his nose, J.T. squeezed his eyes shut and exhaled a heavy sigh. Finally he held out his hands, palms forward. "All right. Why don't we sit down and discuss this calmly?"

"I don't want to sit down. I'm too angry."

Fascinated, he watched her prowl around the room. God, she was magnificent. Vibrant and alive and sizzling with fire.

A small, self-deprecating smile tugged at his mouth, and he shook his head ever so slightly. To think, when they met he had thought her too placid and reserved. Too delicate. What an idiot. This fragile-looking flower was an independent, gutsy woman with the heart of a lioness and the pride of a queen. As long as he lived he would never forget the sight of her chasing after those men and blasting them with a shotgun that was nearly as big as she was.

Even now those usually calm gray eyes were still shooting sparks. She fairly crackled with temper.

Who would have thought that calm exterior masked a

simmering passion, just waiting to erupt? It amazed him that some man hadn't snapped her up.

He frowned. The mere thought of some nameless, faceless man laying claim to Kate set his teeth on edge. Just as well no one had succeeded, he thought with hard determination. In a flash of stunning clarity, J.T. suddenly knew, without the least shadow of doubt, that if any man was going to be the recipient of all that shimmering passion, it was damn well going to be *him.*

And if Zach Mahoney had a problem with that, too bad.

J.T. believed absolutely in fate. All of his life he had been certain that when he met his mate he would know it. He was surprised, though, that it had taken him so long to recognize her. He had been at the Alpine Rose for over a month already.

But he knew now.

She was so agitated she had yet to notice that the belt on her robe had come loose, creating a six-inch gap between the front edges. A smile tugged at J.T.'s mouth as his eyes skimmed over the ankle-length, pink flannel nightgown and creamy skin visible above the scooped neckline. The practical garment shouldn't have been sexy, but it was. He wondered if she wore anything under it, and for a moment allowed himself to imagine what it would be like to strip it off her, inch by inch.

He shook his head to clear it of the erotic picture and zeroed in on her hair. It was the first time he'd seen it unbraided. The thick fall cascaded down her back, and when she turned abruptly to pace back to the other end of the kitchen, it swung out around her shoulders like a shiny golden cape. His fingers itched to dive into that luxurious mane and grab hold, to feel its silkiness slide against his skin.

To keep himself from doing just that, J.T. turned the fire

on under the teakettle. "Why don't I make us some hot chocolate?" he offered, pulling two mugs from the cabinet. "It'll help you relax." He emptied packets of hot chocolate mix into the mugs, then leaned his hips back against the countertop and continued watching her while he waited for the water to heat.

"Okay. So, let's take this one step at a time. First of all, what happened here tonight?"

Kate slanted him a sullen look, her chin lifting. "I heard a noise outside my bedroom window. When I looked out I saw two men, one digging up my garden and the other trying to break into the garage."

"I see. So...you see two men wearing ski masks sneaking around in the middle of the night and you grab your shotgun and go after them? Good grief, woman! Are you nuts?"

"I was protecting my home," she said in a defiant voice.

"And what if they had been armed, too? For all you knew, they could have been dangerous psychos. Murderers or rapists."

"There wasn't much danger of that. They had to be from town. And as soon as I fired off the first shot and sent them running for cover I recognized Cletus."

"You can't be sure of that."

"Please. I've known Cletus since I was six. Nobody else around here runs like that. It comes from lighting charges in the mines, I guess. Once I pegged him, it wasn't difficult to figure out who the others were. Cletus, John Dunlap, Ward Atkinson and Brian Hetch have been thick as thieves all their lives."

"Still, taking matters into your own hands was a damned risky thing to do. You should've woken me."

The baffled look on her face told him that option had not even occurred to her. It was deflating to realize that she didn't think of him as someone to whom she could turn in a crisis. Not yet, anyway, he thought. *But you will, sweetheart. You will.*

"Why would I do that? You're a guest here, not a security guard."

"Roommate," he stubbornly corrected, ignoring the way she rolled her eyes heavenward. "And if some jerks in ski masks are sneaking around here, I damned well want to know it. You should have called the sheriff and let him handle the situation."

"Don't you think I've tried that? It doesn't do any good. Protecting me and my property isn't a high priority for Sheriff Huntsinger. Anyway, these men are his buddies. When he bothers to show up at all, he merely laughs and gives them a tongue-in-cheek lecture and shoos them home."

"Wait a minute. This has happened before?"

"Oh, yes. At least once every winter. That's why I had the security lights installed. When the tourists leave and the town shuts down, the men have too much time on their hands. They get to boozing down at the lodge and rehashing their cockamamie theories and inevitably someone gets the bright idea to search for the money."

"The money?" J.T. tried to look baffled, but she wasn't buying it.

"Oh, please. I'm not an idiot. Did you think I wouldn't know that as soon as you went into town you'd hear the things that are being said about my brother and me? I'm sure the moment the guys learned you were staying here they couldn't wait to fill you in on their version of what happened four years ago."

J.T. started to pretend ignorance, but Kate's unwavering stare stopped him. "Okay, I'll admit I heard about the swindle your stepfather pulled."

"And?"

"And that the feeling among the people down in town is that you and your brother were in on the scam. That the police and the FBI just weren't able to prove it."

"Idiots. The authorities couldn't prove anything because we didn't *do* anything! But we'll never convince the people in this town of that."

She paced to the other end of the kitchen, then swung around. "I'm sure that someone also told you that most of the people in Gold Fever believe the money is hidden somewhere on this property."

"Yeah. They mentioned that, too." The teakettle started to whistle, and J.T. picked it up and filled the two mugs. "Here you go." He placed the two mugs on the table. Kate reluctantly sat down, but she merely toyed with the mug handle and stared at the pale-brown liquid.

She slanted J.T. a look. "And now I'm sure you're wondering, Did they do it? Are my host and her brother con artists and thieves who swindled their friends and neighbors?"

"You're wrong. I wasn't thinking that at all."

She narrowed her eyes and studied his expression. "But you believe them, don't you?"

"Not necessarily. Look, I was just—"

"You were just wondering if I had access to the money, right?" she finished for him in a voice as cold as ice.

"Well…they did say that your brother sneaks into town periodically. The consensus seems to be that he knows the feds are still watching him so he's taking the money a little at a time so they won't get suspicious."

"Zach does *not* sneak into town! He comes to visit me two or three times a year. We happen to be very close."

"According to your neighbors he always arrives in the middle of the night at odd intervals. Never on holidays or weekends, when you would expect families to visit. And he holes up in this house the whole time he's here, never going into town, never speaking to anyone else.''

''Wouldn't you if your former friends and neighbors threatened to turn into a lynch mob whenever they saw you?''

''Maybe. But you have to admit, it does give the appearance of guilt.''

In the space of a heartbeat she went from controlled anger to blazing fury. ''Get out!'' she demanded.

Chapter Six

"*What?*" J.T.'s head snapped back.

"You heard me. I want you to pack your things and get out of my house. Now. And don't worry, I'll give you a refund. I don't want your money." Her voice was low and raspy, barely above a whisper yet vibrating with fury.

"Now wait just a minute. What the hell is the matter with you?"

The legs of her chair scraped the brick floor as she shot to her feet. "I may have to put up with accusations and slurs from the people of this town, but I won't share my home with someone who believes that I'm a thief and a swindler."

Kate whirled around and stalked to the counter, presenting him with her back. "I knew letting you stay was a mistake," she muttered to herself.

Rarely did anything rile J.T. to the point of true anger, but being tossed out by this slender wisp of a woman that he intended to claim for his own did the trick. He stared at her rigid back and saw red.

He bolted out of his chair and reached her in two long strides, grabbing her shoulders and spinning her around.

"Let go of me."

"Dammit, Kate, you're *not* throwing me out."

"I don't want you here."

"Too bad. I'm staying. Now listen to me. I haven't made any judgment about you. I was just repeating what I'd been told, that's all. Until I hear both sides I try never to form an opinion."

"Oh, I see," she snapped. "The jury is still out, is it? If that's supposed to make me feel better, it doesn't."

His own anger faded as quickly as it had flared. Lord, she was something. All fire and ice.

Had he really thought she was cool and dispassionate? Beneath that calm surface was spirit enough for any man. More than most could handle. He stared into those turbulent gray eyes and felt desire—hot, sweaty, tear-up-the-sheets, raw desire—rip through him. He wanted this woman more than he'd ever wanted any woman in his life.

Consumed with need, he couldn't think for a moment. His gaze zeroed in on that lush mouth, trembling now with the force of her emotions, and heat speared straight to his loins.

His chest tightened, making it difficult to breathe. J.T.'s eyelids grew heavy. His hands tenderly squeezed her upper arms, and he leaned closer, his gaze fixed on her mouth as his head began a slow descent.

Just in time, a small spark of sanity kicked in, and he jerked back. Easy, Conway. Easy. Now is not the time.

Much as he wanted her, J.T. knew in his gut that he would have to ease his way into her life. Experience had made Kate wary of everyone. The last thing he wanted was to scare her off.

He was relieved to see that she was still so angry she apparently hadn't noticed his near slip.

J.T. gave her a lopsided smile. "You expect me to take you on faith, huh? Sorry, Kate, but we don't know each other well enough for that."

Which was a bald-faced lie. He didn't believe for a moment that she had fleeced her neighbors and friends. Zach? Well, he'd have to wait and see about him, but only an idiot could look at the wounded outrage in Kate's eyes and doubt her honesty.

Her lips compressed tighter, but he could see her absorb the fairness of his statement, though grudgingly. That merely confirmed his faith in her.

"What I expect is that you would give me the benefit of the doubt."

"I have. I swear it. Just because I listened to the accusations doesn't mean I believe them. Now, why don't you come back and sit down and tell me your side of the story."

"How big of you," she snapped, but J.T. paid no attention and firmly but gently nudged her down into the chair, then took the one next to hers.

"Now then, what happened, Kate?"

Her chin came up another notch. "I never discuss what happened. I didn't do anything, and neither did my brother, so I see no reason why I should have to defend myself to you or anyone," she replied bitterly.

"Ah, Kate. Kate. There's that stubborn pride again."

She sat with her back ramrod straight, her hands clasped together on top of the table, her face set. She was marginally calmer, but not ready to give an inch.

He reached over and pried her hands apart and took them in his, ignoring her glare and her efforts to pull away. "Is this how you answer the charges your neighbors leveled against you? With stony silence? No wonder they're so convinced you're guilty. Hell, Kate, if you don't deny the charges, what are people supposed to think?''

"These people have known Zach and me since we were children. I shouldn't have to deny anything.''

"True. But people do tend to get a little crazy when they've been fleeced out of their life savings.'' He squeezed both of her hands and gave her a coaxing look. ''Now, why don't you tell me what happened. Why is everyone convinced that you and Zach were in on the scheme?''

Kate's eyes were still shimmering with resentment, and for a moment he wasn't sure she would comply.

Finally she turned her head and stared at the blaze in the fireplace. "It's a long story.''

"I'm listening.''

She sighed, her expression softening from anger into resignation. "The Reverend Bob Sweet came to Gold Fever eight years ago,'' she said in an emotionless voice. "The effect he had on the people of this town was incredible.''

"How so?''

"He was the most charismatic preacher anyone here had ever encountered. He could hold a congregation spellbound with only his oratory and the sheer force of his presence.

"To call him handsome was an understatement. He had a shock of white hair and piercing blue eyes, and when he walked back and forth before the congregation giving one of his impassioned sermons he looked like an Archangel, breathing fire and brimstone. He had an aura, I guess you would call it.'' Kate's mouth twisted. "And he knew how to use it. Mere weeks after his arrival here, everyone, even the most profane of the miners, thought that Reverend Sweet could walk on water.

"I'll admit, I did, too, at first. It wasn't long, though,

before I knew better. But as far as the good people of Gold Fever were concerned, the pastor was a saint and a god-send, and anyone who disagreed was a heretic.''

''I take it there were some besides you who disagreed?''

Kate slanted him a look. ''Just one.''

''Ah, I see. Let me guess. Zach?''

''Yes. At the time, Zach was working on a ranch near Ridgeway.''

A thrill of excitement rippled the hair on the back of J.T.'s neck. Ridgeway was no more than an hour's drive from Gold Fever. ''A ranch? You mean as a cowboy?''

''Sort of. You see, from the time Zach was small he wanted to be a rancher, so in college he studied animal husbandry and business. I think Dad was a bit disappointed that he wasn't interested in mining, but he understood and supported Zach's decision. As soon as Zach graduated he went to work at the Double L as assistant ranch manager.

''When our father was killed in a mining accident, Zach took a six-month leave from his job and came home to give Mom emotional support and help her start the Alpine Rose. I had just graduated from college myself and was in the process of looking for a job, but Mom was so grief stricken over losing Dad I thought it would be best if I stayed at home and helped her run the B&B.

''We got through our first tourist season without too many disasters. When we shut down for the winter, Zach finally felt confident enough that Mom and I could handle things and returned to the ranch, but he came home almost every weekend.

''Reverend Sweet moved to Gold Fever the following January. The town had a church building, but, thanks to our remote location and dwindling population, we'd been without a pastor for several years, and I suppose people were hungry for religious guidance. The church was overflowing for his first sermon, and he packed them in every service after that.

"Zach saw through Bob Sweet right away, though. He tried to tell our mother and some others that the man was a charlatan and a con man, but that merely infuriated everyone and made Zach an outcast. No one would hear a word of criticism about the man. It was as though Bob had cast a spell over everyone.

"When he started courting our mother, Zach was furious. He tried in every way he could to get Mom to see the man for what he was, but she was in love—or at least, she thought she was—and nothing Zach said or did could change her mind. They had some terrible arguments during that period."

Kate shrugged. "Mom was an intelligent and educated woman, but she had been a widow for almost two years, and she was lonely and a little scared. She and my dad had been college sweethearts who had married a week after graduation. Then suddenly, for the first time in her life, she was on her own.

"She was flattered by the attention Bob showered on her. Added to that, everyone in town was constantly telling her how lucky she was to have caught the eye of such a wonderful man."

Kate gave an inelegant snort. "What caught the good pastor's eye was this place. He saw this house and thought he'd found himself a rich widow. I believe he actually thought the B&B was just a lark, that Mom had opened it because she had nothing to do and was bored. Anyway, after a whirlwind courtship, Bob and Mom were married."

For a moment Kate seemed to be lost in memories. If the grim set of her mouth was any indicator, they were bitter ones, J.T. realized.

She was silent for so long he was considering whether

or not to prod her when she gave a mirthless little laugh and added, ''Imagine how furious Bob was when he discovered that the only money Mom had was what the B&B brought in. He was so angry I'm sure he would have divorced her, if he could have figured out a way to do it without tarnishing his image as the local saint and a man of the cloth.''

''I think Mom knew within days of marrying Bob that she had made a mistake. But she and Zach had had a terrible row just before the wedding, one that created a rift between them that they were never able to fully heal. After that, she would have died before she admitted that Zach had been right about Bob Sweet all along. Her stubborn pride wouldn't allow her to admit that, maybe not even to herself.''

''Hmm. So that's where you get it.''

''In public, he was charming and saintly and a devoted and loving husband and stepfather. At home he was a domineering, verbally abusive tyrant. I suspect he was physically abusive, as well, although I have no proof, and Mom would never have admitted it.

''I do know that after the marriage she changed. She became withdrawn and quiet. Fearful even. Whenever Bob was home she scuttled around this house like a scared mouse, trying her best not to draw attention to herself.

''That's why I stuck around after she married Bob. I thought about leaving several times.'' She gave J.T. a wry look out of the corner of her eye. ''Thought about it? Lord, I was desperate to get away from Bob Sweet. But I was more afraid to leave Mom alone with him.''

''Did he ever abuse you physically?''

''Just once. He backhanded me across the face when I disagreed with him over something. I don't even remember exactly what it was now, but he hit me so hard he bruised my cheek and split my lip.

"Zach saw the damage during his next visit and demanded to know what happened. He was livid. He stormed into the library and punched Bob."

Kate slanted J.T. a satisfied look. "Knocked him flat on his backside and broke his nose. Zach probably would've beaten him senseless if Mom hadn't intervened. While Bob lay writhing and moaning on the floor, clutching his nose, Zach stood over him with blood in his eyes and warned him if he ever laid a hand on either Mom or me again he'd kill him. Bob knew he meant it."

J.T. stared at her, his jaw clenched so tight his teeth ached. The thought of any man hitting a woman disgusted and angered him. Knowing the man had struck Kate filled him with rage. Good for Zach. If J.T. could have gotten his hands on Bob Sweet he would have pounded the coward into a pulp himself.

"After that he never risked hitting me again, but I'm not so sure about Mom. He had her so cowed I don't think he worried about her telling Zach, especially with the strain that existed between them. But even without using his fists, Bob managed to make my life and my mother's miserable in other ways."

"What kind of ways?"

Kate was so lost in the past she didn't seem to notice that J.T.'s voice had grown tight.

She shrugged. "Constant berating and belittling, threats, vicious tirades, that sort of thing. Mom couldn't stand up to him, and I had no authority, so he took over—the running of the Alpine Rose, Mom's finances, our lives, everything."

"What about your brother? Couldn't he do anything?"

"Zach tried, but there was nothing he could do. Bob had

browbeaten Mom into giving him total power of attorney. It was all legal.

"He already hated Zach for opposing the marriage. And for seeing through him. Bob was accustomed to having people idolize him and fawn over him. After Zach hit him, he became obsessed with striking back at my brother and hurting him in any way he could.

"Bob told everyone in town that Zach was no good and that my parents regretted adopting him. It wasn't true, but the gossip got back to Zach. It hurt him."

"Bob even turned the fight with Zach to his advantage. He told everyone in town that my brother had attacked him without provocation. Bob put on a pious face and said that he'd forgiven Zach but to his sorrow the boy was unrepentant.

"Every chance he got he insinuated that Zach was devious and untrustworthy, constantly getting into trouble. He would shake his head mournfully and tsk-tsk about Zach's so-called violent temper and claim that he was uncontrollable, though God knew, he was doing all he could to straighten the boy out. Bob even made a public plea in church for everyone to join him in praying for Zach to repent his evil ways.

"Bob knew exactly what buttons to push with which people, how to twist and turn everything to his advantage." Kate shook her head. "He even used Zach's career choice against him by spreading talk that Zach thought he was too good to work in the mines. That didn't endear him to the people around here.

"It was all lies, of course. Every bit of it. But everyone swallowed them, and the whole town hated Zach after that.

"Ridgeway isn't that far from here, but Zach visited only rarely after Mom married Bob. I'm sure if I hadn't been here he wouldn't have come back at all."

Careful to keep his voice neutral, J.T. cocked one eyebrow and looked at her with what he hoped was mild curiosity. "Is he still there? At the ranch?"

"Oh, no. Zach saved all he could while he worked there, but he realized that if he was ever going to afford a place of his own he'd have to do something to earn large amounts of money in a relatively short time. So he became a rodeo cowboy. He's been following the circuit for almost seven years now. He's won some big purses, but he still has a way to go before his dream of owning a ranch becomes a reality."

Disappointment settled over J.T. but he kept his expression neutral and steered the subject back to Reverend Sweet and the swindle.

"The Alpine Rose has always done quite well," Kate explained. "But the profits fell far short of Bob Sweet's expectations. He always wanted more."

"I thought preachers weren't interested in material things."

She shot J.T. a pithy look. "*Real* preachers, maybe, but not Bob Sweet. As soon as he found out the true state of Mom's finances he wanted to sell the house, figuring it was worth a small fortune, but he couldn't.

"To shield us from inheritance tax, our father had set up a trust with the house the main asset. Mom was the primary beneficiary and Zach and I were second in line. Bob couldn't touch it."

"I'll bet that ticked him off royally."

She answered him with a sidelong look, and the hard satisfaction in her eyes made J.T. chuckle. Bland and unemotional? This woman? Not hardly.

"Bob's biggest talent was he knew how to work people, how to exploit their weaknesses and vulnerabilities.

"About ten years ago the mines started shutting down,

one after another. The Shamrock held on the longest, but a few months after Bob came to Gold Fever it closed, too. That was a disaster for this town. Most of the miners had to leave to find work elsewhere. Those who stayed had to switch to some other line of work or starve. The result was a lot of resentment and feelings of helplessness and yearnings for the old way of life.''

"Yeah, so I discovered last night.''

"I'm not surprised. You can't spend an hour at the lodge without learning that much.

"It took him a couple of years, but Bob finally figured out a way to profit from the misfortune. He came up with a scheme and convinced everyone it would solve all their problems. He said he'd contacted Burleson Mining, the new owners of the Shamrock, and put out feelers. According to Bob, Burleson had no plans to reopen the mine or reclaim the old equipment abandoned here, but they were willing to entertain an offer. If we all pooled our money Bob was certain that we could purchase the Shamrock at a bargain.''

"I don't get it. How would buying a played-out gold mine help the miners?''

"Oh, there's a bonanza of gold left in the Shamrock. Probably more than has already been taken out. Everyone knows that, including the people at Burleson Mining. They closed the mine because volatile gold prices and high operating costs had cut into their profit margin and investors started pulling out. So the company shut down operations. When, or if, conditions become favorable again, mining will probably resume.

"But according to Bob, the owners were tired of waiting and willing to sell. He argued that if everyone owned a piece of the mine and they all worked together and kept prices down, we could make it worthwhile. Everyone would be shareholders as well as workers.''

"It sounds good," J.T. mused.

"Yes. It might even have worked if someone other than Bob Sweet had been in charge. But everyone had complete trust in him. He was their minister, after all. And the man who was going to return their jobs to them. The people around here handed over every penny they had or could borrow. Even some who I thought had precious little managed to scrape together enough to take part. And not just the locals, either. Bob hit up people all around this part of the state."

"How much did he collect?"

"Just over two million."

J.T. gave a low whistle.

"Ironically, the day Bob left to meet with the mining company officials the whole town turned out to give him a big send-off. The trouble was...there was no meeting scheduled. He never had any intention of buying the Shamrock. We found out later that he'd never even contacted anyone at Burleson Mining."

"When a week passed with no word from Bob, people wondered what was taking so long. Another week went by, then another, before they accepted that their beloved Reverend Sweet had absconded with their money. Which gave Bob plenty of time to flee the country. When the FBI finally caught up with him, he was living the good life on the island of Antigua.

"His arrest and return were videotaped and splashed over the news. Bob took one look at the cameras and used the opportunity to whitewash himself and lash out at Zach one more time."

She shook her head at the memory. "With crocodile tears running down his face he looked straight into the camera and begged forgiveness and sobbed that he had been led astray by his stepson in a moment of weakness. He swore that the scam had been Zach's idea.''

''The authorities picked Zach up for questioning, but other than Bob's word, there was not one shred of evidence connecting him with the scheme. That didn't seem to matter with the faithful of Gold Fever. They preferred to believe Bob Sweet.''

''Why, for Pete's sake?''

''I think it was easier to blame Zach, and by association, me, than to admit that they were rotten judges of character. Also, the money was never found. Bob swore on his Bible that Zach had it.''

''Ah, so that's why they think the money is here.''

Kate nodded and looked away, her face solemn as she stared into the fire once more. ''Mom died shortly after the scandal broke. The doctor said it was heart failure, but I think it was shame. The whole town turned against us after Bob's arrest. I couldn't even get anyone to work here. Mrs. Womack, the lady who helps me with the cleaning during tourist season lives in Ouray.''

''Surely there are some others in town who didn't believe Sweet.''

Kate shook her head and smiled sadly. ''Maybe at first a few had doubts, but six months ago Bob Sweet died in prison of cancer. To the end he swore that Zach planned the swindle and had the money.

''It was his final act of revenge against Zach. Around here a deathbed confession carries more weight than hard evidence.''

''The money isn't hidden on this property, but until it's found elsewhere—which seems unlikely after all this time—my former friends and neighbors will always believe it is.''

He knew there was more to the story and waited for her

to tell him, but she fell silent and stared at the tabletop and nervously traced a pattern on the surface with her forefinger.

Finally J.T. realized he would have to broach the matter himself. "Kate?" he said gently. "You want to tell me about Kurt Hattleman?"

Her head snapped up. "They told you about him, too?"

"Actually, I met him."

"Oh, God." She closed her eyes. When she finally opened them again she couldn't seem to look at him, focusing instead on the cold fireplace ashes, her faraway look full of pain. "Kurt was my fiancé—or at least, I thought he was, but that turned out to be a lie.

"You see, all through high school I had a gigantic crush on Kurt, but he didn't look at me twice. I'm positive he knew. Everyone did. It's impossible to keep a secret in this town.

"Inevitably those adolescent feelings faded. I went away to college and forgot all about Kurt.

"After the scandal, though, he was the only one in town who defended Zach and me, and…well I guess some remnants of the girlish crush remained. I was flattered and happy when he stood up for me, and thrilled by all the attention he showed me. When he said he loved me and wanted to marry me, I believed him."

Her voice cracked on the last, and J.T. ground his teeth as he watched her fight for composure, blinking furiously to contain the tears that threatened.

"Fool that I was, I even let him move in here after we became engaged. I thought we were going to be life partners, standing shoulder to shoulder against all the gossip and ugliness. Then one day I had to go to Durango on an errand. I had gotten just a few miles down the road when I remembered that I had forgotten my checkbook, so I came back for it. I found Kurt wildly searching the house for the money.

"It turned out the people in town had chosen Kurt to court me. They figured if I fell in love with him, he could wheedle it out of me where the money was hidden. When that didn't pan out as they expected, he decided to search for it."

J.T. put his hand over Kate's clasped ones, and when she finally met his gaze he said softly, "I'm sorry, Kate."

She attempted a brisk smile, but the effect was spoiled by the slight quiver of her lips. "Yes, well, I'm older and wiser now."

And that, J.T. thought, explained a lot.

She turned her head and fixed him with a direct look that demanded a straight answer. "And there you have it. That's our side of the story. So now who do you believe?"

Leaning back until the chair balanced on the rear legs, J.T. studied her. She sat with her spine stiff, her face set, braced for the insult she was sure was coming.

Absently he raised his hand to his chest and fingered the medallion fragment beneath his shirt. Was he letting his feelings for Kate and the possibility that Zach Mahoney might be his and Matt's brother color his judgment?

The journalist in J.T. winced at the idea.

No, that wasn't it. He didn't know Zach Mahoney or what he was capable of doing, but years as an investigative reporter had sharpened his instincts about people, and his gut was telling him that Kate could not have been involved in Bob Sweet's scam. Those gray eyes were clear and guileless, shimmering with hurt, and her whole body radiated righteous indignation.

J.T. shrugged. "Seems an easy enough call. It all boils down to Sweet's word against your brother's. Personally, the word of a swindler doesn't mean squat to me. The authorities obviously feel the same. Sweet went to prison. Your brother didn't. That's good enough for me."

"Then…you…believe me?"

"Yeah."

She stared at him, her eyes growing suspiciously moist again, and he wondered why she looked so stunned. Then he realized that it had been a long time since anyone had believed in her.

His heart twisted with sympathy, and a warm rush of emotions too complicated to analyze.

J.T. stared at her tear-drenched eyes and her trembling mouth and could not resist.

The front legs of the chair hit the floor with a thump. Before Kate could move, J.T. leaned across the corner of the table, hooked a hand around her nape beneath the collar of her robe, and put his mouth on hers.

Her breath caught and her eyes widened, but in the space of three heartbeats her eyelids drifted shut. Beneath his hand, J.T. could feel the erratic dance of her pulse. She sat ramrod straight, her hands clamped together in a white-knuckled grip on the table, the quiver of her soft lips against his her only movement.

The kiss was as soft as thistledown, a press of warm lips, a rub, a nibble, the merest touch of tongues. Yet for all its gentleness and brevity, the caress carried a punch that rocked J.T. to his soul. A shudder rippled through Kate, and he knew that she felt it, too.

He pulled back, shaken, but he grinned when her eyelids lifted as though they were weighted with lead. She blinked slowly and tried to focus, and his grin grew wider, cockier.

"Wh-why did you do that?"

J.T. winked. "To show you that I'm on your side. Besides, you looked like you needed it." He rubbed his thumb along her jaw and winked. "Hey, don't look so stricken,

Katy. It was just a little kiss between friends. Nothing to worry about.''

To emphasize the point, he gave her another quick peck on the lips, then stood up and stretched with a lot more nonchalance than he was feeling. ''Now, I don't know about you, but I'm going back to bed for a few more hours of shut-eye. Tomorrow I'll give you a hand with the garden and flower beds.''

''Oh, no, that's all right. Guests aren't expected to help.''

''I thought I told you not to think of me as a guest.'' He touched the end of her nose with his forefinger and grinned. ''We'll have to work on that later.''

He headed for the door into the hall, but when he reached it he stopped and looked back at her. ''Before I go, would you answer one question?''

She tensed again and shot him a wary look. ''What?''

''What are you doing here?''

''Pardon me?''

''Why do you stay here and take the abuse you do?''

Her spine straightened and her shoulders went back in that proud way he was beginning to recognize. ''What else can I do? Sell the house? To whom? The real estate market in Gold Fever is worse now than when Smithson heirs were trying to sell. And my parents put too many years of hard work into this place. I won't walk away and leave it. Anyway, leaving would be like admitting guilt. Plus, this is my home. No one is going to run me out of it. No one.''

J.T. looked at the jut of her chin and the belligerence shimmering in those gray eyes. He grinned and shook his head. ''Ah, Katy, Katy. There's that stubborn pride again.''

Chapter Seven

Rarely did anyone come to Kate's door after tourist season ended. When the Westminster door chimes reverberated through the downstairs a little before eight the next morning, she was so startled she nearly dropped the pan of blueberry muffins she had just removed from the oven.

"Who in the world?"

Kate dumped the muffins into the bread warmer and hurried to the front door. The instant she opened it, her spine stiffened.

"Oh. It's you." Unconsciously Kate squared her shoulders and lifted her chin. She gripped the edge of the door with one hand and the frame with the other. She had no intention of inviting him in. "Is there something you need, Sheriff?" she asked coldly.

Alvin Huntsinger replied with a curt nod, but didn't bother with a greeting. "There's been some complaints about you. I'm going to have to place you under arrest."

"Arrest!" A chill race down Kate's spine. "What for?"

"Assault with a deadly weapon for starters. Maybe even attempted murder."

"Attemp— That's ridiculous!"

"I got four men in town who say otherwise."

"Then they're lying."

"You saying you didn't shoot at Cletus and his friends last night?"

"I fired my shotgun, but I was shooting rock salt. I certainly didn't assault anyone."

"Well now, I only have your word for that, don't I."

"And mine."

The deep rumble of J.T.'s voice was the most wonderful sound she had ever heard. Kate looked around, weak with relief to see him ambling toward her down the central hall. Coming to a halt directly behind her, he stared at the sheriff over her head.

Sheriff Huntsinger frowned, his eyes narrowing. "And who might you be?"

"J. T. Conway."

"Ah, yes. You're that writer fella I've been hearing about."

"That's right."

"And you saw Kate shooting at four men last night?"

"No. I saw Kate fire a warning shot of rock salt into the air."

"Into the air, huh? How do you know she was shootin' rock salt?"

"I examined the shells when I unloaded the gun. You know, Sheriff, in most Western states there's no law against discharging a firearm on your own property if you live out of town on acreage, as Kate does. But I'm quite certain every state has laws against trespassing. Not to mention breaking and entering and vandalism."

"Breaking and entering! Now just hold on a minute," Sheriff Huntsinger blustered. "Those boys just came up here to have a talk with Kate is all."

"At three in the morning? I don't think so."

"While Cletus and the other two were digging up my property, Ward Atkinson was trying to cut the padlock off my garage. If that's not breaking and entering I'd like to know what is," Kate snapped, emboldened by J.T.'s support.

J.T. gave the sheriff one of his charming smiles, but his eyes held challenge. "You know, Sheriff, I have no stake in this. But if it ever came to trial, as a neutral third party, I'd have to testify to what I saw. And I have to say, I think any jury would find that Kate was within her rights in protecting her property. If I were you, I'd tell those guys to forget any idea of pressing charges against her, and just be glad she's not pressing charges herself."

The subtle warning was not wasted on the sheriff. He stared at J.T., his face turning a mottled red, but after a moment he jerked his head in a curt nod. "All right. I'll talk to them."

When he had gone, Kate closed the door and leaned her forehead against it, nearly sick with relief.

"You okay?"

She looked up at J.T. with a wan smile. "Yes. I am now. He wasn't bluffing, you know. He really would have arrested me." She put her hand on his arm. "Thank you, J.T. I'm just sorry you had to stretch the truth for me. We both know I wasn't shooting in the air."

"What stretch? The only shot I saw you fire was when I knocked the gun barrel up."

The mischief in his eyes made her laugh. "So it was."

She exhaled a long sigh of relief, then straightened her shoulders. "Well. Now that we have that settled, let's have breakfast, shall we? I have blueberry muffins in the warmer," she said, heading for the kitchen.

"Mmm. Sounds great, as long as there's coffee to go with them. Uh, Kate...there is just one thing."

She stopped and looked back at him. "What's that?"

"Those shells you were firing...they were loaded with rock salt, right?"

"It's about time you got in touch! Why the devil did you change your cell phone number? I've been trying to reach you for over a week."

J.T. winced and jerked the telephone receiver away from his ear. "Jeez, Charlie, it's nice talking to you, too."

"Don't get cute with me, Conway. I distinctly remember telling you..."

While his editor ranted, J.T. held the cell phone out from his ear and wandered over to the front windows of his room.

Through the lace curtains he saw Kate, working furiously to repair the damage Cletus and his friends had done to the rose beds the night before.

It had snowed during the night, covering the ground nearly a foot deep, and it was still coming down. She'd had to clear the snow off the tops of the beds before she could even begin the repairs. Kate's coat and red knit cap were dusted with the white flakes, but she was determined to save her precious roses.

J.T. shook his head. Stubborn woman. She'd flat-out refused his offer to help. Gotten downright huffy about it. He'd never known anyone, male or female, with so much stiff-necked pride.

"...give an order I expect you to follow it. You hear? Now, where the hell are you, boy? And why haven't you called?"

J.T. ignored the first question. "Sorry. I haven't had a chance," he said absently, smiling as he watched Kate replant an uprooted bush and pat the soil in place around the base with the tender care a mother would give a baby. "Besides, there hasn't been anything to report."

Charlie pounced on the statement like a duck on a june bug. "You're calling now, so that must mean you have something."

"Mmm. Maybe. I don't know. I'm looking into something, but until I have more to go on, I'd rather not talk about it. Mainly I'm just checking in so you won't go ballistic on me."

"Now, look here, Conway, if you've got a hot story brewing I damned well want to know about it."

J.T. sighed and raked his hand through his hair. He was already regretting making the call to his boss. Charlie was like a pit bull: once he got his teeth into something he didn't let go. "You will, don't worry. As soon as I'm sure there is a story I'll tell you all about it. This may turn out to be nothing."

"Yeah, well, you'd better," he growled. "So how's the book coming along?"

"Fine."

It wasn't a lie. The first draft was shaping up, and he'd picked up a lot of usable color and background from the guys at the lodge and technical and historical info from Sean Mahoney's library. However, his story had taken a back seat to the real-life drama that had taken place in Gold Fever four years ago.

All morning he hadn't been able to think about anything else. Or write about anything else. If handled right, a fictionalized version of the crime and all that had followed had the makings of a first-rate novel. He already had five pages of outline written.

Charlie harrumphed, somehow managing to imbue the sound with utter derision. "And how about the search for your other triplet? How's that going?"

Automatically J.T. raised his hand to his chest and fingered the medallion piece he always wore. "Nothing definite yet, but it looks promising."

"Yeah, sure. Which means, you've got bubkus. Why don't you just forget all this nonsense about writing a book and digging up long lost relatives and get back here where you belong?"

"Forget it, Charlie. I'm doing this."

"Yeah, well...if that's all you've got to say, I gotta go. Unlike you, I got work to do."

J.T. chuckled. It was a typical Charlie response. When the man couldn't win an argument any other way, he cut you off. "So long, Charlie."

"Yeah, yeah. Keep in touch, Conway. Ya hear!"

J.T. pushed the power button on the cell phone and flipped it shut, but for several seconds he merely stood there, watching Kate.

What would it hurt if he did a little digging of his own? If he could unravel the mystery of what happened to the money, it would remove suspicion from Kate and Zach. He would be doing them a favor.

And providing yourself with the basis for a blockbuster story, his conscience niggled.

J.T. frowned and tapped the small phone against his chin. So what was wrong with that? It wasn't as if he'd be hurting anyone. The story of the swindle had already made the papers.

He flipped the cell phone open, but still he hesitated, torn, and not sure exactly why.

Finally, ignoring the prick of his conscience, he hit the power button again and punched in the number. "Dammit, what harm could it do?'' he muttered, but as he waited for the connection to complete, he turned away from the window and his view of Kate.

"*Houston Herald.* How may I direct your call?''

"Hey, Josie. It's J.T. again. Put me through to Sunny will you, darlin'?''

"Anything for you, sugar,'' the grandmotherly woman replied.

"Morgue. Roberts speaking.''

"Hi-ya, gorgeous. How's it going with my favorite girl?''

"Save the sweet talk, J.T. What do you want?''

J.T. grinned. Sunny Roberts had worked in the *Herald*'s morgue for over forty years and had run it for the last twenty-two. Sunny was, however, the very antithesis of her name. She had the disposition of a grizzly with an impacted tooth, and a sour puss that would stop a clock. However, when it came to research or locating something in the newspaper's archives, there was no one better. Luckily for J.T., the woman had a soft spot for him in that stone she called a heart, though she would walk through fire before admitting it.

"That's what I love about you Sunny, you have such an even temper. Always rotten.''

"Yeah, yeah. I'm busy, Conway. What do you want?''

"I need all you can find on a swindle that took place in Gold Fever, Colorado, around four years ago. Five, tops. Also, anything you can dig up on a Reverend Bob Sweet. I know he was arrested on Antigua, extradited back here, tried and sent to prison for the crime. I want every scrap of coverage on those events and anything else you can dig up on the guy.''

"Got it. Anything else?''

"No. Wait! Yes.'' J.T. hesitated, and rubbed the back of

his neck, grimacing. "If you can find anything on a rodeo cowboy named Zach Mahoney, send me that, too."

"A crooked preacher and a bronco buster, huh? Now there's a combo for you. What're you up to, J.T.?"

"No good, darlin'," he drawled. "No darned good."

"Now that I'd believe. So where do you want this sent?"

When he'd given her the general delivery address and hung up, J.T. wandered back to the window. Kate had finished replanting and was shoveling the last of the compost and mulch back on the beds.

I won't hurt you, sweetheart, he swore silently. Whatever I find, I won't let anything hurt you.

Kate finished covering the beds and stopped to arch her back, but suddenly she turned toward the road or, at least, what you could see of it.

Around dawn J.T. had heard the snowplow, but another couple of inches had fallen since then, obliterating the road except for the snow furrow along its outer edge.

The sound of a vehicle approaching reached J.T., and he saw a dump truck filled with firewood lumbering up the snow-covered track.

Carrying her shovel, Kate went out to meet the truck when it pulled into the driveway. She exchanged a few words with the driver, and he drove around to the back of the house with Kate following on foot.

J.T. wandered back to the desk and poured himself another cup of coffee from the carafe that Kate had filled for him that morning. Absently sipping the brew, he settled in front of the laptop and pulled up the outline he'd been developing on the swindle.

He worked straight through the next few hours and two more cups of coffee, developing the plot and various subplots, the characters, twists and turns and a few red herrings. Frowning at the screen, trying to come up with a background for his Reverend Sweet character that would explain but not excuse his actions, J.T. reached for the carafe again to refill his cup, but only a trickle came out of the spout.

He muttered a mild curse. Since he was temporarily stumped, anyway, he decided it was as good a time as any to take a break. And to spend some time with Kate while he was at it, he thought with a spurt of pleasure.

Kate was skittish and wary of closeness. And who could blame her, after people she'd known her whole life had turned so thoroughly against her? But he had a plan.

The night before he had immediately begun a subtle but relentless campaign to win her over—touching her frequently, flirting with her, steering their conversation in more intimate directions—all manner of small things that would, he hoped, disarm her and let him sneak in under her guard and ease his way into her life.

J.T. was a patient man. That he would not eventually wear her down never occurred to him.

He suddenly realized that he was ravenous, and a glance at the clock confirmed that he had missed lunch again. Standing, he stretched and rotated his stiff shoulders. After a brief stop by the bathroom, he picked up the carafe and headed for the kitchen.

Whistling a cheery tune, J.T. loped down the stairs, a smile of anticipation on his lips.

His smile faded when he stepped into the kitchen. As always the room was spotless and neat as a pin, but there was no sign of Kate.

He found a plate containing a thick ham sandwich and fruit covered with plastic wrap in the refrigerator. He poured himself a cup of coffee from the pot on the warmer and wolfed down half the sandwich in three bites while standing at the counter. He was working on the second half when a sound from out back caught his attention.

Curious, he finished off his coffee in one gulp and ambled out the back door onto the service porch, munching the sandwich.

He stopped short when he spotted Kate. "What the—"

A mountain of firewood lay smack-dab in the middle of the driveway in front of the garage, blocking the doors. The idiot truck driver had driven around the port cochere, and J.T.'s Jeep, dumped his load and driven off!

To J.T.'s astonishment—and fury—Kate was attempting to move the logs, one wheelbarrow load at a time, to the neatly stacked woodpile at the edge of the terrace.

The unwieldy apparatus wobbled drunkenly from one side of the path to the other while Kate fought to keep it from toppling. At the same time she had to dig in her heels to keep the whole thing from dragging her down the slope.

J.T.'s much-vaunted patience went up in smoke. Stuffing what was left of the sandwich into his mouth, he snatched the man's pea jacket that Kate was so fond of wearing off the hook and slammed out the screen door, thrusting his arms into the sleeves as his long, angry strides carried him across the terrace.

"What the hell do you think you're doing?" he bellowed, intercepting her halfway up the incline.

Kate started and let out a squeak. She had been concentrating so hard on trying to manhandle the loaded wheelbarrow she hadn't seen J.T. approach. A tiny shiver ran down her spine when she took in his thunderous expression, but she refused to be intimidated.

She dropped the wheelbarrow down on its supports, panting as she wiped snowflakes off her lashes with the back of her gloved hand. "What does it look like I'm doing? I'm moving the firewood to the woodpile."

"Isn't the driver supposed to stack it for you? What kind of idiot dumps firewood in a driveway? And why in the name of heaven didn't you call me to help?"

"Yes. An idiot like Lewis Goodman. And I didn't ask you to help because gu—"

"Don't!" He jabbed his forefinger in the air near the end of her nose. "Don't you dare say because guests aren't expected to help out," he warned. "So help me, if you do—"

"If I do, you'll what?" Kate demanded, with a haughty arch of one eyebrow.

J.T.'s eyes narrowed. "Trust me, darlin', you don't want to know." He elbowed her out of the way and grasped the handles of the wheelbarrow. Immediately, Kate tried to take them back.

"No, really, I can manage."

"That's not the point."

"No. J.T., please don't. I can't ask you to do this."

"You didn't ask. I volunteered. And I'm not taking no for an answer. It's one thing when it's gardening, which you obvious love, but I'm not standing by with my hands in my pockets and watch you wrestle with a ton of firewood."

"But—"

"Kate. Kate." He let go of the wheelbarrow with one hand and grasped her chin, bringing his face close to hers. His usual good humor had already reasserted itself, replacing the anger in his eyes. He shook his head and gave her an admonishing look, then followed it up with one of those devastating smiles that temporarily short-circuited her brain.

"Are we going to stand here arguing and wasting time, or are you going to accept my help graciously?"

He leaned closer, blue eyes twinkling, his handsome face

full of friendly mischief. "You're a strong, proud, independent woman, and I admire that. But it's only fair to warn you, Katy, mine, I can be just as stubborn as you any day of the week. I'm Irish, too, you know."

His intimate tone made her heart skip a beat.

The wind tousled his dark hair, and the cold had whipped ruddy color into his tanned face. Already, snowflakes clung to his eyebrows and the ends of his lashes. This close she could smell his scent—soap, shaving cream and maleness mixed with the sharp freshness of the outdoors. The heady combination caused her head to spin.

Kate felt foolish, and she lifted her chin, preparing to stand firm, but the words stuck in her throat as she stared into those sapphire eyes. For all J.T.'s geniality, she could see that he meant what he said: he wasn't going to budge.

Her chin went up another notch. "Very well," she replied with all the haughty dignity she could muster. "There's a wool cap and some work gloves in the pocket of that coat. You'd better put them on."

"'Atta girl." J.T. grinned and winked.

His temper threatened to explode all over again when he hefted the wheelbarrow and started down the path. "Damn, woman, what were you thinking? This thing weighs more than you do."

"I could handle it," she insisted to his broad back as she trailed him down the path. "I've already moved three loads. And I told you, my name is Kate, not Katy!"

As usual, he answered with a chuckle.

They worked steadily for the next three hours, J.T. manning the wheelbarrow and both of them stacking the split logs, but by dusk they had barely cleared half of the pile away from the garage doors.

"We're not going to finish tonight, you know," J.T. said,

when he paused to rotate his arms and stretch his tired back muscles. "Why don't we call it a day?"

"Not yet." Kate glanced at the low-hanging snow clouds as she placed another log on the pile. "We can stack another load or two before it's completely dark."

Maintaining a steady rhythm, she grabbed a chunk of wood, swung around, thunked it down on the stack and twisted for another. She had just picked up a piece when a snowball hit her shoulder and shattered over the side of her face and neck.

Stunned, Kate wiped at the slush and looked at J.T. with her mouth agape.

He grinned and scooped up another handful of snow.

"Why you—" She dropped the wood back into the wheelbarrow with a thunk, then grabbed up a double handful of snow, gave it a couple of quick squeezes and let fly. The missile splatted dead center of J.T.'s chest.

A look of surprise came over his face as he stared down at the splatters of snow, and when he looked up again Kate met his gaze with a smug grin.

"You picked on the wrong girl, city boy. I grew up winging snowballs at Zach."

"Hmm. Nice shot, Katy, mine." Nonchalantly, J.T. looked down and flicked a chunk of snow off the pea jacket. "But now you're gonna have to pay."

Kate let out a yell, they both grabbed for snow...and the war was on.

They pelted each other mercilessly, darting and dodging around the small yard outside the terrace, yelling taunts and dire threats, and whooping and laughing like children. Within minutes they were both covered in snow from head to toe.

Kate dodged one of J.T.'s zingers and yelled an insult.

While he bent to reload, she ducked down behind the end wall of the terrace and packed a giant ball of her own.

"All right, you coward, where'd you go?"

Peeking over the top of the wall, Kate grinned as she watched J.T. turn in a circle. When he was facing the other way she stood up and fired, catching him squarely in the back of the head.

"Aarrghhh!" J.T. slapped at the ice and snow sliding down the back of his neck, and Kate bent double with laughter.

"Oh, now you really are gonna get it." He dropped the snowball he'd just made and started for her. Kate screamed and took off.

He caught up with her around the corner of the house and brought her down with a flying tackle. Twisting with her, he took the weight of the fall, bringing her down on top of him. Before she could scramble free, he rolled her onto her back, and pinned her with his body.

Breathless and giggling helplessly, Kate pushed at his shoulders, but it was like trying to toppled a boulder with your bare hands. Grinning evilly, J.T. scooped up a heaping handful of loose snow, and her eyes widened.

"You...wouldn't!" she gasped between giggles.

"Oh, wouldn't I?"

"No...J.T....don't you dare. Oh, no...please."

The pitiful plea had the desired result. Taking advantage of his hesitation, she shoved his hand upward and buried his face in the snow.

J.T. howled and repaid her in kind, and a wrestling match ensued. They rolled together across the yard in a tangle of arms and legs, shouting and laughing and plastering each other with snow.

When they finally came to a stop at the base of a mountain laurel, J.T. had her pinned beneath him, his legs scissoring hers in place, his hands shackling her wrists deep into the snow on either side of her head. Winded and panting, they laughed helplessly, their vaporized breaths mingling between then.

Then something changed, and their laughter faded.

Awareness shimmered between them like sparkling crystal in the failing light. Everything grew suddenly still, eerily quiet, the only sounds their labored breathing and the thuds of their hearts reverberating in their ears.

Blue eyes gazed into gray with an eloquence that made words unnecessary. All around them, snowflakes floated down in mystic silence.

Caught in the current of their breathing, one flake fluttered between their faces. J.T.'s gaze broke from hers to watch it eddy back and forth, then nestle, light as thistledown, in the corner of Kate's mouth. His gaze flickered to up hers again. Then he lowered his head and lifted the feathery crystal with the tip of his tongue.

A shudder rippled through Kate, and she closed her eyes and moaned. The feel of his warm, wet tongue against her cold skin was the most erotic thing she had ever experienced.

"Kate," he murmured in a raspy voice that wasn't quite steady. Releasing her wrists, he framed her face between his gloved hands. They were coated with snow and ice, but she barely felt the chill as she opened her eyes and looked into the blazing blue of his.

"Kate," he said again as his head began a slow descent. "My beautiful...beautiful...Kate."

Her chest was so tight she could barely breathe, her body so hot she felt as though she was glowing from head to toe, like a fiery ember.

Delicious tingles raced over Kate's skin, and she closed

her eyes in anticipation. When his mouth settled on hers, she sighed and wrapped her arms around him.

She needed this, she thought. Oh, yes, she needed this so much. The warmth, the closeness, the intimate touch of another human being. Of this strong, wonderful, sexy man. It had been so long. So long. Her spirit craved this. Her body yearned for it. Her heart wept for it.

The kiss started out soft, a tender seduction, but passion overtook them and it quickly became hungry and forceful, almost fierce. His mouth rocked over hers, taking, demanding, and she met him, need for need, hunger for hunger. Lips rubbed, tongues swirled and tangled, teeth nipped. Hands roamed and clutched and roamed again.

They lay in the snow, as the weak gray light seeped away.

Kate was on fire. She would not have been surprised to discover that all the snow had melted within a three-foot radius of their entwined bodies.

Need grew to a fever pitch. Just when she thought she would surely die from wanting, J.T. broke off the kiss, raised his head and stared down at her. In the waning light she could barely make out his features, but the blaze in those blue eyes was clearly visible.

"We should go inside," he said in a raspy whisper.

Unable to speak, she could only nod.

In one fluid move, J.T. rolled off her and stood up. The sudden loss of his weight and warmth left her feeling so bereft she almost cried out. Then he grasped her hands and pulled her to her feet.

He dusted the snow off her backside, then put his arm around her shoulders, pulled her tight against his side, and they walked back around to the rear of the house. The snow squeaked and crunched beneath their boots, but neither spoke.

By the time they entered the service porch, Kate's ardor had cooled, and doubt and nerves had set in, along with all manner of self-recriminations.

They paused on the porch to shed their coats, caps, gloves and boots and dust the remaining snow off their clothes. Kate couldn't remember ever feeling so awkward and nervous.

The moment they entered the kitchen she turned to face him with a worried look, her hands unconsciously clasped tight against her midriff. "J.T., I... What happened out there...that is...I should never have let it happen. I'm sorry. It was wrong of me. I'm...I'm just not..."

"You're not ready for an intimate relationship," he finished for her in a low but surprisingly gentle voice.

Kate had expected anger and frustration. Cutting reproach. And she wouldn't have blamed him. She had made no effort to stop what was happening, had, in truth, welcomed it, reveled in it. Any red-blooded male would have interpreted her response as an invitation.

J.T., however, did not appear to be angry. Though his expression was serious, there was only warmth and caring in his eyes.

She wrung her hands and gave him a despairing look. "I'm so sorry, J.T."

"Hey, there's no reason to apologize."

"But—"

Covering the space between them in two long strides, he pulled her into his arms and cradled her close against his chest. "Shh. Shh. It's all right, sweetheart. I'm the one to blame. I knew before I kissed you that you weren't ready for a relationship. I shouldn't have tried to rush you."

Kate was so relieved she let herself relax against him, savoring his solidness, his strength. It felt so good to have someone on whom she could lean, if only for a little while.

Because it did, after a moment she made herself pull away. "You're really not angry?" she asked, looking up at him doubtfully.

"No, I'm not angry." He smiled and smoothed an errant curl back from her temple. "Disappointed. Frustrated as hell. But not angry. But that's okay. When we make love—and trust me, sweetheart, it *will* happen—I want you to be as sure as I am of the rightness of it."

She searched his handsome face, and her heart squeezed at the warmth she saw there. He'd made the statement with such self-assurance, such absolute certainty, that she could almost believe him. Almost.

The familiar glint entered J.T.'s eyes as his smile turned from tender to flirty. He bent and placed a quick kiss on her mouth, then turned her toward the hall door. "Now then, why don't you run upstairs and thaw out under a hot shower, put on something pretty and I'll take you to dinner at the lodge."

"What?" Kate spun back around, her eyes wide with alarm. "Oh, J.T., that's…that's sweet of you, but I couldn't let you do that."

"Why not?"

"I told you—the people in Gold Fever hate me."

"Hate? Come on, isn't that a little strong?"

"Oh, really? Lewis Goodman didn't dump four cords of firewood in the driveway because he's stupid. He did it to strike out at me. And Cletus and his buddies may have been looking for their money, but they knew exactly what they were doing when they destroyed my roses.

"If I was foolish enough to go with you to the lodge, I doubt that they would serve me."

"The hell they won't!" J.T. snarled, and Kate blinked, startled by the suddenly hard menace in his face. "We'll just see about that."

His anger on her behalf warmed her, but she had to make him understand. "No, J.T., listen to me. Even if they would, I'd be afraid to eat the food. The cook would probably lace mine with milk of magnesia, or something equally revolting. But most important, you can't afford to be seen with me socially, not if you want the people in town to keep talking to you. And you need them for the research on your book. That's why you're here, remember."

He looked so guilty at that, she rushed forward and placed her hand on his arm. "Oh, please, J.T., don't feel bad on my account. Believe me, I'm used to getting the cold shoulder in town."

If anything, his frown deepened. "You mean you never have an evening out? Or any social contact with your neighbors? You just sit up here all alone, year after year? That's depressing as hell."

Put so bluntly, she had to agree, though she tried never to dwell on the situation. "It's not so bad, really. I have plenty of company during the tourist season, and by the time it's over I look forward to having the house to myself for a while."

He continued to look doubtful but finally he nodded. "All right, we won't go out. But tonight, I'll cook."

"You?"

"Hey! I'll have you know, I cook a mean burger."

Kate's mouth twitched. "Burger, huh? I should've known."

At the door she turned and studied him.

He arched an eyebrow. "What?"

"I was just wondering... Why are you doing this?"

"What do you mean? Doing what?"

"Being so nice to me. This morning with Sheriff Hunt-singer. Helping me with the firewood. Cooking dinner for me. It seems an awful lot of trouble just to get me in bed.

Especially since I'm quite certain that you could have your pick of women. So why me?''

"I don't want just any woman, Katy. I want you."

"Why?"

"Isn't it obvious? I'm more than just attracted to you. I...have feelings for you. Very strong feelings."

She wanted to believe him. She wanted that very much. But experience had been a harsh teacher. Even though he met her gaze with unflinching directness, there was still that small kernel of doubt she could not overcome. The best reply she could manage was a wan smile and a nod.

She started again to leave, but this time J.T. stopped her. "Katy?"

She cast a wary look over her shoulder. "Yes?"

Leaning against the kitchen counter with his arms crossed over his chest and his usual crooked smile in place, he would have looked the picture of nonchalance had it not been for the way he stared at her.

"One of these days you're going to realize that I'm not Kurt Hattleman."

Chapter Eight

Snowflakes as big as quarters fluttered past the window, drifting silently down to cover everything in a blanket of white. In the warmth of the kitchen, fresh-baked layers of chocolate cake cooled on wire racks. Their heavenly scent mingled with the smell of pine boughs that draped the mantel and the bayberry candles scattered about the house. A cheery fire crackled and popped in the kitchen hearth, and Bing Crosby's rich baritone crooned "White Christmas" on the radio's golden oldies station. From the basement came the sound of intermittent hammering as J.T. made repairs to the basement steps.

Humming along with the radio, Kate whipped a bowlful of double-chocolate frosting, a soft smile curving her mouth.

She couldn't remember when she had felt so content and happy. Perhaps it was foolish of her, but she couldn't seem to help it. She had grown so accustomed to being alone and keeping her distance from people these past four years that she had forgotten how pleasant it could be to have someone to talk to, someone with whom she could share meals, to simply enjoy another person's company.

Pausing, she stared dreamily out the kitchen window, her smile widening a bit. Particularly when that person was J.T. He was not only handsome, he was charming and funny and fun to be around. And he was downright handy.

J.T. had taken it upon himself to do whatever repairs he thought were necessary without bothering to consult her, such as replacing the broken and wobbly steps on the basement stairs, as he was doing today, or replacing a leaky valve on the water heater, or putting new washers in dripping faucets, or unsticking doors.

If she so much as looked as though she might object, he fixed her with his stern "don't you dare" stare. If that failed to stop her, he shut her up by simply planting a mind-blowing kiss on her lips. By the time the sensual caress was over she couldn't have told you her name, let alone objected to anything.

That Irish devil knew it, too, darn him. Whenever one of those kisses ended and he looked into her dazed eyes, his own were always twinkling. He would grin and pat her cheek, then saunter off to do whatever it was he had intended to do in the first place.

After a few such encounters, Kate decided that the prudent thing was to accept defeat and let him work on whatever he wanted. Although, she had to admit, there were times she was tempted to argue, just for the pleasure of letting him stop her.

In the almost eight weeks that J.T. had been there, Kate had learned that his inspiration came in spurts. At times he worked furiously, night and day, like a man possessed. When he ran out of energy or the creative juices dried up—

whichever came first—he would crash, sometimes sleeping around the clock.

During the periods in between the bursts of creative activity, he spent a lot of time in town.

Several evenings a week he hung out at the Miners' Lodge. Somehow, thanks to that glib tongue of his and that irrepressible Irish charm, he'd managed to convince Cletus and his pals that he'd had no choice but to tell the sheriff what he'd seen that night they had dug up Kate's place, and, miraculously, there were no hard feelings over the incident.

J.T. spent hours pouring through the archives of the local weekly newspaper and talking to the people in town.

He also visited the mining museum which was housed in the old jailhouse that had been built in 1875. Technically, the museum was only open during tourist season, but, naturally, J.T. had struck up a friendship with Pete Braddock, who ran the place, and he let J.T. poke through it as often as he liked.

When he was at home and not working on his book he insisted on helping Kate around the house, making repairs, helping with the dishes, shoveling the walkways and the path to the garage, bringing in firewood and building fires.

There was one thing, though, that she would not allow him to tackle.

Kate grinned, remembering the morning he had discovered it was she, not the Gold Fever snowplow driver, who cleared the road that led down the mountain into town.

It hadn't been quite seven in the morning, and she had just gotten into her snow gear and was on her way out the back door when he had entered the kitchen in search of a cup of coffee.

He had obviously just gotten up. His hair had been rumpled, his eyes slumberous, and above the beard stubble that shadowed his jaw his face had still borne crease marks from his pillow.

Barefoot and dressed in old jeans and a hastily pulled-on, wrong-side-out sweatshirt, he looked adorably disheveled, and so darned sexy that for a moment Kate was distracted, and when he asked where she was off to so early in the morning she did not have the presence of mind for an evasion.

"Oh, just out to plow the road," she mumbled absently, staring at him like a love-starved puppy.

"Plow the *road?*" he exploded. He slammed down his coffee mug and glared at her across the room. "You mean *you're* the one I've been hearing out there before dawn every morning after a snow? I thought it was Joe Baxter."

"Joe plows the streets in town. Smithson Mountain is private property." Opening the back door she waved. "See you later."

"Kate, come back here!" he bellowed, but she pretended not to hear.

He caught up with just as she reached the garage and threw open the double doors. The security lights revealed that he had thrown on Zach's old pea jacket and shoved his bare feet into her brother's snow boots, but he hadn't taken the time to lace them. "Kate, I don't want you plowing that road," he gasped. "You go back to the house. I'll do it."

Chuckling, Kate walked into the cavernous old carriage house with J.T. dogging her heels. "Oh, I don't think so."

"Kate, it's still dark out, and there aren't any lights or markings on that road. It's too dangerous."

She climbed up onto the seat of the small snowplow, then looked down at him, still smiling. "Have you ever plowed snow before?"

"No. Of course not. I'm from Houston."

"Uh-huh. That's what I thought. Have you ever even driven a snowplow before? Or a simple tractor?"

"No," he snapped grudgingly.

"Well I have."

"It's still dangerous."

"True. Which is precisely why I'm doing this and not you. J.T., I've been plowing that road since I was fourteen. I know every rock and pothole, every twist and turn. Trust me. I know what I'm doing. I could plow it with my eyes closed. You, on the other hand, would probably go over the side at the first switchback."

She pulled her wool cap farther down over her ears and wrapped her long scarf around her neck and the lower half of her face. After hitting the starter button she flicked on the headlights and the powerful spotlights mounted above her head on the roll bar. "Go on back inside," she shouted over the engine noise. "This won't take long."

Kate chuckled as she placed a cooled cake layer on the cake plate and spread icing over the top. After stacking a second layer on top of the first, she anchored it in place with three toothpicks and scooped up another large dollop of icing.

To give him credit, when she'd returned that morning, and every morning since after plowing, J.T. had not only met her at the door with a steaming mug of coffee, he'd prepared breakfast, as well.

It was only one of many small ways that he pampered her, and she'd be lying if she said she didn't enjoy every minute of it. Being cosseted and looked after, worried over, was a new and novel experience. One to which, she was very much afraid, she could become accustomed to all too easily.

J.T. was attracted to her and he wanted her. Though he

did not try to pressure her into an intimate relationship, he made no effort to hide his desire for her.

He touched her constantly, nibbled on her neck or her fingers whenever he got the chance, looked at her with that predatory gleam in his eyes that sent delicious shivers down her spine, made suggestive comments.

Kate enjoyed his flirting. It had been a long time since she had been the target of those kind of seductive glances, and the feelings they stirred inside her were exciting.

The truth was, she was just as attracted to him as he was to her. And J.T. knew that, as well.

Kate closed her eyes and sighed. No, what she felt was more than mere attraction, she admitted shakily. Exactly what she feared would happen, had: she had fallen in love with the man. She just didn't know what, if anything, she should do about it.

Much as she yearned to make love with J.T., to share that special intimacy that only a man and woman who are truly in love can share, she didn't think she could bear to make another mistake. Kate knew only too well that for a man, wanting and loving were not necessarily the same thing.

And though she felt guilty about it, still lurking in a corner of her mind was that kernel of doubt she couldn't quite dismiss.

J.T. said he cared about her. He acted as though he cared about her. Went through all the right motions, said all the right things.

But then, so had Kurt.

Kate didn't think J.T. was after the money. As far as she could tell, he hadn't known about the swindle before coming to Gold Fever.

Still, she'd been wrong before. Horribly wrong.

Which was why she kept reminding herself that J.T. was

not a permanent part of her life and she would be wise to keep things between them platonic. Come spring, he would be leaving, and she would go back to being alone. She knew she would not survive if she let him take her heart with him.

The telephone rang just as Kate added the third layer to the cake. It was an infrequent enough occurrence in the wintertime that she jumped.

Probably someone calling to book a room for the following season, she thought, wiping her hands on her apron as she went to answer it.

"Alpine Rose Bed-and-Breakfast."

"I'm calling for J.T. Conway," a gruff voice on the other end of the line barked.

Surprise darted through Kate. J.T. had been there almost two months, and this was the first call he'd received. "Certainly. Hold on while I get him."

The ringing of the telephone registered only distantly to J.T. as he hammered in the last nail. He straightened and stood on the new step, jumped on it a few times. Satisfied that it was sturdy, he picked up the toolbox and returned it to the shelf beneath the workbench along the far wall. He had just hung the hammer on the pegboard when the door at the top of the stairs opened.

"J.T., you have a phone call."

Surprise shot through him. Uneasiness followed instantly. Who the devil...? No one except Matt and Maude Ann knew he was there, and when they wanted to talk to him they called his cell phone.

But that was upstairs in his room. Maybe they'd been calling and he hadn't been there to answer. Maybe there was an emergency. Maybe something had happened to one of the kids. Or Matt, or Maudie. Ah, hell, maybe they'd gotten word the adoptions didn't go through.

He beat sawdust off the front of his shirt and jeans and took the stairs two at a time. By the time he reached the top his heart was beating double time. "Who is it?" he asked the instant he stepped into the kitchen.

"He didn't say."

J.T. strode across the kitchen and snatched up the receiver. "Hello. Matt?"

"Hell no. Do I sound like that hard-nosed cop to you?"

J.T. gritted his teeth and raked his free hand through his hair. "Aw, jeez! I don't believe this."

"Thought you could hide from me, did you?" Charlie gloated. J.T. could almost see him, reared back in his chair, grinning around one of his soggy stogies. "You're not the only one who cut their teeth on investigative reporting, you know."

"How did you find me?"

"Boy, by now you ought to have learned that nothing goes on around this newspaper I don't know about."

The clippings! J.T. grimaced, silently cursing himself. He should have known Charlie would see the request on Sunny's weekly activity sheet.

"I read those articles you requested," Charlie said, confirming what J.T. already knew. "From there it was easy to put it all together. So what've you got on this swindle so far?"

"Nothing."

"Dammit, Conway, don't be a sorehead just because I tracked you down. I've known where you were for weeks. I gave you plenty of time to call in, but you didn't. If you have a lead on where that dough is hidden, I want—"

"I told you. There's nothing."

"Yeah, right. You're staying at the B&B with the sister.

Probably romancing her. And you expect me to believe that? I know what kind of effect you have on women.''

Frowning, J.T. glanced at Kate, who was busily icing a cake at the other end of the counter. He turned his back to her and lowered his voice to barely above a whisper. ''I don't care what you believe. Like I told you before, when I'm ready I'll get in touch. Until then, don't call me here again. Got that?''

''Now, wait just a damn minute!''

''I mean it, Charlie. If you don't lay off, all you'll get from me is another copy of my letter—the one that you tore up. Remember?''

''All right. All right,'' Charlie grumbled. ''Don't get your shorts in a wad. But hurry it up, will ya, Conway. The paper hasn't run an article with your byline in two months.''

''Goodbye, Charlie.''

J.T. hung up the wall telephone with a sharp *clunk* but kept his hand on the receiver for several seconds and stared, frowning, into space. Damn, Charlie.

His editor's remarks had left him feeling somehow… unclean.

Dammit, he cared about Kate. Cared, hell. He loved her. He wasn't stringing her along, nor digging for information just to get a story for the *Herald* or material for a novel. He was doing it for her and Zach, as well.

''Is something wrong?''

''What?''

''You didn't seem pleased to hear from whoever that was.''

''Oh. No. No problem there.'' Shaking off the unpleasant sensation Charlie's remarks had brought on, J.T. forced a grin and massaged the back of his neck. ''That was just my editor.''

"Oh, I see."

For the first time since entering the room, J.T. looked around, taking in the warmth and coziness of the scene—Kate with an apron tied over her ankle-length gray wool skirt and wine turtleneck, her glorious hair pulled back and clipped at her nape, busily icing a cake. The delicious smell of chocolate and Christmas in the air. The cheery fire dancing in the hearth, and Mel Tormé's velvety voice crooning "Winter Wonderland" from the radio.

The simpleness, the domesticity of it all, tugged at something deep inside him and filled his chest with a sweet ache. He could live like this, he realized. He wanted this, wanted to share a lifetime of this sort of contentment with this strong, proud and feisty, delicate-looking blond beauty.

All he had to do was convince Kate that she wanted the same.

Going with his feelings, J.T. walked over to stand behind Kate as she finished icing the cake and dropped the spatula into the soapy dishwater. "Mmm, that looks good and smells delicious. How about cutting me a piece?"

"Not on your life. This is for our Christmas dinner tomorrow."

Slipping his arms around her middle, J.T. propped his chin on the top of her head and grinned at her adamant tone.

Kate was determined that Christmas would not be a repeat of Thanksgiving. During the November holiday he'd been so immersed in writing that he hadn't even been aware that it was Thanksgiving. Or that Kate had prepared a special meal, which she had eaten alone in the dining room.

They were going to celebrate Christmas, she had warned him, even if she had to break down his door and drag him by the ear away from his computer.

She had gone all-out, decorating the house from top to

bottom until it looked and smelled like every child's fantasy of Christmas. They had spent an entire afternoon tromping through the woods until she'd found the perfect tree, which he had cut and dragged home. The thing almost touched the twelve-foot plaster ceiling in the parlor. That evening they had decorated the tree together, then had sat on the floor in front of the fire and drank hot chocolate while they admired their handiwork. It was one of the most perfect days of his life, one of those crystal-clear memories that J.T. knew he would retain forever.

Love for the woman in his arms overwhelmed him. Unable to resist, J.T. bent and began to nibble the side of Kate's neck.

"Oh! Now, J.T., stop that," she laughed, hunching her shoulder against the sensual assault. "I'm too busy for this. I have a lot of cooking to do for tomorrow."

"Spoilsport."

She swiped her finger around the edge of the cake plate to pick up a blob of icing, but before she could wash it off under the faucet J.T. grabbed her hand.

She sent him a startled look over her shoulder. "What are you— Oh."

Holding her gaze, he took her finger into his mouth and slowly sucked off the chocolate icing. She gripped the edge of the counter so tight with her other hand that her knuckles whitened.

He felt her tremble, saw the way her mouth formed a soft *O,* heard the helpless little moan that whispered from her throat. The dazed look of arousal on her face sent fire streaking straight to his loins.

He wanted her. Damn, he wanted her. He'd been exercising extreme restraint with her, taking things nice and slow, letting her become accustomed to him, to his presence in her life, to his touch, to the possibility of him as her lover.

The plan was working. She had softened toward him, was comfortable with him now. And he had seen the passion in her eyes when he touched her.

But, sweet heaven, the waiting was killing him.

J.T. was fairly certain that if he pressed he could take her right then, right there. Simply pull her into his arms and hold her tight, kiss her luscious mouth until neither of them could think, and sink with her to the floor.

Tempting as the thought was, however, he knew that neither the time nor the place was right yet. Forcing down the raging desire that racked his body, he removed her finger from his mouth and kissed the back of her hand. "That was delicious," he murmured against her skin before released her.

"Th-thank you."

A blush spread up her neck and face, and she quickly turned back to the sink, but not before he'd noted with a deep sense of satisfaction the tremor in Kate's hands as she plunged them into the dishwater.

Taking mercy on her, and himself, he stepped to one side and leaned his hips back against the counter beside her, legs outstretched and crossed at the ankles, and folded his arms loosely over his chest. "You know, since it's just the two of us, instead of you going to all the trouble to cook a huge meal, why don't I take you out for Christmas?"

"Oh, J.T. that's so sweet of you, but—"

"Yeah. We could drive down to Durango and spend the day. I checked with the weather service. The snow is supposed to end by midnight, and the roads will be plowed by morning."

He saw the a flash of longing in her eyes, but it was quickly squelched. "Thank you for the thought, J.T., but I don't dare leave for the whole day. If I did, Cletus or some of the others would be up here in a flash.''

''They don't have to know we're gone. We'll leave the radio on and the drapes open. You have a timer on the coffeepot. We can hook it up to a lamp in the parlor, just in case we don't get home before dark.''

''I don't know…'' She caught her bottom lip between her teeth.

''C'mon, Kate, it'll be fun. Beside, it'll do you good to get out.'' He ducked his head and waggled his eyebrows at her. ''So whadda ya say? Hmm?''

The day was more than fun: it was heaven.

It started with an exchange of gifts before breakfast on Christmas morning. For days Kate had been itching to open the red foil-wrapped package with her name on it that had mysteriously appeared under the tree, but she contained herself and opened Zach's gifts first.

The packages had arrived only the day before, just an hour or so before he had called to wish her Merry Christmas. In typical brotherly fashion, Zach had sent her a polar-fleece top and a new guest register for the B&B.

She then opened the red foil package, but she did so with such excruciating care that finally J.T. groaned, ''Just tear the damned paper off, will you.''

She laughed and continued her meticulous unwrapping. ''Oh, J.T.,'' she gasped when she finally lifted the lid. ''It's beautiful.'' The box contained an exquisite silk scarf in a misty pattern of cobalt-blue, lavender and Kelly-green swirls. Kate loved it and thanked J.T. profusely. She immediately looped the silk oblong around her neck over her robe and stroked its softness as J.T. tore into her gift to him.

''Oh, Kate!'' He lifted the gift out of the box with something akin to reverence and turned it slowly, his face full of awe.

It was a piece of Western sculpture by a local artist that she'd seen him admire one day when they had gone into town for supplies and the mail. About sixteen inches high, the piece depicted a cowboy on his horse, riding hell-for-leather after a maverick steer.

When J.T. finally looked at her, his eyes gleamed with pleasure. "Kate, this is…" He shook his head and looked back at the sculpture. "I don't know what to say."

"I hope you like it."

"Like it? Sweetheart, I *love* it. It's wonderful." Leaning across the space that separated them, he hooked his hand around her nape and brought her closer for a long, searing kiss. When he raised his head he drew back only inches and looked deep into her eyes. "Thank you, Katy, mine. And merry Christmas."

She blinked in surprise when he withdrew a small flat box from the pocket of his robe and handed it to her. "What is this? You've already given me my present."

"That was just the decoy. In case you were one of those who rattles the boxes or sneaks a peek."

"I would never—" she began, but J.T. cut off her indignant protest with another quick kiss, then grinned.

"Just open it," he murmured.

She did so with her heart pounding. When the velvet jeweler's box emerged, her startled gaze darted to his, but he merely waited, watching her. "Oh! Oh, my!" she exclaimed in a breathless voice when she lifted the lid. "Oh, J.T. it's exquisite."

Nestled against the black velvet lay a dainty, antique necklace made of amethysts set in swirling strands of gold, delicate and lacy as a spiderweb. "But how…? Where…? When did you get this?"

"I found it in Durango, the day I got your flowers. I thought it looked like you. Delicate and beautiful."

"Durango! But you'd been here only a little over a month at that point."

J.T. met her stunned gaze with unblinking directness, his eyes intense. "So? I knew even then what you were coming to mean to me. Now, why don't we put this on you and see how it looks?" He plucked the necklace from the box and moved around behind her.

The delicate web of cool metal settled against her neck and collarbone. Kate's trembling fingertips touched it as she tried to decipher the confusing emotions that roiled inside her.

She wore the necklace with her black turtleneck and long gray skirt for their trip to Durango. They left immediately after showering and eating breakfast. To avoid being seen leaving, Kate lay down in the back seat until they were clear of Gold Fever and climbed into the front once they started up out of the valley.

As the weatherman had promised, the storm had moved east during the night and the sky above the twisting mountain road was a clear, vivid blue. A deep blanket of snow covered everything, sparkling in the sun like a field of diamonds. There didn't seem to be anyone else on the highway, so the snow was still a pristine white, even that which had been piled on the side of the road by the snowplow.

In Durango, they enjoyed a sumptuous buffet dinner at the Strater, a grand old Victorian hotel on Main Street. Afterward, they strolled hand in hand around the quaint Western town, looking in the shop windows and simply enjoying the crisp, sunny day.

Then J.T. took Kate to a movie at the old Gaslight Theater at the end of Main Street. It was the first movie that Kate had been to since she'd left college, and she thoroughly enjoyed sitting in the darkness with her hand in J.T.'s, losing herself in the story unfolding on the screen.

A purple twilight had fallen when they emerged from the theater, but Kate was too happy to be concerned about arriving home after dark.

The mellow happiness lasted almost all the way home.

Savoring the end of a perfect day, they were both quiet. Mozart flowed softly from the CD player. The only other sound was the crunch of the tires on the snow-packed road. They met only two other vehicles as they wound their way back through the snowy mountain passes, making it feel as though she and J.T. were the only two people left in the world.

For most of the trip Kate simply relaxed with her head back against the seat and looked out the window at the eerily beautiful sight of moonlight on the craggy, snow-covered peaks and deep valleys.

They had just crested Turnbow pass and began the descent down the twisting road into the valley when J.T. broke the silence. "There's Gold Fever," he murmured as the lights of the town came into view far below.

"Mmm." Kate smiled dreamily as the sound hummed from her throat. She was feeling too lazy and content to say more.

"You know, I've been thinking," J.T. said casually, bringing the Jeep to a crawl to negotiate a hairpin curve. "Do you have any idea at all what Reverend Sweet might have done with that money?"

The question shattered Kate's contentment like brittle glass. She sat up straight, her body going rigid. Her heart felt as though it were being squeezed by an iron fist.

What a fool she had been to think he was different. She should have known. Turning her head away, she stared blindly out the window and pressed her lips together, fighting the urge to cry. "No. How could I?"

"I thought there might be some clue among his things. I assume when he left town for his bogus meeting with the mining company he left most of his belongings behind. He wouldn't have wanted to arouse suspicion."

"He did, but the FBI went through everything," she replied in a flat voice, but J.T. didn't seem to notice her coolness. "They found nothing. After Bob was convicted and sent to prison, I burned all his things to get them out of the house."

He grimaced. "Too bad. Oh, well, it was just a shot in the dark. If we could locate that money and return it to the investors, you and Zach would no longer be under a cloud of suspicion."

Kate's head snapped around. She stared at him through the darkness. "You mean if you found the money you would give it back?"

"Sure. It isn't my money." He slanted her a glance that appeared to be part surprise and part disappointment when he saw her expression in the dim glow from the dashboard. "Don't tell me you wouldn't?"

At first she was so overwhelmed with emotion the question didn't register. She gazed at him, her heart swelling with elation and pride, and a rush of love so strong it made her chest hurt.

Her prolonged silence deepened J.T.'s scowl. "Aw, c'mon, Kate. Don't tell me you'd keep the money?"

"What? Oh! No, of course I wouldn't. It's just that…I thought you…that is…"

"Oh, I see." He cast another glance her way, but this time his face looked as though it were carved from stone. "You thought I'd take the money and disappear, didn't you? That I was no better than Bob Sweet. Thanks a lot,

Kate.'' He gave a bark of mirthless laughter. "That pretty much tells me what you think of me.''

"No, J.T., I didn't mean that. I—''

"Forget it. It's not important.''

Kate opened her mouth to say more, but he reached over and cranked up the volume on the CD player, making conversation impossible.

In only minutes they arrived at the Alpine Rose. To Kate it seemed like hours. She spent the whole time berating herself.

J.T. was angry—angrier than she had ever seen him, and who could blame him? How could she have doubted him? Lumped him in with Bob Sweet and Kurt?

Over and over these past weeks J.T. had shown himself to be an honorable man, but she had been so filled with bitterness and suspicion she had not been able to fully accept that.

And now she'd hurt him. Insulted him. Somehow she had to put things right.

Even as angry as he was, when he parked the Jeep under the port cochere, J.T. behaved with rigid politeness, assisting her out of the vehicle and unlocking the door for her, then stepping back to let her precede him inside. However, as soon as he closed and locked the door behind them he bade her a curt good-night before she could apologize.

"J.T., wait! Please, I have to talk to you,'' she cried, but he headed for the stairs with a tight jaw and long angry strides.

"J.T.! Please, don't be this way! J.T., wait!''

Catching up with him at the top of the stairs she grabbed his arm before he could storm away to his room. Her eyes pleaded with him. "I'm sorry, J.T. I'm so sorry. I know you're not like Bob Sweet or Kurt. It's just that... well...except for my family, everyone I've ever known and trusted has betrayed me. I guess I've come to expect it."

"Dammit, Kate, I told you I wasn't Kurt Hattleman. I would never lie to you. Never use you. I love you! Haven't you figured that out yet?"

"You...you love me?" Kate stared up at him, her heart swelling with hope and burgeoning happiness.

"Ah, hell." He grimaced when he realized what he'd blurted out. "Look, I didn't mean to say that. Not yet, anyway. The last thing I want is to rush you or scare you, so just forget I said it, okay."

"But I don't want to forget it. Not if you mean it."

J.T. went absolutely still, not quite able to believe he'd heard her right. "What?"

"I know, it's crazy. We haven't known each other long enough, but that doesn't seem to matter, because I do lov—"

Employing his favorite method of shushing her, he swooped like an eagle before she could finish and covered her mouth with his.

As he snatched her into his arms and brought her tight against him, Kate went up on tiptoe and locked her arms around his neck, giving in to the kiss with an eagerness that brought a low growl from J.T.'s throat.

At first touch, the hungry kiss exploded into a red-hot passion that threatened to consume them. Mouths rocked and hands clutched and groped, bodies strained, but still they could not get close enough.

Their breathing grew rough and rapid. Their hearts pounded. Small, desperate sounds of frustration and want escaped them. Emotions and desires that had been building for weeks burst free. Frantic, they strained together, wanting more, much more, but their hunger for each other was so great they were loath to part.

Suddenly J.T. broke off the kiss, drawing a moan of protest from Kate. Breathing heavily, he stared down at her flushed face, at the passion swirling in her eyes, and a hard shudder ripped through him as he fought to hold in check the fierce need raging inside him. "Kate, are you sure? Are you very sure?" he gasped between ragged breaths. "This is your last chance. We either stop now, while I still can, or not at all."

His whole body clenched as he waited for her reply and he watched each nuance of her expression.

Her eyes had a dazed look, and it took a moment for his words to penetrate, a moment that seemed like forever to J.T.

Finally a smile curved her mouth and she reached up and bracketed his face between her palms. "I'm sure. I've never been more sure of anything in my life," she whispered. "Make love to me, J.T."

It was all he needed to hear. J.T. bent and scooped her up, and as Kate looped her arms around his neck he fastened his mouth to hers and carried her down the hall toward her room, his long strides eating up the distance.

The kiss continued even as he opened her door and strode with her across the oriental carpet to her four-poster bed. There he paused before setting her down. "I do love you, Kate. Believe that."

"Oh, J.T." Her chin quivered as emotion overwhelmed her. Threading the fingers of both hands through his hair, she gave him a wobbly smile.

The mattress gave beneath his bent knee as their mouths fused again. Then they were stretched out on the bed together, legs entwined, hands exploring in constant, restless motion.

As they kissed, Kate snatched his shirttails from the waistband of his slacks, slipped her hands underneath and frantically ran her palms over his back, her fingers digging into the firm flesh, her nails lightly scoring. When her fingertip danced down his spine and delved beneath the waistband of his slacks, J.T. could stand no more.

He sat up, pulling her to a sitting position, too. In one desperate motion he grabbed the hem of her sweater and snatched it off over her head.

The garment and the delicate, antique necklace went flying as he eased her back down onto the pillow and pressed his face to the swell of pale flesh above her lacy bra. He strung kisses over the satiny softness, reveling in the low moans that purred from Kate's throat, loving the feel of her, the scent of her.

With the tip of his tongue, J.T. traced a line of fire along the top edge of the black lace.

"Oh, J.T." Kate's spine arched, and she clutched both fists in his hair, urging him closer, her head thrashing from side to side on the pillow.

When he reached the shadowy cleft between her breasts, his tongued plunged, but instead of smooth warm flesh, he encountered something hard-edged and cool hanging from the fine chain around her neck.

"Mmm, what's this?" He raised his head lazily to examine the object, then froze and stared down in horror at the jagged piece of silver that lay nestled between her breasts.

The size and shape exactly matched the missing section of the medallion. If put together with the pieces he and Matt wore, the three would form a whole.

Chapter Nine

"No. *No!*" J.T. stared in horror at the medallion piece lying against Kate's creamy skin and felt a gorge rise in his throat.

"J.T.? Darling, what is it? What's wrong?" Concern marked Kate's face. She raised her hand and touched his cheek, and he jerked back as though he'd been scalded.

Scrambling to his knees, he scooted back until they were no longer touching.

His gaze shot to Kate's face, then back at the medallion piece, then to Kate's face again, panic and revulsion roiling through him. Distantly he registered the confusion in her eyes, the rising hurt, but he couldn't think beyond the nightmare that was staring him in the face.

His head moved from side to side. "This isn't right...I can't...we can't... Oh, God!"

"J.T., what is it? Are you ill?"

Kate sat up, and J.T. shot off the bed.

He retreated to the middle of the room, and stood shaking his head and raking his hands through his hair. He stared at Kate and fought to control the bubble of hysteria that was swelling in his chest.

He wanted to go to her, to hold her close and wipe away that stricken look, but he couldn't. He didn't dare touch her. Not now. Not ever again.

The thought brought a moan from deep in his soul. He closed his eyes and pressed the heels of both hands against his temples. Oh, Lord, this couldn't be happening!

"J.T., please. You're scaring me. Why are you acting this way?"

His eyes popped open. He looked at Kate's pleading face, her kiss-swollen lips, the flush of passion still on her face, and felt his stomach turn over. Shaking his head slowly, he backed away. "I—I'm sorry, Kate...I...this isn't...we can't... I've got to get out of here. I'm sorry. I'm so sorry!"

"J.T., wait! Where are you going?" Kate cried, but he was already out the door.

Stunned, she sat in the middle of the bed with her arms crossed over her breasts and listened to his footsteps pounding away down the hall. Seconds later his door slammed.

Then there was only silence.

In the shortest possible space of time Kate had gone from being deliriously happy and aroused to cold, bereft and alone. For a moment she was too stupefied to feel anything but shock. She looked around, dazed and bewildered, unable to move.

Slowly, however, one truth seeped through her confusion—one inescapable, undeniable, humiliating truth. J.T. had rejected her.

For whatever reason he obviously had changed his mind and no longer wanted her.

Red-hot pain expanded inside her like shock waves radiating out from an explosion. Kate held herself tighter and swore she would not cry. She would *not.*

But not even her fierce pride could hold the pain at bay. A dry sob shook her whole body, then another and another.

She fought for control, but despite all her effort her chin began to quiver, and though she tried to press her lips together, they wobbled uncontrollably. Scalding tears soon filled her eyes. When they began to spill over she surrendered with a wail of pain and threw herself facedown on the pillow and sobbed.

"My sister. Kate is my sister! Mine and Matt's triplet sister!"

Every time J.T. said the words, the pain cut deeper, but he forced himself to repeat them over and over, hoping the agony would help to sear the truth into his brain. Because, God help him, he didn't want it to be true.

J.T. paced back and forth across his room, raking his hands through his hair, rubbing the back of is neck, cursing under his breath. Dammit! He needed to hit something. Hard.

He halted in the middle of the floor, pressed the heels of his hands against his eye sockets and made a low sound of pain. What a fool he'd been. What an utter fool! Why hadn't it occurred to him that Kate, not Zach, might be his sibling?

At the very least, he should have realized that if Zach was adopted, then Kate probably was also.

What a mess. Which just shows what happens when you think with your heart instead of you head, he thought viciously.

He and Matt had known there was a possibility their sibling might be female. It was fairly common for fraternal triplets to be made up of both sexes, and he and Matt were obviously fraternal. They bore no more resemblance to each other than most brothers, and had even less in common.

But because of that damned message on the Internet, he assumed his missing sibling was another brother. Plus the talk he'd heard in town and a few remarks that Kate had made had led him to believe that she was the Mahoneys' natural child.

Or maybe that was simply what he'd wanted to believe.

Exhausted, mentally and emotionally, J.T. gave up pacing and flopped down across the bed on his back. He focused on the ceiling without seeing the fancy plasterwork or the painted cupids. Absently he rubbed his hand over his chest. His heart felt as though it had been clubbed into a bloody pulp.

Dear Lord, how was he going to live without Kate? Worse, how could he bear to accept her as his sister? See her now and then and never be able to touch her, pretend that his feelings for her were brotherly.

And as horrible as J.T.'s pain was, he knew that Kate's had to be just as bad, maybe worse. She, after all, had no idea why he had walked out.

And he had no idea how he was going to explain it to her. What could he say that wouldn't shock and repulse her?

She probably had no idea that she was one of a set of triplets. She might not even know she was adopted, for Pete's sake. It was unusual these days for adoptive parents to withhold that information, but it still happened.

In addition, he dreaded Kate's reaction when she realized he'd deceived her. She was an intelligent woman. She was sure to put two and two together and figure out that he'd come there looking for his sibling. The odds that he had just happened to choose this particular town and this particular B&B were just too astronomical. Even if she believed in fate, that was stretching it a bit.

He had to find a delicate way to tell her the truth. Until he knew how best to handle the situation—hell, until he could come to grips with it himself—he wasn't going to say anything.

She would probably hate him for it. She probably hated him already, but it couldn't be helped.

Actually, it was probably for the best if she did, he thought, rubbing his chest again. Hate would be a whole lot easier to take than this agony. He felt as though someone had driven a stake through his heart.

The next morning Kate had barely entered the kitchen when she heard J.T. leave the house through the side door and drive away in his Jeep.

Just as well, she told herself as she stoically ground coffee beans and started the pot brewing. She wasn't ready to face J.T. just yet. She still felt too fragile, too wounded. Too vulnerable. After that marathon crying jag, she looked, and felt, like hell.

One glance at her puffy face and red-rimmed eyes and J.T. would know that she'd spent half the night crying. She couldn't tolerate his pity. That would be the ultimate insult.

She made herself a piece of toast and poured a cup of coffee, but when she sat down to eat she merely picked at the bread and stared off into space. Over and over during the night she'd asked herself what had gone wrong. Had she done or said something to repulse him?

She'd played the scene over in her mind at least a dozen times, but she was no closer to figuring it all out than she'd been the night before. The only thing that was clear was that J.T. no longer wanted her.

No matter the cause, or how much it hurt, she had no choice but to accept that.

J.T. did not return to the Alpine Rose until late that night. Nor did Kate catch so much as a glimpse of him for almost two weeks. Each morning he left early and did not return until late, long past the time she usually retired for the night.

A couple of times when Kate went into town to pick up her mail, she saw his car—once parked in front of the newspaper office and once in front of the Miners' Lodge, but there was no sign of him around.

Had she not cleaned his room daily she might have thought he'd moved out, but his things were still there, and there were always soiled towels in his bathroom and other small signs of his occupancy.

Kate spent New Year's Eve alone watching an old black-and-white Clark Gable movie on television. On New Year's Day she cooked a ham and the traditional pot of black-eyed peas for luck, but she ate the meal alone. After that she dragged out a thousand-piece jigsaw puzzle—one of her favorite winter pastimes—but she was too agitated and tense to settle, and after only a short while she put it away again. The rest of the day was spent prowling the house, looking for something to do.

As the days passed, Kate's reaction to what had happened between her and J.T. underwent a gradual change. After days of self-doubt and assuming she was to blame, her pride asserted itself once again, and she adamantly refused to accept that.

She had gone over and over that scene in her mind, and by heaven, she had done nothing wrong. Nothing.

Kate began to wonder if the whole thing hadn't been deliberate on J.T.'s part. Maybe he was just a trophy hunter, one of those vile men who liked to prove he could have any woman he wanted. Maybe he got his jollies by humiliating women. Or maybe he was one of those who enjoyed the chase more than the actually lovemaking.

Whatever his reason for doing what he'd done, by the second week in January, Kate's humiliation had turned to simmering anger. Though she had been glad of the reprieve in the beginning, she was now heartily sick of J.T.'s disappearing act.

Whether he liked it or not, they were going to talk about what had happened and clear the air.

That evening Kate settled in the parlor with a book and a cup of coffee, determined that no matter how long it took, she would wait up for J.T. and waylay him before he had a chance to disappear into his room.

She tried to concentrate on the book, but she was so keyed-up and alert for the least sound of his return that she found herself reading the same passages over and over and still not retaining a word.

By midnight Kate had consumed a whole pot of coffee and there was still no sign of J.T. In desperation she turned on the television.

The next thing she knew she awoke with a start, shivering with cold. It was a little past two in the morning, the fire in the fireplace had burned out, snowy lines filled the television screen and static came from the speakers.

J.T.! Kate bolted out of the chair, switched off the TV and hurried down the hallway. ''Oh, no,'' she groaned when a quick check out of the side door revealed his Jeep in the port cochere.

Kate considered storming up the stairs and banging on his door until he answered it, but she discarded that idea almost immediately. When she confronted him she wanted to do it calmly and with dignity.

Trudging up the stairs to bed, she tried to come up with a way to force him to talk to her, but she was too weary to think. Feeling absurdly like Scarlett O'Hara, Kate told herself she'd worry about that tomorrow and collapsed into bed.

The next morning Mother Nature came to Kate's aid.

She awoke at her usual time, about an hour before dawn. She felt wooden-headed and achy from too little rest but knew she would not be able to go back to sleep: her internal clock had been set years ago.

Climbing out of bed, Kate lifted her arms above her head and stretched, then, as she did every morning in winter, she padded over to the window and peeked out to check the weather.

When she pulled back the curtain, her eyes widened. Beyond the panes the world had been reduced to a swirling maelstrom of white. The blizzard that had been predicted on the TV weather report the previous evening had roared in with a vengeance.

A slow, self-satisfied grin curved Kate's mouth. J.T. wasn't going anywhere for several days.

Kate was waiting when J.T. came downstairs. She'd propped the kitchen door open, and when he passed by, heading for the side exit, she walked over and stood in the doorway and watched him.

Blowing snow hit him in the face when he opened the door. He halted abruptly and stared. Even beneath the shelter of the port cochere the blizzard winds whipped the snow into a frenzy.

"Wherever you were heading, forget it. You won't make it to the road in that."

J.T. whipped around. "Kate! I, uh…I didn't see you there."

"Yes. I can see that." He stood with his hand still gripping the knob of the open door, looking uncomfortable, and she could swear he had paled when he saw her. "The road into town is impassable. Why don't you just come in the kitchen and have some coffee."

"Impassable? You didn't plow it this morning? Look, if you're too busy I'll be happy to do it for you."

"J.T., besides being dangerous, it's pointless to plow in a heavy storm like this." She nodded toward the open doorway. "In case you haven't noticed, we're in a white-out. Visibility is so poor I wouldn't be able to *find* the road, much less plow it. It would be suicide to try. Even if I could plow without going over the side, by the time I reached the bottom, the road would be covered over again."

"But…I need to go to town."

"I did warn you about winter in the high country, remember? Now, would you mind closing the door before we freeze?"

"Oh. Sorry." He did as she asked, then turned with a feeble attempt at a smile. "Well, I guess I'll go back to my room and get some work d—"

"J.T., we need to talk."

"Talk? You mean…now?"

This time there was no doubt: he definitely paled.

"Yes, now."

"I'm, uh…I'm kinda busy, Kate. Can't it wait?"

"I've been waiting for over two weeks. I think that's more than enough." She fixed him with a level look. "You owe me an explanation, J.T."

Looking as though he would rather be anyplace but there, he grimaced and turned his head to the side to stare down the hall. Finally he sighed and looked back at her. "All right. I guess it's time to get this over with."

Kate would have felt better about the whole thing if he hadn't looked as though he were going to his own execution, but she wasn't about to back out now. Turning, she led the way into the kitchen. While J.T. shed his coat and hung it on the back of a chair, she poured two mugs of coffee.

"Have a seat," she offered, placing the drinks on the table.

"If you don't mind, I'd rather say what I have to say standing up."

Oh, dear. Was it that awful? Kate watched him pace, noted the agitated way he kept raking his hand through his dark hair, and she felt the knot of sick dread in her stomach tighten. She took a sip of coffee, wrapped her cold hands around the mug to keep them from shaking and plunged in.

"Why did you do it, J.T.? Why did you leave me like that? You'd been pursuing me almost from the day you arrived, then, just as we were finally about to make love, you ran out. Do you have any idea how much that hurt? How humiliated I felt?"

"I'm sorry. I'm so sorry, Kate. Believe me, the last thing I wanted to do was hurt you."

"Then why did you do it?"

His jerky steps carried him to the back door. He stared out through the glass as though looking for an avenue of escape. "I didn't have a choice. I had to."

"*Had* to? Why?"

J.T. tipped his head back and looked up at the ceiling, his face contorted with what looked like pain. Finally he turned to face her fully, and Kate almost cried out at the living hell in his eyes.

"I couldn't make love to you, Kate, because...because you're my sister."

Kate goggled at him, speechless. She couldn't have been more shocked if he had confessed to being a murderer.

The absurdity of it was too much. She simply couldn't help herself. She burst out laughing.

For over two weeks J.T. had agonized over telling Kate the truth. He'd imagined dozens of scenarios and ways she might react. Laughter wasn't one of them.

Yet there she sat, doubled over in gales of laughter. She laughed so hard and so long she lost her breath and nearly choked, and J.T. began to feel affronted.

"This is *funny* to you?"

"N-not...fu-fu-funny. Just...ri-ridiculous," she sputtered in between helpless peals.

"Dammit, Kate, will you stop that laughing! I'm serious. You and I are brother and sister."

Shaking her head, she wiped her eyes with her fingertips and struggled to contain her mirth. "Not unless my parents had a son they never told me about," she choked out. "And I have to tell you, that doesn't seem likely."

"You don't understand. I have proof."

"Proof? Oh, J.T., that's impossible," she insisted, trying without much success to stop her lips from twitching.

"No, listen to me. You, me and our brother, Matt Dolan, we're triplets. Our mother gave us up for adoption when we were two years old. She required only one thing of our adoptive parents, and that was they we were always to wear these."

Reaching into the neck of his shirt, he pulled out the silver chain that held his medallion piece and dangled it for her to see. "She gave us each one. When you put the three pieces together they form a whole medallion. That's how Matt and I learned we were brothers. We discovered that we wore similar pie-shaped fragments that fit together perfectly. When I saw the piece you wear, I knew you were our missing sister.''

"Ah, I see. When we were in bed, about to make love, you saw my medallion.''

J.T.'s stomach roiled at the appalling memory of what they had almost done. "Yes.''

"I see. No wonder you turned that sickly shade of green and ran out.''

Frowning, J.T. watched her, waiting for the shock and horror to hit her, but to his amazement her lips began to twitch again, and a sound suspiciously like a chuckle bubbled up. Then another, and another. When she could no longer hold back, more gales of laughter rolled from her throat.

"Dammit, Kate! What's the matter with you?''

"I'm sor-ry. I'm sorry, I ca-can't help it.''

"Well, I'm glad you're enjoying this. Personally, I feel like a gutted fish.''

"Oh, J.T.'' Instantly contrite, Kate jumped up and put her hand on his arm. "I didn't mean it that way. It's just that this whole thing is a silly mistake. I'm not your sister, J.T. For starters I'm not adopted.''

"But your medallion piece—''

"Is a copy.''

He froze.

"A copy?'' he repeated weakly.

"Yes, a copy. Look, I'll show you.'' She reached into the neckline of her sweater and fished out the piece of silver. "Your piece has some sort of symbol on one side and fragments of writing on the other, right?'' At his nod, she held out her own. "Mine doesn't. See?''

His knees gave way, and he sank down onto the chair she had just vacated.

Immediately Kate knelt beside him and took his hands in hers. "J.T., listen to me. The real medallion piece belongs to my brother. I told you how close we are. We have been from the day I was born.

"You see, after ten years of marriage produced no children, my parents adopted Zach, but as often happens, three years later they had me. From the moment they brought me home from the hospital Zach was the proudest, best big brother any girl could have, and as a child I idolized him. I still do.

"Naturally, when I was old enough I was told all about the adoption, how my parents had chosen Zach to be their son, and about the medallion fragment that his birth mother had asked that he always wear.

"As a kid I was fascinated by that piece of silver and the mystery behind it. To tell the truth, I was envious. I wanted one of my own. I guess I thought having it made Zach special.

"I was thirteen when he left for college, and it broke my heart to lose him. To console me, he had a copy of his medallion made for me. He told me that as long as we both wore them, the bond between us would never be broken, no matter how many miles separated us."

Her mouth quirked in a self-conscious half smile. "As an adult, I know it was just a gesture to ease the transition for me. That's the kind of brother Zach is. But it still gives me comfort. I wear it all the time, the same as he wears his."

Not yet allowing himself to fully accept what he wanted so badly to be true, J.T. eyed her cautiously. "Then you're saying...you're not my sister?"

"That's right." Kate's lips twitched again, but he was too relieved to care. "I am most definitely not your sister."

"Thank God." J.T.'s shoulders slumped as his breath rushed out in a long gust.

"However," Kate added, drawing his attention again. "Apparently Zach is your brother."

"Yeah, apparently so. And I'm sure I'm going to be really happy about that later, but right now all I can think about is how wonderful it feels to know that I don't have to let you go."

Freeing one of his hands, he cupped her cheek. "Ah, Katy, I know I hurt you, but believe me, these last two weeks I've suffered pure living hell thinking you were my sister." He shook his head, his adoring gaze wandering over her face, touching each feature. "Because, no matter how many times I told myself it was wrong, I couldn't stop loving you."

"Oh, J.T. I love you, too." she whispered, giving him a melting look. She cupped her hand over his and nuzzled her cheek more firmly against his palm. Her misty eyes glinted like liquid silver, and her smile wobbled. "I've been so miserable. I thought you didn't want me anymore."

"Didn't *want* you?" He pulled her up and into his lap, looped his arms around her hips and looked deep into her eyes. "That will never happen," he declared fiercely. "I'll still want you when I'm ninety."

"Oh, J.T." His name came out on a sigh, and her eyes fluttered shut as their lips met in a long, smoldering kiss.

Kate's heart soared. Joy overwhelmed her, filling her being until every cell in her body tingled. After the past two weeks of misery and heartache, she never expected to be in J.T.'s arms again, to kiss him again, to experience the pleasure of his touch.

And the pleasure was exquisite.

She went limp in his arms, melting into the kiss with an abandon she had never dared before, holding nothing back.

Clutching his hair with both hands, she gave herself up to the moment, luxuriated in the voluptuousness of it.

When at last their lips parted, J.T. strung a line of nibbling kisses over her cheek, her chin, the tender underside of her jaw. Eyes closed, Kate sighed and let her head loll back to give him better access to her neck.

As his lips explored that long, graceful arch, one by one, he opened the buttons on her shirt.

The draft of cooler air against her heated skin brought a flash of sanity. Even so, as J.T. dipped his head to nuzzle the soft swells of flesh above her bra, her thoughts threatened to scatter, and she had to struggle to focus.

"J.T....I...we..."

"Mmm?"

A low moan purred from Kate's throat as the tip of his tongue drew a moist line along the lacy edge of her bra. A delicious shiver followed, and her fingers dug into his shoulders when he delved into the cleft between her breasts.

"We're in the kitchen," she gasped. "Sit-sitting on...a chair."

At first she thought he wasn't listening, but then he slowly raised his head. His face was flushed, his hair disheveled, his eyes hot and slightly out of focus. Nevertheless he looked around, and after a moment he smiled and nodded. "So we are."

"Oh! What're you doing?" she squeaked when, in one fluid motion, he rose with her in his arms and started toward the door.

"I'm taking you upstairs to bed. You're right. While I have no problem with being innovative or adventurous, I want our first time together to be in a comfortable bed. Besides, I'd like to finish what we started. We're going to take up where we left off."

"Ah, I see. Well that's fine with me, but I *can* walk, you

know,'' she said, smiling seductively as he swept up the stairs, carrying her as though she weighed no more than a down pillow.

''Uh-uh. Not on your life. This time I'm not letting you go until I've had my way with you, woman.''

''Ohhh. I do love a masterful man,'' she purred. She traced the swirls in his ear with her forefinger and had the pleasure of feeling him shudder and almost stumble.

''You're gonna pay for that, woman,'' he growled, and strode purposefully down the second-floor hallway and shouldered open the door to her room.

J.T. crossed the room to her four-poster, and without any hesitation or hint of what he intended, he tossed her up in the air.

Kate screamed as she felt herself falling through space, but the sound cut off as her back hit the mattress and she bounced. ''Gotcha, now,'' he crowed, pouncing on top of her before the second bounce was over.

''J.T., you devil!'' They rolled together across the bed in a tangle of arms and legs. ''Fiend!'' Kate cried, giggling helplessly and slapping at his busy fingers, which were already working on the snap on her jeans. ''Sex maniac!''

J.T. scrambled to his knees. ''Damned right!'' he responded gleefully as he peeled off her jeans and tossed them over his shoulder.

''Well there's no game that two can't play,'' she gasped, climbing to her knees, as well, and going to work on his jeans.

In record time, amid much tugging and wrestling and laughter and occasional pauses to kiss and caress, they were both naked. Gasping for breath and still chuckling, they fell together onto the pillows. Stretching out beside Kate, J.T. hooked his leg over hers to anchor her in place.

Then their gazes met and locked, and the time for laughter ended.

They went absolutely still, staring into each other's eyes, their hearts pounding in the thick silence that suddenly surrounded them.

"Kate," J.T. whispered. His hand trembled ever so slightly as he touched her cheek, and the look of awe and love in his eyes made Kate's heart tremble. "Ah, Katy, mine, I do love you so."

And then he kissed her with such exquisite tenderness she thought surely she would shatter. She wrapped her arms around him and pulled him closer, running her palms over the muscles that banded his broad back and shoulders as hot tears seeped from the corners of her eyes and dripped into the hair at her temples.

Here was the one, perfect love she had been waiting for all of her life. Joyous, intense, all consuming. And completely unconditional.

If she ever had any doubts about the depth of J.T.'s feelings for her, he banished them in the moments that followed. With excruciating tenderness, he explored every inch of her, worshiping her with his eyes, his hands, his lips.

He lavished attention on her breasts, kissing and nuzzling them, laving the rosy nipples into aching pebbles with his tongue, nipping and suckling them until she writhed and burned with need. Arching her back, Kate clutched his shoulders, her head thrashing from side to side on the pillow. "Please, J.T. Oh, please," she sobbed.

"Oh, no. Not yet, sweetheart. I've been waiting for this for weeks. We're not going to rush."

Ignoring her pleas, he continued his silent adoration. Taking his time, J.T. touched, tasted and kissed every inch of her, from her hairline to her toes. He explored her abdomen, her ribs, her tender underarms and the backs of her knees, all the while inhaling her scent deep into his lungs, as though imprinting the very essence of her on his psyche.

Kate tried to do some exploring of her own, but he wasn't through with her yet. "Relax, sweetheart," he murmured, and he rolled her over and started the process again. In the end she was so weak with desire all she could do was surrender and let herself be swept along on the delicious tide of passion and pleasure.

J.T. kissed her nape, her shoulders, her shoulder blades. He trailed his fingers down the shallow trench that marked her spine, lingering over each tiny knob. He kneaded and nipped the rounded flesh of her bottom, the backs of her thighs. He kissed her ankles, the soles of her feet and each individual toe.

Just when she thought she would go mad, he rolled her to her back once again and worked his way back up her body, paying homage all along the way with murmured words of praise and lingering kisses.

Then at last he was there, braced above her, kissing her mouth again, this time with a hungry demand that she answered eagerly, instinctively parting her thighs. He shifted into position and entered her with a slow, smooth stroke that drew a moan of pleasure from the core of her being.

Outside the windowpanes the blizzard raged in swirls of icy white. Inside all was warm and cozy. A cheery fire burned in the fireplace, illuminating the room with a soft glow and painting the entwined couple's bodies golden as they moved together in the age-old rhythm.

For a time the sounds of rustling sheets, long, pleasured sighs and moans and murmured endearments whispered through the stillness as they loved each other. Then their breathing grew more rapid, their moans more desperate until finally their hoarse cries rang out.

Then a hush fell, and the only sounds in the room were the rasp of labored breathing, the crackle of the fire, wind howling around the eaves, and the erratic screech and thump of a bare tree branch scraping a windowpane.

Chapter Ten

Replete, Kate lay in J.T.'s embrace, her arm draped across his chest and one leg hooked over his. With a contented sigh, she snuggled her cheek more comfortably on his shoulder, wound a curl of his chest hair around her forefinger—and yanked.

"*Ow!*" He jerked and grabbed her wrist. "What was *that* for?"

"For deceiving me." She tipped her head back so she could look into his eyes. Several pieces of hair had come loose from her French braid, and the long, curling locks floated around her face, giving her the look of a wanton angel. "I don't know how you knew where to look, but I don't believe for a moment that coming here was just a lucky stroke of fate. I'm not that dumb or that naive. You came here looking for Zach, didn't you?"

He winced. "Not entirely. I am a writer. And I am writing a book set in this area."

Two books, he amended silently, but he thought it wise to keep that to himself, at least for now. There was no point in telling Kate about the second one until he finished it. *If* he finished it. At this point that was by no means a certainty.

In the beginning the story had gone along great, but he was now totally blocked. What he needed was a satisfying resolution, not the limbo the story was in real life.

What he *really* needed was to find that money and prove that Kate and Zach had nothing to do with Bob Sweet's scam.

"As for Zach, I admit that I wanted to find out if he was my brother, but I didn't know when I came here if he was or not. I was just following up a lead I'd gotten." He explained about the message he'd posted on the Internet bulletin board and the flood of responses it had brought, and how the one about Zach had been the most promising.

"So, you didn't know about the swindle and the missing money before you came here?"

"Not exactly."

Her eyes became mere slits. "What does that mean?"

"The message hinted that Zach was under suspicion in a criminal investigation, but didn't give specifics. Here, I'll let you read it."

Releasing Kate, he rolled to the side of the bed and groped for his pants, which lay in a heap on the floor. He fished his wallet out of the back pocket, removed the paper and handed it to her. "This is all I had to go on. It's not much, but I figured since I needed to do research, anyway, I could check out Zach while I was here."

Sitting up, Kate modestly pulled the top sheet up over her breasts, anchored it under her arms, and unfolded the paper. Grinning, J.T. leaned back against the pillows with his fingers laced behind his head and enjoyed the view from behind.

"There's no name on this."

"Yeah, I know. My guess is it was sent by someone local. Probably someone hoping to get the whole thing stirred up again."

When she finished reading, Kate looked at him over her shoulder. Her eyes had softened and a smile curved her mouth. "You really didn't know about the money."

"No, but I'll tell you, that message gave me a few uneasy moments. The idea of a brother of mine being involved in a crime didn't sit well."

"No, I don't imagine it did." She studied him in silence, her gray eyes direct and serious. "And how do you feel now?"

"Now?" He gave her a smoldering look and trailed his forefinger down her spine, all the way to the shadowy cleft at its base. Her delicate shiver brought a slow smile to his lips. "Now I know you and love you, and I know damned well that neither you nor Zach had anything to do with Bob Sweet's scheme."

"Oh, J.T."

Modesty forgotten, Kate dropped the sheet, flung herself at his chest and twined her arms so tight around his neck she nearly choked him. The feel of her soft breasts pressed against his chest made him catch his breath.

"Thank you, my darling. You have no idea how much it means to me to hear you say that." When she drew back her smile was wobbly, her eyes swimming with emotion. "It's been so long since anyone has believed in Zach and me."

"That's all changed now," J.T. vowed. Cupping his hand against her cheek, he looked deep into her eyes. "I'll always be here for you, sweetheart. You can count on it."

She settled against him again and nuzzled her cheek against his chest, sighing as J.T. absently ran his fingers up and down her arm from her shoulder to her wrist and back.

"How do you think Zach is going to react when we tell him?" he asked after a while.

"With a go-to-hell stare and stony silence."

"Great. Another hard-nose like Matt. Just what I need."

Kate chuckled. "He's not that, exactly. Zach is just intense and private. He doesn't allow many people to get close to him. Even as a boy he was the strong, silent type, and since the scandal he's turned into even more of a loner. Now he's also suspicious and slow to trust."

"That's understandable, given what's happened to the two of you. But, whether Zach likes it or not, he has two brothers, and he needs to know that. Maybe he won't be interested in developing any family ties with Matt and me, but one way or the other, the three of us need to make contact. If for no other reason than to learn what's etched on the medallion. Matt and I hope that it will help clear up some questions about our mother and perhaps our family history, as well. Which is why I think you and I should go to wherever Zach is and break the news to him."

"Both of us?"

J.T. grinned and gave her arm a squeeze. "Yeah. He'll probably take the news better coming from you. And I figure, if you're there, he's less liable to punch my lights out when he finds out how things are between us."

"Coward," she teased.

"Damned straight." J.T. rubbed the spot on his ribs where she'd poked him, then he lifted her hand and nibbled the end of her fingers, watching with satisfaction as her gaze went slightly out of focus and her breathing became choppy. "I'm a lover, not a fighter," he murmured in a seductive voice.

"Mmm, you are that. But I wouldn't count on my presence saving you from Zach if I were you," she teased. "Where his little sister is concerned, he's very protective."

"Oh terrific. I'm going to track down my long-lost brother so he can take a swing at me."

"Actually, you don't have to go anywhere. Zach will be coming here in a few weeks. He always tries to make it home for his birthday."

"February sixth, right? He'll be thirty-five."

"How did you— Oh! Of course! It's your birthday, too."

"Yeah. And Matt's."

"The other brother. Tell me about him."

J.T. made a sound something between a snort and a chuckle and stared into the distance, absently stroking Kate's arm. "We have the same build and are the same height, but he has black hair and blue eyes. He's tough as nails, but to his credit, he's madly in love with his wife, Maude Ann.

"They married just three months ago. She's a psychiatrist who runs a foster home for abused and neglected children. Matt fell in love with the whole brood, and at his insistence they've filed to adopt the five kids who are living there now."

"He sounds like a wonderful man."

"Yeah, I guess he is…in his own way. He's a bit crusty and abrupt, but he's okay.

"Right after graduating from college Matt joined the Houston Police Department and quickly worked his way up to detective. Then, a few months ago, he got shot in the line of duty. Six months earlier he'd been wounded in the same leg. He recovered fully that time, but the last shooting did some major damage and left him with a permanent limp. After almost thirteen years on the force he had to retire.''

"How awful for him.''

"Yeah, I thought so, too, at first, but he seems to have adjusted. He enjoys helping Maude Ann operate the foster home, and he's nuts about those kids.''

"Did you search for Matt, too, the way you did for Zach? Or did he find you?''

"Neither. We discovered we were brothers purely by accident. Matt and I had known each other for over eleven years, but we had no idea we were related. For that matter, neither of us had any idea we had siblings.''

"You were friends? How wonderful.''

"Whoa, wait a minute. I said we knew each other. We weren't exactly what you'd call friends.''

Kate looked horrified. "You didn't *like* each other?''

J.T. grimaced and groped for an explanation. "We weren't enemies. To tell the truth, I've always liked and admired Matt. He's tough, but he's as straight and honest as they come, and he was one helluva cop. But he and I have always been...I guess you'd call it friendly adversaries.

"A few months ago we accidentally discovered that we both wore similar pieces of silver on chains around our necks. When we put them together they fit like pieces of a puzzle and formed two-thirds of a medallion. The missing third told us we had another sibling somewhere.

"The writing on the back and the symbol on the front of each piece matched up exactly—but two thirds wasn't enough to decipher the whole message. However, it did convince us that we were brothers. That was a shock for both of us, I can tell you.''

"But surely your relationship changed once you knew.''

"Some, I guess, but...well, to tell you the truth, I'm not

sure Matt and I will ever be close. We're too different. We have different personalities, come from different backgrounds, had different upbringings, different life experiences.''

Kate was silent for a moment, and he could tell that she was troubled. Finally, in a subdued voice she said, ''The same will be true with Zach, you know.''

She tipped her head up to look at him, her eyes brimming with concern. ''Oh, J.T., it breaks my heart to think that you and Matt and Zach might end up as strangers to each other. Brothers should be share a bond. Especially triplets.''

''Hey, sweetheart, don't worry about it. Just because Matt and I aren't close doesn't mean that Zach and I won't be.'' Although, from what she'd told him about her brother, J.T. didn't hold out much hope of that happening. ''But, look, if it doesn't work out, we'll just have to deal with it. Matt, Zach and I have led different lives. We can't change that.''

Suddenly J.T. rolled over with Kate in his arms until her back was against the mattress. Lowering his head, he began a sensual assault on her neck.

''Mmm. I just wish I could—'' he paused to nibble her earlobe ''—do more for you. Like find the money and—'' he traced the delicate swirls of her ear with the tip of his tongue and smiled when he felt her tremble ''—clear both your names. Too bad you burned all of…Reverend Sweet's things.'' Slowly, while his hand skimmed up over the curves of her hip and ribcage to cup her breasts, J.T.'s mouth strung nibbling kisses along her collarbone, then downward, homing in on the silky skin between her breasts. ''They may have contained…clues.''

Eyes closed, Kate shifted restlessly. Her breathing was rapid, and she clutched J.T.'s head with both hands, her fingers moving frantically through the dark strands.

Then, in the midst of the swirling passion, she suddenly experienced a blinding flash of clarity, and her eyes popped open.

"Oh!" She stiffened. "Oh, my! I just remembered something!"

Taking J.T. by surprise, Kate shoved at his shoulders and rolled him off her.

"What the—" he began, but she had already popped up like a cork and scrambled off the bed. "Ah, hell. Katy, have a heart. Whatever it is can wait. Come back to bed."

"No, you don't understand." She hurried over to her closet and grabbed her blue velour robe and slipped into it. Her heart pounded with excitement. How could she have she forgotten? "I just remembered that I do have something of Bob's. After he died the prison warden sent me his personal affects."

"Great. We'll look at them later." J.T. raised up on his elbow and held out his other hand to her. "Right now, I have something else in mind."

"No, I have to look at them now." To think, all these months, the answer to where the money was hidden could have been sitting up in her musty attic. Kate tied the sash on the robe with shaking hands and sent him a pleading look. "C'mon, J.T. I won't be able to think about anything else until I look at the contents of that box."

He sighed and rolled his eyes. "Okay, okay. We'll give 'um a look." He climbed from the bed and pulled on his navy jockey shorts and jeans. Stuffing his arms into the sleeves of his flannel shirt, he stepped into his athletic shoes and motioned for her to lead the way.

"There's not much. Just one small box," she informed him excitedly, hurrying down the back hall and up the servants' stairs to the attic. "I started to toss it in the garbage but when I peeked inside I saw his family Bible. Burning clothes is one thing, but I couldn't quite bring myself to destroy a bible. So I stuck the box in the attic and forgot about it.''

On the third floor she led him along a narrow, dark hallway, past a dozen or so cubbyhole rooms that had once housed a staff of servants, to a door at the end that led into the open area of the attic.

As they stepped into the cavernous darkness Kate waved her hand over her head, snagged a light chain and gave it a yank. The bare bulb hanging from the ceiling cast a weak circle of light by the door, where a feather boa, a beaded 1890s style dress and an enormous hat with ostrich feathers hung from a leaning coatrack. At its base sat a pair of high button shoes, and nearby was a lady's fainting couch and a marble-topped Victorian table with a fringed lamp on top that looked as if it belonged in a bordello.

J.T. studied the items with a grin. "Lemme guess. This was your playroom. I'll bet as a kid you spent rainy days up here playing dress up, right?''

"Yes, I did," Kate replied, refusing to be flustered by the teasing light in his eyes. "These days, little Jennifer Womack plays up here. She's the granddaughter of the lady who helps me with the housekeeping during tourist season.''

"I'll bet you were adorable in that hat.''

"That's right. I was," she said with a pert lift of her chin. "Little girls love to play dress up, and an attic is like a wonderland. Now where did I put that box?'' she said, poking through the maze of discards as they worked their way deeper into the shadows. "Look for one with a Colorado State Prison shipping label on it.''

"Okay. About what size is it?'' he asked, and walked straight into a cobweb that stretched from a rafter to the floor. "Holy—''

Sputtering and cursing, he flailed his arms and fought to free himself, while Kate giggled. When he finally scrubbed the sticky stuff from his face he shuddered. "Jeez, you could get eaten alive up here," he grumbled, but Kate laughed harder.

"You think that's funny?"

"Oh, J.T., it was just a little spider."

"Little, my eye! Did you see that thing go scuttling up to the rafters? It was big as a saucer."

Still slapping at his clothes, he glanced around. "Just look at this stuff. You could open an antique shop with what's up here. Or a haunted house."

Spread out over the shadowy reaches of the attic stood sheet-shrouded furniture, fringed lamps, an antique baby pram, a cracked cheval mirror, paintings and old tintypes in baroque frames, piles of leather trunks and boxes and a plethora of other items that were no more than hulking shapes in the gloom.

"Here it is!" Kate shouted, pointing to a box on the top of a waist-high stack. Hope and excitement expanded in her chest until she could barely breathe. *Please, let there be something in there that would help them.*

Her nerves stretched taut as J.T. hefted the box and carried it back to the table beneath the light. "Mmm, you were right, there's not much here."

He lifted out the Bible and began examining it while Kate watched, her heart pounding.

The leather binding on the Bible showed years of wear, but in the lower right-hand corner, in gold, were the initials, R.J.S. A wide, locked strap fastened the book, but the key dangled from a velvet ribbon looped around the strap. The key was large and ornate, like something from the Middle Ages, engraved on both sides with a bow, twining vines and flowers.

J.T. unlocked the fastening and flipped through the pages, examining the lining and the edges, but he found nothing unusual—no hiding places, no incriminating notations in the scriptures, no notes tucked inside, just the usual handwritten family tree at the back and a laminated bookmark of the "Lord's Prayer."

"Nothing here. What else is in there?"

"Not much. Bob's razor, a brush and comb, a watch, the diamond ring he had on when he was arrested, his wallet. It's empty except for his driver's license and an expired credit card."

"I suppose the authorities went through all this stuff before they shipped it to you."

J.T. picked up the watch and turned it over. He used his pocket knife to pop open the back, but there was nothing inside but the works. He unscrewed the crystal and lifted off the face, but found nothing there, either.

"Yes, I imagine so. I know after Bob was arrested a swarm of FBI men came here and searched the house from the attic to the basement."

J.T. and Kate examined every item but found nothing. Finally, thoroughly deflated, they dumped everything into the box and put it back where they'd found it.

"I guess this was a waste of time," Kate sighed as they descended the attic stairs to the second-floor hall. "I was so hoping—"

She gave a shriek as J.T. swooped her up.

"J.T., you idiot! What are you doing?"

He grinned into her startled face and strode down the hall with her in his arms. "Well, you see, I have this fantasy."

Depressed and disappointed, she was not at all in the mood for amorous games, and she opened her mouth to tell him so, but one look into those mischievous eyes and she felt a smile tug at her lips. Kate sighed. The man was irresistible.

Tipping her head back, she arched one eyebrow. "Oh, really?" She looped her arm around his shoulders and toyed with the short hairs at his nape, lightly scoring his skin with her nails. "A fantasy, huh? And how long have you had this fantasy?"

"Since the day I arrived."

"Oh, really? That long? And it involves me?"

"Oh you know it, sugar. You're the star."

"Mmm. Well, in that case I feel I should tell you that you've just passed my room."

J.T. didn't so much as slow down. His grin merely widened as he strode to the other end of the hall and into his own room. He quickly crossed the rose-patterned rug to the enormous bed. Kate expected he would fall onto the bed with her in his arms, or give her one of those caveman tosses onto the mattress as he'd done earlier, but instead he sat down on the edge of the high bed and cradled her on his lap.

Smiling at her puzzled expression, he picked up the end of her untidy French braid, pulled off the elastic band and began to unwind the intricate plait. "I love your hair," he murmured. "The smell of it. The feel of it against my skin."

As though to demonstrate, when the thick braid was fully undone he dove his fingers into the shiny mass. He rubbed several strands between his thumb and fingers, buried his face in it and inhaled deeply, lifted it, watched with heated eyes as it twined and slithered through his spread fingers. "Beautiful," he whispered. "Absolutely beautiful. You have no idea how many times I've wanted to do that." He untied the sash and pushed her robe off her shoulders and arms, and grinned as he watched hot color rise from her chest all the way up her neck and face to her hairline. "You're adorable when you blush, you know that?"

"Well, you know what they say about what's good for the goose," she retorted sassily, stripping away his flannel shirt.

Chuckling, J.T. twisted around and placed Kate on the bed. Then he climbed onto his knees beside her and spread her long hair out across the pillow, arranging it just so. When he was done he sat back on his heels and drank in the sight. "Since the afternoon I arrived and you showed me into this room, I've fantasized about how you would look in this bed. How you would look with all that glorious hair spread out across the pillows."

Kate arched one eyebrow. "The first *afternoon?*"

"Mmm. By now I must have imagined how you would look lying there like that at least a hundred times."

"A hundred? Oh, J.T., you can't really expect me to believe that. You've been here just over two months."

"You're right. Make that two hundred."

She started to laugh, but the sound cut off when she saw his serious expression.

He climbed from the bed just long enough to shuck out of his jeans and jockey shorts and pull off his shoes, then he was back, stretching out beside her. "I gotta tell you, reality is every bit as good as I imagined. Better even."

Propping up on one elbow, J.T. cupped her breast and ran his thumb back and forth over the nipple, smiling as he watched it pucker. "I've wanted you from the moment I saw you. And I've loved you almost as long. I was just waiting—hoping really—that eventually you'd love me back."

"Oh, J.T." She stared at him, stunned, and so touched she could barely breathe. Emotions came gushing up inside her like a geyser, filling her heart to overflowing. "Oh, my darling, I love you, too,'' she declared and looped her arms around his neck, bringing him down to her for a long, heated kiss.

Their mouths rocked together hungrily as both sought to express feelings too strong and deep for words, but still it wasn't enough. Teeth nipped and scraped, lips rubbed and nibbled, tongues swirled and mated, and all the while their hands frantically roamed and clutched.

When they came up for air, J.T. dragged his open mouth across her shoulder, dewing her skin with his warm, moist breath, but when he started moving down her chest, she was having none of it.

''Oh, no, you don't.'' Taking him by surprise, she shoved at his shoulders and sent him tumbling onto his back.

Before he knew what happened, Kate flung herself on top of him. She sat up partway, astraddle his hips, the heels of her hands pressing his shoulders to the mattress, and smiled.

''You did the seducing last time,'' she said in a throaty voice. ''Now it's my turn.''

Surprise and bemusement flickered across J.T.'s face, followed quickly by a look so roguish she almost laughed out loud. They both knew that he could dislodge her in one quick movement, but he assumed a tragic look and sighed dramatically. ''It appears I have no choice. You've overpowered me. I'm at your mercy.''

Ignoring her hands pressing against his shoulders, he flung his arms wide in abject surrender. ''Go ahead. Have your way with me. Just please...be gentle.''

He managed a tragic little catch in his voice at the end, but despite his pathetic tone, the look in his eyes was so sensual, Kate felt fire lick through her belly.

''Uh-uh.'' Shaking her head, she put her forefinger

across his mouth. "I make the rules here, not you. Remember that."

"Uh-oh. I think I'm about to be ravished."

"You got it, big boy," she said in her best Mae West voice. "Now lie still and you won't get hurt."

Sprawled naked atop him, Kate could not help but be aware of his body's response, and she experienced a thrill of power that was new to her. It was exciting—and scary, and for an instant she was shocked at her own boldness. Then she looked into that handsome, wickedly sensual face and saw the laughter and challenge in his eyes, luring her, daring her to follow through.

Kate tipped her head back at a haughty angle and narrowed her eyes. The gauntlet had been thrown, and the stubbornness that was so much a part of her nature would not let her quit now.

Smiling provocatively, she settled more completely on top of him, lowering her upper body until her soft breasts brushed against his chest. J.T.'s expression didn't change, but every muscle in his body tightened. Pleased with herself, Kate gazed at him from beneath half-closed eyelids and moved ever so slightly from side to side, dragging her nipples through the thatch of dark curls on his chest.

His eyes darkened and narrowed. "Oh, very good, sweetheart," he murmured in a strained voice. "Very good."

Kate's sense of power burgeoned like an inflating balloon, and with it so did her boldness. She wiggled and shifted, rubbing her body against his in a slow undulation. She heard his sharp intake of breath and smiled.

Trailing her pointed tongue through his chest hair, she drew an intricate, wet pattern on his skin, then scraped the tiny nub she found there with her teeth, all the while watching for his reaction.

J.T. remained with his arms outstretched, still and submissive. Only the shudder that rippled through him and the glitter in his eyes gave him away.

Seducing, Kate decided, was quite enjoyable and liberating. Emboldened by her success so far, she really let herself go. She nipped at his shoulders, his neck, his earlobes, his jaw. Exploring his face, she ran her thumbs over his eyebrows, feathered them over his lashes. She traced his lips with her forefinger, explored a tiny scar she discovered beneath his chin, investigated the swirling pattern in each ear.

She scooted down his body and traced a wet circle around his navel, blew on it, then jabbed her tongue inside the tiny cavity, and she smiled when she felt him jerk.

Sitting back on her heels between his legs, Kate traced the silky line of dark hair that shot downward from his navel to the thatch of dark curls at the base of his aroused sex. With her fingertips, she explored his hipbones, trailed a feathery line along the junctures where his legs met his torso, then down along the insides of his thighs, the backs of his knees.

For several tormenting moments, she touched him everywhere...except where his taut body silently begged her to touch. Then she wrapped her hand lovingly around him, and J.T. groaned. "Oh, yes, sweetheart! *Yes!*"

Kate smiled slowly. "You like that?"

"Yes. Sweet heaven, yes!"

"And this? Do you like this, too? Hmm?"

"Yes! Yes! Don't stop!"

Straddling him, Kate leaned forward. Her gray eyes were stormy with passion as they stared down into his, and J.T. groaned again as she lowered herself onto him.

"Ahhh, Katy. Kate!"

Chapter Eleven

The day before Zach was to arrive another blizzard struck. He telephoned from Albuquerque to let Kate know he would wait out the storm there and drive up as soon as the roads were cleared. However, the storm raged for five days without letup, dumping over seven feet of snow. All roads and highways in the San Juan Mountains were closed, all air traffic in and out of the area airports grounded.

When the storm finally blew itself out, it took J.T. and Kate a whole day to dig themselves a path to the garage and another to clear the road into town, and even then, the highway snowplows hadn't reached Gold Fever. No sooner had they finished digging out, than another storm hit.

After waiting in Albuquerque for a week, Zach telephoned to tell Kate that he couldn't lose any more time hanging around waiting for the weather to clear. He had to head for Texas and the Houston Fat Stock Show and Rodeo. As it was, he only had a few days to get there in time to enter the competition.

Kate was disappointed, but she understood. The Houston Rodeo was one of the biggest in the country, with some of the biggest purses, and Zach couldn't afford to pass it up.

While still on the phone, in an aside to J.T., she explained the problem and offered to let him talk to Zach and tell him about their kinship, but J.T. declined. He didn't want to break such stunning news over the telephone.

Left with no choice, Kate and J.T. decided they would fly to Houston as soon as weather permitted. She did not, however, mention the plan to her brother.

Though J.T. and Kate were anxious for him to be reunited with Zach, they were happy about having some time alone together, and they made the most of it. Trapped in their private aerie, high on mountainside, they reveled in their isolation.

Giving free rein to their passions, they made love frequently. When that spark leaped between them, they simply surrendered to it, wholly and with a wild abandon that Kate had not dreamed she was capable of exhibiting.

Her experience with physical intimacy was limited. Until J.T., she'd had no knowledge of the varied moods of love, but under his tutelage she explored them all—joyous, serious, intense, frantic, playful and everything in between.

They made love on the giant bed and on Kate's feminine four-poster. They got into a tickling match that resulted in a lot of laughter and an awkward but thoroughly delightful episode on the stairs. In the shower they shared the most erotic passion Kate had ever experienced, their warm, soap-slicked bodies sliding against each other in a primal rhythm beneath the relentless spray.

One night a silly argument culminated in hard, fast, almost rough loving on the sofa in the parlor. Another night, while the blizzard howled outside, they made slow, sweet love on the hearth rug with only the dancing fire illuminating their entwined bodies.

Then there was a memorable evening when they were cooking dinner. What had begun as a quick kiss ended up a sizzling embrace that shut out the rest of the world. Within seconds they were both naked, with Kate astraddle J.T.'s lap on a kitchen chair.

By the time they had found fulfillment and collapsed together in satisfaction, the steaks they were cooking looked like charred hockey pucks and the veggies in the steamer had turned to mush. J.T. cursed a blue streak, and Kate dissolved into a fit of giggles. They ended up eating bologna sandwiches for dinner.

And neither of them cared in the least.

In between the sizzling lovemaking, they talked endlessly. Kate told J.T. about growing up in Gold Fever, how she and Zach had run wild over the forest-covered mountains, how she'd learned to ski at the tender age of six, what it was like to grow up in an isolated small town, to know all your neighbors and have them know you.

One afternoon, as they lounged on the sofa before a roaring fire, J.T. told her about growing up an adopted only child in an affluent family. He recounted often-hilarious stories about his studious college professor father and his funny, free-spirited and brilliant mother, who was a pediatrician.

He told her of the flashes of memory he often had of times before his birth mother gave him and his brothers up for adoption, and about Matt's recurring dreams of a tearful woman in the mist waving goodbye.

He explained that while he seemed to have weathered the separation with little apparent trauma, Matt had dealt with a lifelong feeling of abandonment, which was why he resisted change of any kind. That, J.T. felt, was one of the reasons the two of them had not been able to develop a closer relationship.

As she listened to it all, Kate's tender heart ached for the three little boys who had been separated so young.

When J.T. noticed the tears in her eyes, he quickly changed the subject and launched into a story about his beautiful, brilliant sister-in-law, Maude Ann, and her determination to provide a loving foster home for abused and neglected children.

"She calls the place Henley Haven, in honor of her first husband, who was also a police officer," he explained. "Tom Henley was killed in the line of duty.

"The first time Matt was wounded his boss coerced him into recuperating at the Haven. Lieutenant Werner is Maudie's godfather, and he knew that she would look after him. The stubborn cuss had been refusing to let anyone help him when he left the hospital, even though he was so weak at the time he could barely stand."

"Mmm. Still, I can understand how he felt," Kate murmured, snuggling her head into a more comfortable position on his shoulder.

J.T. rolled his eyes. "Now, why am I not surprised? Could it be because I'm talking to the number-one Miss I-Want-to-Do-It-Myself in the whole state? I swear, you and Matt have just about cornered the market on pride."

She poked him in the ribs, and he grunted. "There's nothing wrong with pride. Besides, I prefer to think of it as independence."

"Whatever," he said, taking the precaution of clamping his hand over hers. "Anyway, Matt fought against the arrangement, but his lieutenant gave him no choice. Then he fought against his feelings, but that was just as futile. He fell in love, not only with Maude Ann, but with all the kids who were at Henley Haven at the time.''

Beneath Kate's ear a chuckle rumbled in J.T.'s chest as he rubbed his hand slowly up and down her arm. ''Matt was one tough cop, and he's gruff and intimidating, but under that crusty shell, he's an old softie. When two of the kids were transferred out of Maude Ann's care by Child Protective Services it really tore him up. I think it was the first time he realized that they could lose any one of the kids at any time.''

The more Kate heard about Matt and Maude Ann, the more convinced she became that she was going to like them. So would Zach, if he would just give them a chance.

''Now waiting for the courts to make a decision about the adoption is nerve-racking. I don't know what the holdup is. Every one of those kids has been permanently taken from their abusive parents by the courts and made a ward of the state. You would think they'd be happy that a great couple like Maude Ann and Matt want to adopt them.''

Kate tipped her head back on J.T.'s shoulder and saw that a look of concern had replaced his usual happy-go-lucky expression. ''You love those children, too, don't you?''

''Yeah, I do. I've always been a sucker for kids. All kids. I'd like to have a houseful of my own someday. But these five have lived through some hellacious things that no one should have to endure. They deserve the love and the stable home that Matt and Maudie can give them.''

Emotion clogged Kate's throat. If she hadn't already been hopelessly in love with J.T., she would have tumbled on the spot. That such a strong, utterly masculine man so obviously loved children was deeply touching and wonderful, and as she gazed up at his profile, her heart melted like a chocolate candy bar in the hot sun. ''I'm sure the adoptions will go through soon,'' she whispered, loving him so much her chest hurt.

"Yeah, you're probably right. I hope so, anyway.''

The one thing J.T. did not tell Kate about, during their many talks, was his long career as a newspaper reporter for the *Houston Herald*. In his experience, particularly when it came to their personal lives, people tended to resent the press. He had never understood why. After all, they were merely doing their jobs.

Knowing how intensely private and proud Kate was, he was fairly certain she would react negatively if he told her. So, for the time being, he figured what she didn't know wouldn't hurt her. Until he could present her with his finished manuscript and prove that he meant her and Zach no harm, he thought it best to keep that bit of information to himself.

If now and then J.T. experienced a niggle of doubt about what he was doing, he quashed it by reminding himself that he had freedom of the press on his side.

Four days after Zach's call, J.T. and Kate awoke to sparkling clear skies and the insistent chirping of his cell phone. Snagging the instrument off the bedside table, he barked a morning-grumpy "hello,'' listened for a second, then jerked straight up in the bed.

Kate's heart gave a leap at his suddenly ashen face.

"Maude Ann? Is that you? Are you crying? What is it? What's wrong? Maudie, I can't understand a word you're saying. Stop crying and slow down and tell me.

"Matt! Thank God. What's wrong with your wife?''

Sitting up now, too, Kate chewed her bottom lip and anxiously watched J.T. Gradually his eyes widened, and a grin as big as Texas spread across his face. "That's great! Congratulations! But why the devil is Maudie bawling? I thought she'd be happy.'' He put his hand over the receiver and mouthed to Kate, ''The adoptions went through.''

Instantly his attention switched back to Matt. ''She's *crying* because she's happy?'' J.T. looked heavenward and shook his head. ''Lord, will I ever understand women? Look, if you can ever get her to stop blubbering, give Maudie and the kids a kiss for me, will ya. And tell them we'll celebrate when Kate and I get there.''

There was a pause, and then, from J.T., ''Actually...'' He glanced out the window at the bright sunshine and grinned. ''Soon. Maybe even tomorrow, or the next day if we can get a flight out of Durango. Yeah, Kate's coming with me.'' Another pause, and then J.T. added in a more subdued voice, ''It turns out that Zach Mahoney *is* our brother, Matt. At the moment he's busting broncs in the Houston Rodeo, so Kate and I will be there as soon as we can get a flight.''

Two days later the roads were open again. Kate arranged for Mrs. Womack and her granddaughter to stay at the Alpine Rose. She and J.T. then drove to Durango, where they boarded a plane for Denver and made connections to Houston.

Matt and Maude Ann met them at the airport. Kate was nervous, not only about breaking the news to Zach that he was one of a set of triplets, but also about meeting J.T.'s family.

Her first look at Matt Dolan as they stepped from the jetway into the terminal did nothing to ease her edginess.

J.T. had described his brother as tough and intimidating. As far as Kate was concerned, that was an understatement. Even though he leaned on a cane, there was nothing weak or disabled about the man. He looked strong and tough. And dangerous.

Matt and J.T. were the same height and general build. There was a faint resemblance between them, Kate realized as they approached the couple, though it was not one you would notice unless you were looking for it. J.T.'s hair was a dark, rich brown and Matt's was black as coal. Both had chiseled features, but Matt's face had a craggy, go-to-hell look, whereas J.T.'s was drop-dead gorgeous.

Though both men had blue eyes, J.T.'s twinkled with mischief and good humor, where Matt's were fierce and piercing as an eagle's. When he turned that harsh gaze on her, she had to fight to suppress a shudder and force her feet to keep moving in his direction.

"Hey, it's good to see you two!" J.T. exclaimed as they reached the couple. Kate hung back as he and Matt exchanged greetings and a handshake that were just shy of stiff, but when J.T. turned to his sister-in-law he let out a whoop. Kate barely got a glimpse of the leggy redhead before he enveloped her in a bear hug and lifted her right off her feet.

"Maudie, you sexy thing, I swear, you get more beautiful by the day. Why don't you give us a kiss. It'll drive that tough guy you married crazy."

"Idiot!" Laughing, Maude Ann planted a smacking kiss on his cheek.

Kate sneaked a quick look at Matt and saw that, indeed, his eyes had narrowed into dangerous slits, but he made no move toward the pair.

J.T. finally put Maude Ann back on her feet and looked at her fondly. "So how's the new little mother?"

"Terrific. I can't tell you how good it feels to know that the children belong to us now. By the way, the kids send their love. They can't wait to see you."

"The feeling is mutual. Soon as we get this business over with we'll drive out to the lake to see the little rug rats.

But first…'' He grasped Kate's hand and drew her forward. "This is Kate Mahoney. Zach is her adopted brother."

Matt nodded and murmured a polite, "Nice to meet you, Kate," but Maude Ann surged forward with her arms outstretched and enveloped her in a warm embrace.

"Kate. I'm so glad you're here. I've been dying to meet you. J.T. has talked about you so much during our phone conversations, I feel that I know you," she said before Kate could get a word in. "I think it's absolutely wonderful that Matt and J.T. are gaining not only another brother, but a sister as well."

"Well, uh…" Kate cast an uneasy glance at J.T., and he stepped closer and put an proprietary arm around her shoulders.

"Correction, gorgeous. Matt may have gained a sister, but I promise you, my feelings for Kate are far from brotherly."

"Ahhh, I see." Maude Ann jabbed her elbow into her husband's ribs. "See. Didn't I tell you something was going on between them?"

"So you did, sweetheart." Matt looked at J.T. and rolled his eyes. "It's woman's intuition. I've been learning all about it lately."

Kate almost goggled as she watched a slow smile curve Matt's mouth and crinkle the corners of his eyes. The transformation was stunning, changing Matt's harsh, go-to-hell face into one so ruggedly handsome and sexy that just looking at him would make any female's heart do a back flip. Until that moment Kate had been wondering what a warm and beautiful woman like Maude Ann saw in a somber man like Matt Dolan, but no longer. The man wasn't just good looking, he was lethal.

"Well…what now?" Matt asked.

"First Kate and I check into our hotel and drop off our bags, then we go find Zach and break the news."

The rodeo was held in the Astrodome in southwest Houston, and the fat stock show exhibits took up all of the adjacent Astrohall. Near the back entrance to the hall, a large area of the parking lot had been roped off as a campground for the contestants who traveled from one rodeo to another in RVs. There, too, were the pickup trucks and stock trailers and temporary corrals filled with rodeo animals.

Kate, J.T. and the Dolans arrived an hour before the evening rodeo performance, which Kate knew meant they would most likely find Zach in his motorhome.

The guard at the entrance to the area was reluctant to let them in, but Kate finally convinced him that she was Zach Mahoney's sister by producing a picture from her wallet of the two of them together.

The air all around the area was redolent with the fecund smells of animals, hay, feed and manure. As they maneuvered through the corrals they were bombarded with the *chink-chink* sounds of spurs, neighing horses and the incessant bawling of cattle. Mingled in the cacophony were the Western drawls of the cowboys milling about, CW music blasting from the campers and pickups, and the distant sounds of city traffic.

They wandered through the jumble of corrals, trailers and pickups for almost fifteen minutes before they located the camping area and Kate spotted Zach's motor home.

The others held back a bit while she knocked on the door. It was opened almost at once.

"Yeah, whadda you— Kate!"

"Surprise!"

"Kate, what're you doing here?" Even as Zach asked

the question he hurried down the metal steps and snatched her up in his arms. "Lord, it's good to see you, Sis."

She hugged him back, her heart swelling with love and pride. All of her life, Zach had been her rock, her hero, her protector. "It's good to see you, too."

Grasping her shoulders, he held her away and ran his gaze over her, frowning as though he expected to see visible signs of damage. "What's wrong? Why did you come here?"

"Calm down. Nothing is wrong." She smiled and touched his tanned cheek. "We came to tell you something, Zach. Something important."

"We?" His gaze narrowed even more and shot past her to the others. "What do you mean? Who are these people?"

Kate reached out and took J.T.'s hand. "This is J.T. Conway. And this is his brother and sister-in-law, Matt and Maude Ann Dolan."

Zach zeroed in on J.T., frowning as he took in the way his hand remained clasped with Kate's. "Conway. You're that writer Kate's told me about, aren't you? The one who sweet-talked his way into staying at the Alpine Rose through the winter."

Kate sighed. Her brother's tone bordered on belligerent. So did his scowl and his aggressive stance. He couldn't have made his disapproval clearer if he'd hired a skywriter to spell it out in letters a hundred yards high.

"Yes, I am."

"What are you doing here with my sister?"

"Za-ach," Kate groaned. "There's no reason to take that tone."

"No, that's okay, sweetheart. We probably should set things straight before we go on." J.T. met the hard glint in Zach's eyes with one of his own. "The main reason I'm with Kate is because I love her. And you might as well know right now that if she'll have me, I intend to marry her. You got any objections to that?''

''J.T.!'' Kate gasped, before her brother could answer. She stared up at J.T. with her mouth agape, so thunderstruck she couldn't utter another sound. Happiness gushed up inside her in a warm tide, filling her pounding heart to overflowing.

''Sorry, sweetheart. I didn't mean to spring it on you that way, but Zach seems to have some concern about my intentions. I just wanted to make my position clear.''

''Di-did you mean it? Do you really want to marry me?''

''More than I've ever wanted anything in my life.'' He brought her hand to his mouth and kissed it, smiling at her over the top, his eyes full of love. ''So? Will you marry me, Kate?''

Her chest was so tight Kate felt as though she might burst at any second. She smiled up at him with all she was feeling shining in her eyes. ''Yes,'' she whispered. Then, laughing, *''Yes!''*

J.T. bent his head and kissed her, long and lavishly. Distantly Kate heard Maude Ann sigh and Matt clear his throat, but she was too lost in bliss to care that they had an audience or that they were standing in a parking lot that smelled of animals and manure. J.T. loved her and wanted to marry her, regardless of the controversy that surrounded her and Zach.

When he finally broke off the kiss he raised his head just inches and smiled, looking deep into her eyes. His own were warm with emotion and that familiar sparkle of mischief. ''We'll continue this later,'' he promised in a sexy murmur.

Zach's hard stare didn't soften in the least as he turned

his pale gaze on his sister. "Are you sure this is what you want? You haven't known this guy very long."

She beamed at him, then turned back to J.T. with a dreamy smile. "Oh, yes, I'm sure. I'm very sure."

Matt cleared his throat. "Touching as that was, shouldn't we get on with the real reason we're all here?"

Zach's gaze sharpened as he looked from Matt to J.T. "There's more? You mean you didn't come here just to announce your intentions to marry my sister?"

Before J.T. could answer, a battered-looking cowboy ambled by. He nodded to Zach and touched the brim of his Stetson with two fingers. "Howzit goin', Zach?"

Zach glanced at his sister's glowing face. "Fair to middlin', Pete." He returned his attention to J.T. "Well?"

"Look, is there someplace private where we can all go to talk?"

When her brother didn't answer immediately, Kate added her own plea. "Please, Zach. This is important."

"All right, I guess you can come inside. But I don't have much time. I have to be in the arena soon to get ready for my event."

Entering the motor home, they found themselves in a tiny sitting area located directly behind the driver's cab. To the rear of that was a minuscule galley with a banquette and table and still farther back a short hall with what appeared to be a bathroom on one side and a closet on the other. At the very back of the vehicle the open bedroom door gave a glimpse of a neatly made bed and a well-used saddle and bridle on the floor next to it. Though tiny, Zach's home was neat and clean, Kate noted with a touch of pride.

The Dolans sat down on the sofa, and Kate and J.T. took the club chairs that sat at right angles to it. Leaning his narrow hips back against the kitchen counter, Zach folded his arms over his chest and swept them all with a narrow-eyed look, starting and ending with J.T. "So what's this all about?"

J.T. glanced at Matt, and he nodded. "Go ahead. You tell him."

"Tell me what?"

J.T. met Zach's gaze squarely. "There's just one way to say this and that's straight-out. We're here because Matt and I have reason to believe that you're our brother."

"*What?*" Zach shot away from the counter and faced them with his fists planted on his hips, his face tight with annoyance and suspicion. "That's a crock. What're you people trying to pull?"

"No, Zach, let him explain," Kate urged. "It's true. There's proof."

"Proof? What kind of proof can he have? You're my only family. These guys are pulling some kind of con, and you've falling for it, Sis."

"Just listen to him for a minute, Zach," she pleaded. "Please. Do it for me."

He hesitated, his mouth folded into a grim line, but finally he nodded. "All right, shoot. But I'm warning you, this had better be good."

"You're birthday is February sixth, right?"

"Yeah, but since I was supposed to come home to celebrate the day with my sister, you already knew that."

"You were born here in Houston at St. Joseph's Hospital, at a little after seven in the morning, right?"

"Yeah," he drawled warily, showing the first sign of surprise.

"And you were adopted by the Mahoneys at age two?"

"Yes, but that information is a matter of public record. I don't know yet why you went to the trouble to look it up, but it proves nothing."

"How about this? Your birth mother made two stipulations when you were given up for adoption—that you go to an Irish-American family and that you always wear around your neck a jagged piece of silver, a fragment of a medallion.''

"How did you know tha—"

"It's pie-shaped and about an inch and a half long. There is some sort of symbol on the front and writing etched on the back, but not enough to make out what it says."

Zach stared at him.

The air inside the RV was suddenly thick and tingling with electricity.

"We know it's difficult to believe. Trust me, we understand exactly what you're feeling right now," Matt said, speaking up for the first time. "J.T. and I had a hard time accepting it, too, but it's true. Here, see for yourself." Reaching inside his shirt, he lifted out his medallion piece and whipped it off over his head. J.T. did the same.

Both men rose and stood in front of Zach. "See, they fit together," J.T. said, and joined his piece to Matt's to form two-thirds of a disc. "We think yours will fill in the missing section."

Zach stared at the two pieces of silver, then at Matt and J.T. Without a word, he reached inside his shirt and pulled out a chain from which dangled a pie-shaped piece of silver. He pulled the chain over his head and slipped the metal fragment between the two others.

They fit together perfectly.

"Well, I'll be damned." Zach looked at J.T., then Matt. "*We're* brothers?"

"Triplets actually."

"The hell you say."

Kate chuckled and shook her head. Her brother's skepticism was easy to understand. Though the three men were the same height and had the same broad-shouldered, nar-

row-hipped build, there the resemblance ended. Matt and
J.T. did not look that much alike, but they both had dark
hair and coloring and vivid blue eyes. Zach's hair was so
blond it was almost white, a startling contrast to his tanned
skin.

The three brothers were all ruggedly masculine, each in
his own way. Matt had a harsh, street-tough look about him,
and J.T. a chiseled handsomeness. Zach, however, had that
weathered toughness of a Westerner—skin tanned to a
leathery brown and etched with fine lines around his eyes
and deeper ones running from the corners of his mouth to
his nose. He had a strong, square jaw, straight nose, cheek-
bones sharp enough to cut and deep-set, green eyes that
glittered like gems in his sun-scorched face giving him the
sharp, wary look of a wolf.

"Yeah, I know. We don't look much alike, do we?" J.T.
said with a chuckle. "We're fraternal triplets, not identi-
cal."

Kate looked anxiously from one man to the other, waiting for them to express some sort of emotion, but they
merely continued to eye one another.

She wanted to knock their heads together and shout at
them, but at the same time she ached with sadness and pity.
That these three men who had begun life together, who
should, by all rights, share a strong bond, now seemed unable to close the distance that time and different life paths
had created was heartbreaking.

Kate glanced at Maude Ann, and she could see that the
other woman was feeling just as exasperated and helpless
as she. Maude Ann, however, had been dealing with Matt's
and J.T.'s standoffish behavior toward each other far
longer, and she had run out of patience.

"Oh, good grief," she snapped. "Don't just stand there
all stoic and macho. *Do* something. Hug. Kiss. Slap some

backs. At least shake hands. You're *brothers,* for pity's sake.''

Matt gave his wife a stern look. When he turned back to his brothers his mouth quirked. ''You'll have to excuse Maudie. She gets emotional at times.''

Maude Ann threw up her hands and rolled her eyes. ''I give up. You three are hopeless.''

''I agree with Maude Ann. What is the matter with you men? Especially you, Zach. This is a wonderful event. You've just been reunited with your brothers. Can't you show a little enthusiasm?''

''Kate, don't push,'' he said in a warning voice. ''Five minutes ago I didn't even know I *had* brothers.''

She made an exasperated sound, and she and Maude Ann exchanged a commiserating look. ''Fine. Be pigheaded. But at the very least shouldn't you see what the writing on that medallion says?''

''Hey, she's right,'' J.T. said. ''I'd almost forgotten about that.''

''Yeah, me, too,'' Matt agreed. ''Let's put the pieces together over here on the table where the light is better and have a look.''

The two women quickly slid onto the bench seats on either side of the table so that they could see, too.

Crowding around the end of the tiny table, their shoulders touching, the three big men bent over and each placed his medallion piece on the table, faceup. Standing in the middle, Matt put a finger of each of the three sections, slid them together and drew his hands back.

''An R with a curved line under it? What does that mean?'' Maude Ann asked.

''It means the Rocking R,'' her husband supplied. ''It's a cattle brand.''

"Yeah. I've heard of that outfit," Zach murmured. "It's a big spread up in Montana."

"Turn it over. Let's see what's on the other side." Even as he spoke, J.T. flipped the silver pieces over and fitted them together again. Etched in block print was the address of the Rocking R Ranch. Beneath the address were the words Your Heritage.

"This must have been your birth mother's home," Kate said, touching her fingertip to the medallion.

"Maybe," J.T. murmured. "Or it could have been our father's, whoever he is, and she just wanted us to know."

"In that case why didn't she just give us each a medallion?" Matt growled. "Why cut one up into thirds? If J.T. hadn't accidentally spotted my piece we would probably never have known that we were related or that this place existed."

"I'd say it was a mother's desperate act. She was probably praying you would find one another when you were grown," Maude Ann said. "Knowing the Texas adoption system, they wouldn't have allowed her to give each of you a whole medallion with that information on it. Especially not thirty-three years ago."

"Yeah, well...at least now we have a place to look for some information about our mother. I, for one, want to know why the hell she gave us away." J.T. straightened and rubbed the back of his neck. "The question is, what's our next move? Do we write? Or call? Or do we all go there together?"

"Right now the only place I'm going is into the arena," Zach announced, glancing at the wall clock. "Bronc riding starts in less than half an hour. I gotta go see what horse I drew and check him out." He started for the door, but J.T. stopped him.

"Zach, wait. Look, we need to talk. Why don't we meet

you for a late dinner after the performance? You name the place.''

He hesitated, his guarded look flickering over all of them. Then he nodded. ''All right. Meet me at Delgado's at ten. It's on Post Oak Lane.''

''Letters and telephone calls seem too impersonal for something like this,'' J.T. said as he cut into his steak. ''It makes it too easy for someone to fluff off your request for information. If we want to get some answers about our mother, then I vote we go to the Rocking R, all three of us together.'' He paused before putting the bite into his mouth and waved his knife for emphasis. ''Who knows what we'll run into up there. We should present a united front.''

''I don't know. Montana is a long way from here. I don't want to leave Maude Ann and the kids for too long.''

''Don't worry about us. Jane and I can handle the children. You go with J.T. and Zach.''

Matt started to argue, but Maude Ann put her hand on his arm and stopped him. ''Darling, you know that until you learn about your mother and find out why she gave you up, you'll never be totally at peace. You want to put those dreams of yours to rest, don't you? Well, this is your chance.''

''How about you, Zach?'' J.T. asked. ''You game?''

Watching her brother, Kate held her breath. Though the three men had exchanged bits and pieces of information about themselves over drinks and throughout the meal, most of it had been merely surface stuff—where they'd gone to school, where they'd lived, what they did for a living. None of them seemed the least inclined to touch on anything truly personal or meaningful. There was an awkward constraint between the three that they either couldn't

or wouldn't try to overcome. They reminded Kate of three
wary dogs, slowly circling one another.

She sighed. She loved her brother dearly, but he was
intensely private and tended to put up a wall between himself and others. As close as they'd always been, there were
some areas of his life that were off-limits even to her. These
past four years he had become even more closed off.

Judging by J.T.'s and Matt's behavior, they were almost
as cautious and untrusting.

"I guess I could forego one rodeo and make the trip.
But it'll be better for me if we do it about a month from
now. I'll be in that area then, and I can meet up with you
in Clear Water."

"That'll work for me. How about you, Matt?"

He nodded, and they returned their attention to dinner.

Kate sighed again. At this rate they weren't ever going
to connect with one another the way brothers should.

Over the remainder of the meal they made their plans
and exchanged telephone numbers, but other than that the
conversation remained desultory and impersonal. Kate was
trying to come up with something to shake things up when
a deep voice from the other side of the restaurant boomed
J.T.'s name. They all looked up to see a short, bald man
approach their table.

"Charlie!"

The man slapped J.T. on the back and took a soggy cigar
out of his mouth. "Good to see you, Conway. It's about
time you came back. When did you get in? And why didn't
you let me know?"

Scraping back his chair, J.T. bolted to his feet and
dropped his napkin on the table. He towered over the
paunchy little man, but Kate could have sworn that he
looked almost frightened. "I'm not back, Charlie. This is
just a quick visit."

"You mean you're going back to that one-horse mining town? Dammit man, I got a newspaper to run. I can't hold your job at the *Herald* forever, you know."

"Uh, look, Charlie, this is not the time for this discussion. I'm with friends and I'd rather not—"

"Sure, sure. I didn't mean to interrupt. Just wanted to say hello." The portly man turned to leave, then looked back and jabbed his wet stogie in J.T.'s direction. "Just remember, I'm still waiting for that article on the Gold Fever scandal that you promised me."

Chapter Twelve

Kate felt all the blood drain from her face. "You're a reporter."

"No, Kate, listen to—"

"You lied to me. All this time you've been lying. You're not a novelist. You're a reporter. One of those bloodsucking muckrakers who swarmed all over our property and wouldn't give us a moment's peace. You think you have the right to poke your nose into other people's lives and print half-truths and innuendoes. It doesn't matter to you who you hurt or what you have to do to get it, just as long as you end up with a juicy story that will sell newspapers. *That's* really who you are, isn't it, J.T.?"

"No, Kate—"

"You wormed your way into my home under false pretenses. Even your search for Zach was secondary, wasn't it? You really came to Gold Fever to write about the scandal, didn't you? To dig up all the old dirt and point the finger at Zach and me again, never mind that he's your own brother."

J.T. winced at the bitter accusation. "No, Kate, that's not true. Give me a chance to explain, sweetheart."

The Dolans exchanged a worried look, but discreetly said nothing. Zach sat rigid, his face stony as his icy gaze bore into J.T.

J.T. dropped back into his seat and reached for Kate's hands, but she snatched them away and clasped them together in her lap. She stared at him, her eyes full of scorn and anger and hurt.

"I didn't lie to you, sweetheart, I swear. I'll admit I was a reporter, but I gave that up to do what I've always wanted to do, and that was write books. I swear I came to Gold Fever to write a novel. I have two stories roughed out already."

"You quit your job? The way that man talked it certainly didn't sound like it to me."

She watched the flash of guilt race over his face, and her last faint hope vanished.

"Well, technically, I'm on a leave of absence," he admitted ruefully, then hurried to add, "But I'm not going back to the *Herald*. I swear it. I just haven't told Charlie yet."

"You son of a—" Zach exploded out of his chair and extended his hand for Kate. "C'mon, Sis, let's get out of here."

J.T. put his hand on Kate's arm, but she rose with fragile dignity, refusing to look at him. He sprang up, as well. Over the top of her head he glared at his brother. "You stay out of this, Zach. This is between Kate and me."

Zach's jaw jutted. "Like hell. Periodically some sleazy journalist like you comes to Gold Fever and starts poking around. And every time something is printed about the swindle, Kate's good name and my own get dragged through the dirt. But that's not the point here. There's something you need to learn about family, *brother*," he sneered. "And that is they stick together. You hurt my sister, you got me to deal with."

The message came through loud and clear: they may be related by blood, but as far as Zach was concerned, Kate was his family.

"C'mon, Sis, let's go." Zach put his arm around her shoulders and started to lead her away, but Kate held back.

"No, wait. There's one thing I want to know first." She fixed J.T. with an unwavering stare. "I've never asked before. I figured it was your business, and if you wanted me to know you'd tell me, but now I'm curious. These books you're writing, what are they about?"

J.T. shifted uncomfortably. "Look, Kate, just because I'm writing a book doesn't mean it'll get published. I've never sold a manuscript before. Oh, sure, I have a few contacts in the publishing world, but that's no guarantee."

"What are the stories about, J.T.?" she persisted.

"I told you, I'm writing a novel set during the heyday of hard-rock mining."

"And the other one?"

"Kate—"

Her chin came up, and J.T. sighed. He raked a hand through his hair. "It's a fictionalized version of the what happened four years ago. But I was going to let you read it before I submitted it to a publisher," he added in a rush. "I swear I was, sweetheart. You have to believe me. I would never do anything to hurt you. Don't you know that?"

Kate felt as though she'd just been stabbed in the heart. The pain in her chest was so awful, for a moment she couldn't speak. "But you have," she managed finally.

"And the truly sad part is, you don't even seem to realize just how much."

The stricken look on J.T.'s face should have pleased her, but it didn't. The pressure in her chest was so great she felt as though she might shatter into a million little pieces at any second. She could barely muster the strength to move, but she slipped her arm through Zach's. "I'm ready to go now."

Zach paused and jabbed his forefinger at J.T. "You can forget marrying my sister, Conway. Just stay away from her. If you don't, I swear I'll break you in two."

Kate didn't know where she found the strength, but somehow she managed to put one foot in front of the other and walk away.

"Kate, wait!" J.T. started after the pair, but Maude Ann grabbed his arm.

"No, J.T., don't."

"Dammit, Maudie, let me go. I've got to stop her."

"I don't think that's a good idea right now. She's upset. They both are."

"With good reason," Matt growled, earning himself a warning look from his wife and a glare from his brother.

Maude Ann squeezed J.T.'s hand. "Give her a little while to calm down, then talk to her. Besides, you don't want to start a fight with Zach. That won't earn you any points with Kate, and that's what it will come to if you don't back off."

Every instinct J.T. possessed prodded him to ignore Maude Ann and rush after Kate, but some small part of him knew she was right. Frowning, he glanced down at his sister-in-law, then at Kate's retreating back. When she and Zach disappeared through the door, J.T.'s shoulders slumped. Sighing, he sank down onto his chair, propped his elbows on the table and dropped his head into his hands.

"I can't believe you didn't tell that girl the truth."

"Shut up, Matt."

"Matt, please," Maude Ann began, but he ignored her and plowed right on.

"This sort of thing is exactly why you and I have been butting heads for twelve years. You're always poking your nose where it doesn't belong. You used to interfere with police investigations right and left and print all sorts of half truths and speculation, and now you're probing into what was the most hurtful event that Kate and Zach have ever lived through."

"If you don't mind, I'm not in the mood to get into another debate with you about freedom of the press."

"Freedom of the press, my arse. That's the flag you guys always wave to excuse your actions whenever you step over the line. Anyway, this isn't about the Constitution, you jerk. This is about betraying the woman you claim to love."

J.T. head snapped up. His blue eyes stabbed into Matt's like shards of ice. The urge to do violence raged inside him. "Back off, Dolan," he snarled.

Matt threw his napkin down on the table and stood up.

J.T. shot to his feet, his stance full of aggression, jaw outthrust.

"Oh, for heaven's sake. Will you two stop it!" Maude Ann got between them and flattened a palm against each man's chest. "I mean it. Right this second. I will not— absolutely *will not*—spend the rest of my life separating two grown men who can't get around each other without acting like children. Now *sit down.* Both of you. As soon as I can get the waiter's attention I'll pay the bill, then we're getting out of here. Until then, not one word out of either of you."

Half an hour later, even though Maude Ann had bullied them into apologizing to each other, Matt and J.T. were still barely speaking. When the Dolans dropped J.T. off at his hotel, Maude Ann gave him a pep talk and kissed his cheek, but Matt merely grumbled a sarcastic, "Good luck," and drove away the instant J.T. climbed from the car.

J.T.'s heart pounded as he cross the lobby and rode the elevator up to the eleventh floor. He'd rehearsed what he would say over and over in his mind all the way back from the restaurant. This time he would make her listen to him, make her see that his book posed no threat to her and Zach. If anything, she should be happy, because he had portrayed her and Zach as the good guys who'd been falsely accused. If that didn't prove she could trust him, he didn't know what did.

It was dark in the room when J.T. let himself in. "Kate, are you awake?" Groping along the wall, he found the light switch and flipped it on...and froze.

After registering at the hotel, they hadn't taken time to do more than stash their bags in the room before dashing off to find Zach.

He stared in disbelief at the empty space where her suitcase should have been.

Kate was gone. She and Zach had been no more than ten minutes ahead of them, but she had already grabbed her things and gone. For a moment J.T. could barely breathe. Then anger rose up inside him and galvanized him into action.

It didn't take a genius to figure out where she'd gone, and with a curse he spun around and raced from the room.

Fifteen minutes later J.T. stood in the camping area behind the Astrodome, staring in disbelief at the empty space where Zach's RV had been just a few hours earlier.

Frustration and fear swirled inside him. Frantic, he glanced around and spotted a light on, in the RV two slots down. It was after midnight, but he didn't care. He hurried to the camper and banged on the door. From inside he heard a muffled curse. A few seconds later the door was jerked open, and a lanky, barefoot man wearing only an unzipped pair of jeans glowered at him through the screen door.

"I don't know who you are, mister, but you'd better have a helluva good reason for banging on my door this time of night."

"Sorry to disturb you, sir, but I need to find Zach Mahoney."

Instantly a taut wariness replaced the annoyance on the man's face. "Zach ain't here. He left."

"I can see that, but I thought maybe you might know where he went."

The man gave him a narrow-eyed once-over. "Even if I did, why would I tell some stranger who comes pounding on my door in the middle of the night? Mister, I don't know you from Adam."

"I'm Zach's brother, J.T."

If anything, the steely eyed cowboy's expression grew more remote. "Izzat right? Didn't know Zach had a brother. You got any proof a' that?"

J.T. ground his teeth. He had plenty of identification, but nothing in the name of Mahoney. "Not with me, no, but—"

"Can't help you."

"No, wait—" he began, but the door slammed in his face.

J.T. cursed and ground his teeth. He cast a grim look around at the other campers. There were no lights shining from any of the windows. Briefly he considered banging on doors anyway, but he discarded the idea. If the taciturn cowboy was any example, he would get no information from anyone in this tight-knit group.

Furious, he stomped back toward the taxi he'd left waiting in the parking lot. All right, fine. He might not be able to find Kate, but one thing was certain: sooner or later, she had to return to the Alpine Rose.

J.T. arrived at the B&B just before dark the next evening. His hope that he'd find Kate already there was dashed when he landed at the Durango Airport and saw that her SUV was still in the parking lot.

Knowing that, even if she had beaten him back, he hadn't a hope in hell of her fetching him from the airport, J.T. had called ahead and arranged for Cletus to pick him up.

The gregarious man was full of curiosity and started bombarding him with questions the minute they climbed into the battered pickup. "Hey ole buddy. I sure was surprised when you called. Didn't even know you'd gone somewhere."

"I had to make a quick business trip." J.T. hoisted his carryall higher over his shoulder and pushed the glass terminal doors open and stepped out into the Colorado sunshine.

"So…where'd you go?"

"Houston."

J.T. slung his carryall into the back of Cletus's pickup and climbed inside the cab. He'd hoped his brief answers would be sufficient, but Cletus wasn't satisfied. When he continued to probe, J.T. pleaded jet lag, slouched down in the seat, put his head back and closed his eyes. He didn't open them again until Cletus brought the truck to a stop before the Alpine Rose.

Without Kate, the huge house seemed like a mausoleum. His manuscript was finished except for the resolution and wrap-up, but he no longer had any stomach for the project. Day after day, J.T. rattled around the house, too restless to work and unable to settle long enough to read or watch television or do anything else.

He tried working on the jigsaw puzzle Kate had left half-finished on a table in the parlor, but after about thirty seconds it was all he could do not to sweep all one thousand pieces off onto the floor. He spent most of every day roaming from room to room and checking out the windows every few minutes, hoping to see her SUV climbing the road from town.

He had taken the precaution of moving his car into the carriage house, fearing if Kate spotted it in the port cochere, she would not return to the house. When the telephone rang he let the answering machine take the calls for the same reason, although he always raced into her office to try to hear who was calling. Most of the time there was only silence at the other end of the line, and he suspected it was Kate, calling to make sure he had left.

The solitude gave J.T. plenty of time to think about all that had happened and his part in the events. At first every time he played back in his mind the things that Kate had said to him, the things Matt had said, he refused to accept that he'd done anything wrong. After some intensive soul searching, however, he couldn't hold on to his denial any longer.

Matt had been right—for years J.T. had been using freedom of the press to excuse his actions. Charlie had wanted sensationalized stories, and J.T. had given them to him. Somewhere along the way, however, in his mind and his conscience, the line between a reporter's right to pursue a story and the individual's right to privacy had gotten blurred.

Gazing out the parlor window at the snow, J.T. snorted and rubbed the back of his neck. Damned if he hadn't become the very kind of arrogant bastard he despised.

Reporting was supposed to be impartial and unbiased, a presentation of the facts, but he doubted that was entirely possible. Even with the best of intentions, a reporter's stories were subconsciously colored by his own beliefs and values.

The plain truth was, every reporter had his own perspective, his own particular agenda, and it was ridiculously easy to manipulate public opinion. A certain tone, a few cleverly worded phrases and veiled innuendoes could nudge a reader's thinking in the direction you wanted it to go. In the twelve years J.T. had worked for Charlie he had honed the skill of manipulation until it was second nature to him.

Damn! Looking back he realized that he had always behaved as though he had some sort of divine right to dig around in people's personal lives and write about whatever he found—sometimes, even what he merely suspected—for all the world to see, no matter how violated it made the people involved feel, no matter who it hurt.

And he had hurt Kate.

J.T. sighed. Matt had been right about that, as well. Writing about the swindle without Kate's knowledge had been a betrayal. The crime and its aftermath had been painful and humiliating for her and Zach. For four years she'd held her head high and endured her former friends' and neighbors' scorn and anger and false accusations with dignity, her only hope being that with time they would eventually realize she and her brother had done nothing wrong. Of *course* she didn't want the whole mess stirred up over and over again.

At the very least he should have talked to her, told her that he wanted to write a novel based on the crime, before actually starting the book. She was the woman he loved, for Pete's sake!

But that smacked of getting permission, something a hot-shot reporter like him considered unnecessary, even offensive. He was used to barreling his way in and getting a story, and if someone was hurt by the fallout…well, that wasn't his problem.

In his entire career, J.T. admitted ruefully, the only person who had ever dictated to him regarding a story had been his sister-in-law, Maude Ann. In hindsight, he knew she had been right to do so, but he had chafed under the restraint at the time. And obviously he hadn't learned a damned thing from the experience.

All along the way he had handled things badly with Kate, he acknowledged with brutal self-honesty. From the get-go he should have told her he was a reporter, been open and totally honest with her. Instead, as usual, he'd been so intent on what *he* wanted, he hadn't let himself consider the situation from her perspective or given a thought to how she might feel. Nor had it occurred to him that, once she learned the truth, she might believe he'd never loved her at all, that he had sweet-talked his way into her life and strung her along merely to get the story.

All in all, J.T. came to the humbling and inescapable conclusion that he had behaved like an arrogant, self-involved idiot, and Kate had every right to hate his guts for what he'd done.

Now it was up to him to put things right. She had to forgive him. She *had* to, he told himself over and over. Still, deep down, it terrified the hell out of him that her pride wouldn't let her give him a chance to make up for the pain he'd caused.

On a bitterly cold day, a week after his return, as much for something to do as out of curiosity, J.T. climbed the stairs to the attic and dug through Bob Sweet's belongings one more time. He picked up the Bible first and turned it over and over in his hands, checking the lining, the edges, the thickness of the padded leather binding, turning each individual page, but he found nothing out of the ordinary.

With a sigh he put the Bible back into the box and turned his attention to the other items. He inspected each one in minute detail, but something about the Bible kept niggling at him and his gaze returned to the black leather-bound book over and over.

Finally, as J.T. was going through Bob Sweet's wallet for the third time, he realized what it was about the Bible that was bothering him: it was a standard size, about seven by ten inches, yet, in proportion, the lock and key that secured the strap were huge.

J.T. tossed the wallet back into the box and picked up the Bible again. The key dangled from a ribbon looped around the strap. He held it up closer to the bare bulb overhead, turning it slowly. Frowning, he angled the key this way and that. Barely discernible among the ornately etched vines and flowers was a tiny hole, partway through, no bigger than the shaft of a pin.

J.T. stared at the key, a thoughtful frown creasing his brow. Acting on a hunch, he left the attic and carried the Bible downstairs to his room.

First he removed the ribbon from the strap and straightened out a paper clip, but the diameter was too large to fit into the hole on the key. Frustrated, he looked around for something else to use. Then he remembered the sewing machine in Kate's room and the needlepoint pin cushion that sat on top of the machine cabinet, and he hurried down the hall. Ignoring the pang of guilt for invading her private domain, he quickly pulled a straight pin from the cushion and went to stand in the natural light coming through the window. He inserted the pin into the minuscule hole and pushed. Immediately the ornate face of the fat key popped open.

"Oh-ho, what have we here?" J.T. murmured to himself. In the hollowed-out space was a smaller key. When he lifted the key out, beneath it, folded up like an accordion, was a small piece of paper about two inches long.

J.T. smoothed out the pleats and held the paper toward the light. As he read, a slow smile spread over his face.

"Gotcha."

Relief poured through Kate when she saw that J.T.'s Jeep was no longer parked beneath the port cochere. Before starting up the mountain road she had driven slowly through every street in Gold Fever, checking to be sure he wasn't there.

She had stayed away for two weeks, hoping he would pack up his things and leave. Apparently, he'd taken the hint.

Despite what he'd done, the thought that he was gone from her life forever made her already-aching heart contract with pain, but she gritted her teeth and refused to let the tears come again. She'd cried a river over J.T. already. Besides, it was for the best.

Too tired and dispirited to put the car away, Kate parked under the port cochere in J.T.'s usual space and let herself in through the side door.

As she passed the kitchen she remembered that she hadn't eaten since the previous morning. She hesitated, then shrugged and trudged on down the hallway toward the stairs. She was too tired and too sick at heart and it was too much of a bother to prepare a meal. Besides, she wasn't hungry.

She reached the bottom of the stairs and put her hand on the newel post just as J.T. stepped out of the library.

"So you're finally back."

Kate nearly jumped right out of her skin. She spun

around, her heart pounding like a wild thing. ''J.T.! What're you doing here?''

She stared at him, quivering inside, her entire being besieged with a combination of outrage and hurt and helpless longing.

He stood at ease just outside the library door, watching her, his hands in the pockets of his gray wool slacks, his tanned skin and vivid blue eyes enhanced by the cream turtleneck sweater that molded his broad shoulders and chest.

Oh, dear Lord, why couldn't he have left? *Why?* Did he have any idea what he was doing to her?

Learning that J.T., like Kurt, had merely been using her had nearly destroyed Kate. Nothing—not her mother's marriage to Bob Sweet, not the unfair treatment of her former friends and neighbors, not Kurt's perfidy—nothing else had ever wounded her so deeply.

It had taken her two weeks to drag herself up out of a bottomless pit of despair and pull herself together—two weeks of tears and humiliation and unbearable heartache, of merciless reevaluation and stern self-castigation before she found the strength to hold her head up and get on with her life.

Poor Zach. Powerless to help her, he had nearly gone insane with worry as he'd watched her struggle. They had been following the rodeo circuit, but Zach had been so concerned about her that he hadn't done well in the competition. For his sake, as much as for her own, she'd decided it was time to come home and pick up the pieces of her life.

Now, just the sight of J.T., standing there looking so impossibly handsome and dear, undid all her hard work, because, God help her, even after what he'd done, her heart still ached for him.

Why did he have to be so cruel?

"I'm staying here, remember? As I recall, my rent is paid through April."

Kate's chin came up. "I'll be happy to give you a refund. I stayed away for two weeks, hoping you'd have the decency to clear out before I returned."

"Honey, you could have stayed away for a year and I'd still be here waiting for you." He started forward slowly, his blue eyes fixed on her, warm and entreating. "I love you, Ka—"

"Don't! Don't you dare say that to me!" she snarled. "I don't know how you have the nerve. It was all a lie. All part of your scheming and manipulating." She was shaking inside so hard she could barely stand, but she couldn't let him exploit her feelings for him again. She wouldn't.

She squared her shoulders and fixed him with an uncompromising stare. "Pack your things and get out. I don't want you here." The harsh words revealed only bitterness and anger and none of the foolish longing that was tearing her apart, for which Kate was profoundly grateful, even a bit proud of herself.

J.T. flinched, but despite her nasty tone his voice remained gentle and coaxing. "Honey, we have to talk."

"We have nothing to talk about." She turned her back and started up the stairs, her head held high. "I'm going to my room to unpack. When I come downstairs again, I want you gone. I never want to see you again. Is that clear?"

"Kate, listen to me. We *have* to talk. I think I've discovered where Bob Sweet hid the money."

She jerked to a stop. Her suitcase slipped from her nerveless fingers and dropped with a thud onto the first landing.

She swung around. "You what?" Her face stiffened. "Is this another one of your tricks? Because if it is—"

"It's true. I swear it." Quickly he explained about the key. "Inside was a smaller key and a receipt from a mini-storage company on the island of Antigua."

"Antigua?" Excitement shot through Kate like a burst from a Roman candle. "That's where Bob was arrested!"

"Yeah, I know. The receipt is dated two days after Sweet left Gold Fever, and it shows that he paid five years rent in advance. My guess is he was afraid there would be too many questions asked if he showed up at a bank with that much cash. Plus he was probably afraid the authorities might be able to trace him through a bank account or a safety deposit box. So he stashed the money in a ministorage unit the day he arrived in Antigua."

Kate hurried down the stairs. "Give me the key and the receipt."

"Oh, no. Not on your life."

"But I have to go to Antigua and retrieve that money so we can return it."

"I couldn't agree more. But I'm going along. And to make sure that I do, until we find that money, the key and the receipt stay with me."

"But—"

"You can argue all you want, sweetheart, but that's how it's going to be. Besides, you and Zach need me as a witness. Otherwise nobody's going to believe you didn't have the money all along and finally just suffered a case of guilty conscience."

"Oh, dear. You're probably right." Kate tried, but she couldn't think of a single thing to refute his logic, and her shoulders slumped as she realized that she would somehow have to endure J.T.'s company for a few days longer.

"Don't bother to unpack your bag. I checked with the airlines days ago. We can get a flight out of Durango tonight with connections in Denver and Miami. I suggest you phone Zach and tell him to meet us at the Miami airport tomorrow morning. And tell him to bring his passport.''

''All right, yes. I will. Right now.'' She was so keyed-up and excited she could barely think as she headed for the telephone in the library.

''Kate.''

She stopped and looked at him over her shoulder. J.T. watched her intently, his eyes sad and pleading, his expression, for once, utterly serious. ''Yes?''

''What I did was thoughtless and stupid, even selfish, but I swear I never meant to hurt you. And no matter what you believe, I do love you.''

For the space of several seconds she stared at him, trying to read the truth in his eyes. He looked sincere, but she no longer trusted her judgment where J.T. was concerned. She could think of nothing to say that would alleviate the awful tension between them or wipe out the hurt. Finally she simply nodded and disappeared into the library without uttering a word.

Zach was no more pleased than Kate that J.T. was going to Antigua with them. He had been furious when he learned that J.T. hadn't checked out of the Alpine Rose.

The instant J.T. and Kate stepped off the jetway, Zach snatched her into his arms as though he were saving her from a vile monster, and sent J.T. an icy stare over the top of her head. When he'd finished hugging her, he grasped her shoulders and eased her back, his worried gaze sweeping her in a quick inspection. ''You okay?''

''Yes, I'm okay,'' she replied quietly. She didn't pretend not to know what was behind the question. Zach had wanted her to stay with him as he traveled from rodeo to rodeo until the Alpine Rose reopened for the season. When she had insisted on returning to Gold Fever he had been worried that she was not yet emotionally strong enough to cope on her own. Now he was concerned that seeing J.T. again had reopened her wounds and undone what little progress she'd made.

Kate knew that the only thing keeping Zach from taking a swing at J.T. was that they needed him to lead them to the place where Bob may have hidden the money.

The belief was confirmed when Zach fixed his brother with a stony look and said, "We don't need you, Conway. Hand over the key and the address, and Kate and I'll take it from here."

"Forget it. You don't seem to understand that I'm calling the shots. I could have checked this out by myself, you know. The only reason I'm letting you and Kate come along is because I know how important this is to you both."

A muscle worked along Zach's jaw. He stared at J.T., his green eyes icy. "Okay, fine. But when this is over and that money is turned over to the authorities, I don't want you coming anywhere near my sister. You hear me?"

"Oh, I hear you, all right," J.T. said with a shrug and a crooked smile. "But that doesn't mean I'm going to do as you say."

"Why you—"

"Stop it right now. Both of you." Kate quickly stepped between them and placed her palms flat on their chests to hold them apart. "For heaven's sake! We're in a public place," she all but hissed.

A quick glance around revealed that several people were eyeing them curiously. Kate looked from one bristling man to the other, her eyes narrow. "Zach, I appreciate your support, but I don't need a protector. And as for you," she said, turning to J.T., "stop antagonizing him. We have a plane to catch and a serious matter to attend to when we get to Antigua. We don't have time for this foolishness. Now, let's go.''

She stalked away down the concourse toward their connecting gate. Glancing over her shoulder, she saw the brothers exchange hard looks before starting after her.

The flight was uneventful. Because they'd booked at the last minute they could not get seats together, a circumstance for which Kate offered up a silent thanks. With the two men separated, at least they weren't lashing out at each other. She was also grateful to have a respite from J.T.'s nearness.

Sitting next to him on the flight to Miami, the way his arm and knee had repeatedly bumped hers, his scent, the warmth of him, had sent goose bumps racing over her skin and stretched her nerves taut as a piano wire.

Kate had slept little during the red-eye flight, and she was bone tired. With a sigh she put her seat back and closed her eyes.

When they landed in Antigua, the car that J.T. had reserved was waiting.

''Wouldn't it be easier to hire a taxi?'' Zach argued. ''A local will know how to find this place.''

''Maybe. But if we find what I think we're going to find, I don't want anyone else around to see.''

The warm sunshine and balmy breezes were a far cry from the weather in Gold Fever, but Kate was too tense and anxious to appreciate either. The turquoise water and pristine, white sand beaches they drove past barely registered on her. All she could think about was what they might find when they reached their destination.

The ministorage wasn't far from the airport. It was a fairly new construction, six rows of garage-type units made of cinder block with steel overhead garage doors. Unit 42D was on the fourth row, and the latch was secured by a heavy steel padlock.

A strained silence surrounded them as they climbed from the car. Both J.T. and Zach paused to look up and down the row, but there was no one else around.

J.T. pulled the key from his pocket and grasped the padlock. "Well, here goes."

One twist, and the lock turned with a smooth click and opened.

Bending, Zach grasped the handle and raised the door, and they stepped inside together. Coming from the bright sunshine into the gloom of the windowless storage room made it difficult to see at first. When their vision cleared Kate experienced a moment of bitter disappointment. Looking around, all she saw was empty space.

Then she spotted the suitcase on the high shelf along the back wall.

"Look!"

J.T. hurried over and pulled the case down. He set it on the floor and squatted on his haunches, and Kate and Zach knelt down on either side of him as he released the catches and spread the case open.

"It's empty." Kate groaned and sat back on her heels. Disappointment and depression settled over her like a blanket of wet cement. "We came all this way for nothing."

"Wait a minute." J.T. measured the inside depth of the case with his fingers, then did the same to the outside. "I thought this was too heavy to be empty. It has a false top and bottom."

The brocaded silk lining was smooth and had been expertly installed to look almost seamless. Unless looking for it, no one would have suspected it hid a false bottom. J.T. ran his hands around the inside, then pulled out his pocket knife and used the point to pry up the stiff bottom. Zach pulled out his own knife and went to work on the top. It took only seconds to pop them free.

When they were removed Kate sucked in a sharp breath. ''Oh, my word.''

''Yes!'' Zach spat out with hard satisfaction.

Packed into the one-inch spaces beneath the removable top and bottom were tightly packed, banded bundles of one-thousand-dollar bills.

Chapter Thirteen

Slidell County was large, but it encompassed only a few sparsely populated mountain towns. The entire sheriff's department consisted of Sheriff Alvin Huntsinger and his deputy, Delbert Wright. When Kate, J.T. and Zach walked into the sheriff's office in Gold Fever the next afternoon, both men were slouched in their seats, shooting the breeze, their booted feet propped on their desks.

Sheriff Huntsinger looked around with the beginnings of a smile, but the good-ole-boy greeting he'd been about to deliver turned to a scowl when he saw who his visitors were. His gaze immediately zeroed in on Kate's brother.

"Well, well, well. If it isn't Zach Mahoney. I'm surprised you have the nerve to step inside this office."

"We're here on business."

"What kind of business?" the sheriff growled. Then he grimaced. "Aw, hell. Don't tell me Cletus and his friends have been nosing around your place again. Look, Kate, I told you before, those fellas don't mean any harm. They're just looking for what's rightfully theirs.''

''And I keep telling you, there is nothing on our property that belongs to them, but you won't listen.''

''This isn't about your trespassing friends, Sheriff,'' J.T. put in quietly.

''Then what is it about?''

J.T. motioned to Zach, who stepped forward and placed the suitcase on the sheriff's desk. Ignoring the older man's splutters of protest, Zach opened the case, and he and J.T. pried out the false bottoms and tossed them aside.

''Great jumpin' Jehoshaphat!'' The sheriff's booted feet hit the floor with a thud, and a second later so did the deputy's.

''Would you look at that!'' Delbert squawked. ''Man-o-man, I ain't never seen so much money, Sheriff!''

''It's the money Bob Sweet stole.'' Zach's voice came out low and tight with barely suppressed fury, but neither the sheriff nor his deputy seemed to notice.

''By heaven, I always knew you had it. What's the matter—'' Sheriff Huntsinger sneered ''—couldn't live with your guilty consciences any longer?''

Zach bristled and doubled his fists, but before he could light into the sheriff, J.T. intervened.

''You're wrong. Zach didn't have the money.''

The sheriff tore his gaze away from the suitcase and eyed J.T. with a cynical expression. ''Izzat so? The law's been looking for that money for four years, and now all of a sudden these two come waltzing in here with it? It sure looks to me like he's had it all along.''

''Sorry, Sheriff, but all this time that money has been sitting in ministorage on the island of Antigua.''

''Mmm. You don't say. Tell me…what's your stake in

this, Conway? You're an outsider. None of this has anything to do with you.''

''Let's just say I believe in treating people fairly. All I've heard since I arrived in this town is how Zach corrupted Bob Sweet, and how Zach and Kate had the money that your crooked preacher swindled from the people in this area. Yet there was no evidence to support those claims and the FBI didn't think either Zach or Kate was involved.

''So I got curious. I went through the box of personal effects the prison sent to Kate after Bob Sweet died. Hidden inside the key to his Bible I found another key and a receipt in Reverend Sweet's name for five years rent on the ministorage. The three of us flew to Antigua yesterday and retrieved the money.''

''That's a little thin, Conway. The FBI and the prison staff went through the pastor's things with a fine-tooth comb and didn't find one clue. You expect me to believe you found something they couldn't?''

J.T.'s face hardened. ''Are you calling me a liar, Sheriff?''

Kate blinked. Though barely above a whisper, his voice purred with soft menace. For an amiable man, when J.T.'s temper was roused it was something to behold.

The sheriff swallowed hard and shifted in his chair, and Kate could have sworn he turned a shade paler.

''No, no. Nothing like that. I'm just saying how it looks, that's all. And even if what you say is true, it doesn't prove anything. Zach could've stashed the money there and used the pastor's name to throw the blame on him.''

''Dammit, Huntsinger! I've told you a hundred times, I had nothing to do with fleecing this town!''

''Bob Sweet said different.''

Too furious to speak, Zach made a frustrated sound and swung away. He stalked to the window and stared out, his hands clenched at his side. Shooting Alvin Huntsinger a scorching look, Kate moved to stand beside her brother and put a comforting hand on his arm as she murmured softly to him.

"Give it up, Sheriff," J.T. said. "Until yesterday, neither Kate nor Zach had ever been in Antigua."

"Humph! So you say."

"It's easy enough to check, using airline and visa entry records. And I'm sure a handwriting expert will tell you that the signature on that receipt is Bob Sweet's."

"Dammit! A man doesn't lie on his death bed. Especially not a man of the cloth."

"He does if he's a malicious lowlife with a vendetta against someone." J.T. leaned across the sheriff's desk and jabbed his forefinger at the end of the man's nose. "Bob Sweet was no more a man of the cloth than you are. He was nothing but a con artist and a thief. If you and the rest of the people in this town don't have the gumption to admit you were taken in by a scumbag, too bad. I'm not going to stand by and let you pin the blame on Zach and Kate. All you've got is the word of a lying, cheating con artist, and, trust me, in a court of law, that's not worth a rat's behind."

"Yeah, well, we'll see. I'll need to check out that key and that receipt, so hand 'em over."

"Sorry, the FBI wants those. Since they're in charge of the case, we called the local office in Durango during our layover in Miami. A whole gang of special agents is on the way. Actually I'm surprised we got here first."

J.T. looked back and forth between the sheriff and his deputy. "The only reason we told them to meet us here is that I wanted you and everyone else in this town to learn the truth firsthand. Maybe then you'll feel some shame over the way you've treated Kate and Zach all these years."

"Now see here!"

"No, *you* see, Sheriff. It's time for you and the good people of Gold Fever to take off the blinders and accept the truth.

"And while we're waiting for the FBI, I suggest that you and your deputy start counting that money. We're going to want a receipt."

"A *receipt.*"

A nasty grin spread across J.T.'s face. "That's right, Sheriff. Not that we don't trust you, you understand, but...well...you know how it is."

While Sheriff Huntsinger sputtered and fumed, Special Agent Diana Grayson, head of the area FBI office, strode in, followed by about a dozen more agents.

"My men and I will take over from here, Sheriff," she said in a brisk tone. "Davis, Strahan, Petrikoff and Nelson, take charge of the money. Duran, you and Wilson take however many men you need and secure the exits. The rest of you will conduct interviews." She turned from issuing orders to her men and looked from J.T. to Zach. "Now then...which one of you is Mr. Conway?"

Three hours later they were finally allowed to leave the sheriff's office. Kate was so exhausted she could barely keep her eyes open on the drive up the mountain to the Alpine Rose. Judging by their silence, so were Zach and J.T. Other than catnaps on the planes, it had been almost forty-eight hours since any of them had slept.

"I realize we were interviewed separately so they could compare our stories, but why did we have to go over the whole thing so many times?" she asked wearily, to keep from falling asleep as much as out of curiosity.

They had been separated and interviewed individually over and over, each time by a different team of agents.

Though couched in different ways, the different agents had asked the same basic questions. She assumed that J.T. and Zach had received the same treatment. By the time Special Agent Grayson was satisfied that they were telling the truth, Kate had been ready to scream.

"They were looking for inconsistencies or little slipups," J.T. replied in a fatigued monotone.

"Yeah. I bet some agent is on his way to Antigua right now to check out that storage rental," Zach added dully.

J.T. gave an amused snort as he brought the SUV to a halt beneath the port cochere. "I'll lay odds that as we speak some poor slob is getting his butt chewed out for missing that hidden latch on Sweet's Bible key."

Too tired to do more than chuckle, they climbed from the vehicle and trudged inside. Once they'd shed their coats and hung them on the antique hall tree beside the door, an awkward silence descended.

"J.T., I, uh…I want to thank you for all you've done for us," Kate offered hesitantly. "Zach and I would never have found that key ourselves. In less that a year the lease on the storage unit would have run out, and the manager would have confiscated the unclaimed contents. If he had found the money, I don't have much faith that he would have turned it over to the authorities."

Zach shifted from one foot to the other, frowning as he studied the toe of his boot. "Yeah, Kate's right," he muttered, with something less than graciousness. "And thanks for sticking up for us back there with the sheriff."

"I wasn't trying to earn your gratitude. I did what I did because I love Kate."

Zach looked up then, straight into J.T.'s eyes. "Try telling that to someone who hasn't spent the past two weeks watching her cry. Just because we're grateful, don't think that changes anything. I still want you out of here tomorrow."

"Zach!" Kate cried. "After all J.T's done for us, we can't just throw him out."

"This isn't about what he's done *for* us, Kate, but what he's done *to* you."

"Kate, sweetheart, don't listen to him. I made a mistake in not telling you the whole truth from the beginning. I admit that. But I wasn't stringing you along in order to get a story. I would never use you like that, I swear it. I do love you. You have to believe me."

She looked at him sadly, her heart aching. "I'd like to, J.T. but I...I just can't. I'm sorry."

"Kate, please—"

"J.T., don't you see? I can't be completely sure of your motives for anything. Even these past two days. As much as I appreciate what you did, I can't quite believe it was merely an act of love on your part. After all, you stand to benefit, too."

He scowled. "How do you figure that?"

"Now you have an ending for your book, don't you? A part of me will always wonder if that was the real reason you helped us."

"How can you even think that?"

She gazed at him solemnly, her head tipped to one side. "Tell me something. Are you going to write the newspaper article that your boss wanted?"

J.T. grimaced and shifted uneasily. "Look, sweetheart, what difference does that make? The whole thing is going to hit the papers, anyway. By tomorrow there'll be reporters swarming all over this town."

"And, thanks to our little jaunt, you have the jump on them."

"Dammit, that's *not* why I helped you!" Sighing, he ground his teeth and raked his hand through his hair.

"So you say. But I'll never know that for sure, will I?" She waited a beat, then added, "I assume you'll finish the book, now, too."

He hesitated. Then he seemed to stand a little taller as he lifted his chin at a determined angle. "Yes."

Until that moment Kate had not realized how much she'd wanted to be wrong, that in her heart she had been hoping, praying that he would somehow be able to convince her that she had misjudged him, that regardless of how it seemed, he had not and would not betray her. Ever.

But with that single word, the last kernel of hope shriveled and died inside her.

Kate swallowed hard and fought to hold back the tears that threatened to fill her eyes. She had already cried a river over J.T. She would not shed any more.

Somehow she managed a wobbly smile. "I see. Then there's nothing left to say, is there?" Turning away, she slowly climbed the stairs, her back ramrod straight, her head high. Neither man watching from the foot of the stairs would ever know how much that dignified exit cost her.

"Like I told you before," Zach said when Kate disappeared into the upstairs hall. "I want you out of here tomorrow."

J.T. met his brother's hard stare with equal determination. "Too bad. Unless you're prepared to throw me out bodily, which I wouldn't advise you try, you're just plumb out of luck, Bro. My rent is paid through April, and I'm staying."

Kate slept twelve hours straight, only to discover that J.T.'s prediction had come true. She awoke around ten to a horrendous pounding on her front door, the telephone ringing off the wall and a small army of reporters on her doorstep.

Zach wanted to run the clamoring horde off with a shotgun, but Kate had learned four years ago that the quickest way to get rid of them was to give them what they wanted. Bracing herself for the ordeal, she stepped out onto the front porch and gave them a brief account of the facts and answered questions for as long as she could stand to do so.

As soon as she went back inside and shut the door, the reporters scattered like a covey of quail, and moments later a string of vehicles raced down the mountainside. Throughout the remainder of the day there were a few stray calls, and once a reporter rang their doorbell, but for the most part the siege was over.

Kate had expected J.T. to rush into town and fax in his story, as well, but according to Zach, who was a habitual early riser, he hadn't left the house. Then she realized that J.T. had probably phoned in his exclusive last night, hours before the other reporters had arrived in Gold Fever.

He stayed holed up in his room all that day and the next. Except for dirty dishes in the sink each morning, there was no sign of him until the third afternoon following their return.

Though Zach was missing some important rodeos, he stubbornly refused to leave her alone in the house with J.T. They were sitting in the parlor before the fire, enjoying a cup of coffee when J.T. walked in.

He looked awful: his face was shadowed with a three-day growth of beard; his clothes were rumpled; and dark smudges formed half circles under his eyes. Kate would have been surprised to learn that he'd slept more than a few hours since their return.

Regardless of his appearance, her heart gave a little kick at the sight of him. He'd hurt her terribly, and she didn't trust him, but, God help her, she couldn't seem to stop loving him.

That didn't mean, however, that she had to let him see how vulnerable she was where he was concerned. With what she considered admirable poise, she looked at him and raised one eyebrow. "Is there something I can do for you?"

"If you're looking for lunch or breakfast you're too late," Zach growled.

"I don't want anything to eat. But there is something you can do for me. I'd appreciate it if you'd both read this."

"What is it?" Zach demanded, scowling at the three-inch stack of paper J.T. plopped onto the end table beside his chair.

"The manuscript for my book," he replied, handing another one to Kate. "I finished it, and I'd like you both to read it."

Looking at the stack of papers she was holding as though it were a snake, Kate pressed back deeper into the sofa. "I'd rather not. Really."

"Me, neither." Though Zach was a voracious reader who consumed three to four books a week, he acted as though J.T. was trying to saddle him with an onerous chore.

Ignoring Zach, J.T.'s gaze bored into Kate. "Please, sweetheart. This is important. Read it, and when you're done, if you still want me to leave, I will."

"I…" She looked from his pleading face to Zach.

He shrugged and picked up the manuscript. "Okay, sure. If it'll get rid of him, I'll read it."

Chewing on her bottom lip, Kate glanced uncertainly at the stack of paper in her lap, then back at J.T. "All right. I'll read it, too."

By the middle of the first page, Kate was hooked. By

the end of the first chapter she had almost forgotten why she'd objected to the book in the first place.

J.T. had an engaging writing style that flowed as smooth as silk and a gift for imagery and creating believable, well-rounded characters and taut situations. From the first line the tension and intrigue built steadily.

Apparently, Zach was just as captivated by the book as Kate. For the next three hours they did not exchange a word. The only sounds in the room were the crackle and pop of the fire, an occasional clink of a china cup against a saucer and the rustle of pages being turned over.

In the beginning Bob Sweet appeared to be charismatic, kindly and devout, a true shepherd of his flock. As the story progressed, however, J.T. gradually and chillingly exposed the preacher as ego driven and power hungry, a manipulative, greedy hypocrite, and an abusive husband and stepfather. Most frightening of all, however, was the hypnotic, Svengali-like power he weilded over his congregation.

A master at mind control, from the pulpit, Reverend Sweet brainwashed the unsuspecting people of Gold Fever with his impassioned and mesmerizing sermons.

When he hatched a plan to reopen the mine and restore jobs and pride to the locals, he became almost a God to them.

J.T. portrayed Kate and Zach as innocent victims who endured years of shame and persecution at the hands of their former friends and neighbors and the news media. In the last quarter of the book, when they were vindicated, events were presented in a way that rendered a blistering indictment against the townspeople, who had wronged them for years.

While Kate and Zach read, J.T. roamed the wide central hallway outside the parlor. Occasionally he came into the room to add another log to the fire or refill their coffee cups or turn on lamps as dusk began to fall, but the little chores were merely excuses to check out their expressions or see what page they were on. His frequent reconnaissance forays became so annoying that Zach finally lost patience.

"Dammit! If you want me to finish this, stay the hell out!"

J.T. retreated to the guest parlor across the hall and stationed himself where he could see when they had finished.

Even though Kate had lived the story and knew how it would end, J.T. had made the events seem much more exciting and interesting than she remembered. She found herself so engrossed she could not have put the manuscript down for anything short of a catastrophic event.

When Kate finally turned over the last page, she felt dazed. The book was not at all what she had expected. Instead of a sensationalized account of the swindle, designed to pander to the insatiable and twisted curiosity of the masses, it was an insightful and chilling examination of mind control and the inherent dangers of cults and the "herd mentality."

Zach had finished reading, as well, and when Kate looked up he was watching her, his expression thoughtful.

"Not exactly what I expected," he murmured.

"No. No it isn't, is it?"

J.T. appeared in the doorway. He looked tense as his gaze darted back and forth between them. "Well? What do you think?"

She thought the book was excellent, but what she felt was *torn*. He had woven an intriguing tale of greed, power and hatred, and he had treated her and Zach fairly. If the story had been about anyone else she would have thought it fantastic. Absolutely wonderful.

But it wasn't about someone else. It was about her and Zach, and in it J.T. had laid bare for all the world to see the most hurtful and humiliating experience of her life. All she wanted to do was forget the whole sorry mess and put it behind her. Her pride balked at the thought of strangers all over the country reading about the ordeal.

There had been no way to escape the media coverage. For the past few days every major newspaper and telecast had rehashed the case. Embarrassing and intrusive as that had been, at least she had the comfort of knowing that, not only did those reports merely skim the surface with sketchy recitals of the facts, interest would soon fade as the newsmongers moved on to the next breaking story. It was different with a book, particularly one with the depth and potential of J.T.'s.

Kate glanced at Zach, but he gestured, silently deferring to her.

"First of all, I suppose I should thank you for setting the record straight."

"You don't have to thank me for telling the truth, Kate. What I want to know is what you think of the story."

"It's quite good. I won't be surprised if it turns out to be a bestseller. I'm sure your editor will be pleased."

J.T. heard the bitter coolness in her voice, and the knot in his stomach pulled a little tighter. Quite good? Hell, he knew the story was an excellent piece of work, probably the best thing he'd ever written. So good, in fact, he figured odds were high that his ole buddy at Hubbard and Rhodes would probably jump at the chance to publish it, particularly given his own involvement in the case. If that happened it would be the fulfillment of his lifelong dream.

Yet, that no longer seemed to matter. Erasing the hurt and anguish in Kate's eyes had become much more important.

"I doubt that. I didn't turn in that article to the paper. I didn't even write one. Matter of fact, I quit my job."

"You quit?" He saw the surprise flash in her eyes, but she controlled it quickly and assumed a neutral expression.

"Yeah. Charlie's probably cursing me to hell and gone right now. Instead of the exclusive he expected, the *Herald* was about the only major paper in the country that didn't have an on-the-scene report of the story."

"Well, I wouldn't worry. I'm sure the book will be a big success."

"Maybe it would be…if I were going to sell it."

"Wh-what? What are you saying?"

He had her attention now. She stared at him as though he'd lost his mind. Zach silently watched them, his eyes sliding back and forth between his sister and J.T.

"I'm saying I'm not going to submit the manuscript to a publisher."

"I don't understand. The book is sure to sell. It's what you've been working for. Why are you doing this?"

"I've been doing some soul searching and, well, I realized you were right. I love you, Kate. More than I've ever loved anyone or anything. But even if I could convince you of that, I know if I sell this book you'll always wonder if that was true in the beginning, or if I had just been using you to get the story.

"Even if you decide not to give me a second chance, I don't ever want you to doubt my love for you, Kate. That's why I won't be submitting the book."

"You'd do that for me?" she asked, with a look of wonder in her eyes that gave him hope.

"That and more. I've erased the manuscript from my computer's hard drive and destroyed the backup diskettes." He bent and scooped up the pile of manuscript papers from her lap. "Once I burn these two copies it will no longer exist."

"*Burn* them? But— J.T., what're you doing!" She shot

out of the chair as he tossed the pages into the fire. "Stop that! Are you mad?"

Grabbing a poker, Kate worked frantically to rake the papers out of the fire, but she was too late. The greedy flames curled the pages into black ashes before she could rescue so much as a single one.

"Oh, look what you've done!" she wailed. "How *could* you?"

"I have no choice. You're more important to me than any book." He reached for the stack of papers that Zach had piled on the end table beside his chair, but Kate darted in front of him and blocked his way.

"Don't you dare touch those!"

"Kate, don't you understand? It's just words on paper. I can write other books, but there is only one you."

She shook her head. "I don't care. I can't let you destroy that book. It's too good. Tell him, Zach!"

"I have to agree with Kate. I hated the idea of you writing the story as much as she did, but I have to admit, this is one helluva tale. Besides, haven't you heard? It's a crime to burn books."

J.T. rolled his eyes. "I don't believe this. Kate, will you be reasonable. You don't want that book published, so what's the point in keeping it?"

"Why did you bother to finish it if you weren't going to submit it?"

"Kate—"

"Tell me why, J.T."

He sighed. "I finished it because I wanted to prove to you, and to Zach, that I would never intentionally write anything that would hurt or embarrass either of you. That, and…"

"And?" she prompted when he hesitated.

"It was just something I had to do," he admitted reluctantly. "But I've got all that out of my system now, so there's no reason to keep it around. I don't understand why you're making such a fuss about me burning it."

"Oh, J.T." Smiling tenderly, Kate stepped close and placed her palms flat against his chest. The soft look in her eyes as she gazed up at him made him catch his breath. Cupping his cheek, she looked deep into his eyes and murmured, "I won't let you destroy the book for the same reason you want to burn it. Because I love you."

"Kate." His throat closed up on him, and he froze, watching her, not daring to hope.

"Don't you understand, my love," she continued softly. "The book is important to you. It's part of you. You poured your heart and soul into it. I love you too much to let you destroy it."

"You love me?" he asked softly, zeroing in on the only thing that mattered.

"I never stopped."

"Ah, Katy," he whispered as he pulled her tight against him. "Sweet, stubborn Katy, mine, I love you, too. I always will."

His mouth swooped down on hers, and with a moan she twined her arms around his neck.

Neither of them noticed when Zach left the room, or that he took the manuscript with him. They were too lost in each other.

They held each other tight, their bodies straining to get closer. The knowledge of how close they had come to losing each other trembled through them, adding a sharp poignancy to their embrace.

The voracious kiss was hot and wet and open-mouthed. Both desperately sought to assuage the misery and hurt they had endured and make up for the long, miserable weeks of their estrangement.

When at last the kiss ended, they still clung to each other: Kate with her eyes closed, her cheek resting against his chest, her arms wrapped around his lean middle; J.T. holding her tight against him, head bent and his cheek snuggled against her temple.

They stayed that way for an interminable time, content and silent, swaying ever so slightly together, basking in the profound sense of relief and the flood of feelings too intense for words.

"Does this mean you'll marry me?" J.T. finally asked, and he felt her smile against his chest.

"Mmm, just try and stop me."

"I wouldn't dream of it," he said with a chuckle as happiness poured through him.

She laughed, too, squeezing him tight, but after a moment she eased her hold and leaned back in his arms to look into his eyes. Her smile wobbled a bit, and he saw her throat work as she swallowed hard, but her gaze didn't waver. "In a few years—after I've gained some distance and the memories aren't so sharp—we'll send your book to your publisher friend."

J.T. felt his heart turn over. Though her expression had that determined look he had come to recognize, he saw apprehension, as well, and he knew then the depth of her love for him, and he was humbled.

Shaken, he stared into those vulnerable gray eyes and knew he was the luckiest man alive. Tightening his arms around her, he brought her closer, and his head began a slow decent. "Ah, Katy, mine, you're a dream come true," he whispered an instant before his mouth settled over hers once again.

* * * * *

Don't miss Ginna Gray's
incredible Mira Books debut!

Turn the page for a sneak preview of

THE PRODIGAL DAUGHTER

On Sale September 2000
Only from Mira Books

One

In Ruby Falls, Texas, population 3,418, the sleek Viper convertible stood out like a tuxedo at a barn dance.

Heads turned and jaws dropped when the stunning redhead roared into town behind the wheel of the hot car, her long hair streaming behind her like a fiery banner, "The Best of Kenny Rogers" blaring from the speakers.

The car's emerald green exterior was only a shade darker than her eyes, a fact that escaped few of the gawkers who followed her progress through town.

Though currently hidden behind a pair of Christian Dior sunglasses, there was scarcely a person in the country, or even the world who didn't know the exact color of those famous eyes. Periodically over the past seven years, Maggie Malone's face, usually wearing a sexy smile while those fabulous eyes danced with wicked amusement, had graced the cover of every major magazine in the U.S. and Europe.

Noting the stunned faces all around, Maggie experienced a rush of satisfaction. The reactions were exactly what she'd hoped for when she'd made arrangements to have the Viper delivered to the DFW airport in time for her arrival.

Seven years ago she'd left Ruby Falls in disgrace, but by heaven, she was returning a success. And nothing drove that point home better than a classy fireball of a car.

Reaching the courthouse square in the center of town, Maggie braked at the red light with a little squeal of tires and a huff of exasperation. After only a few seconds, though, she shook her head, a hint of a smile on her lips.

Drumming long, cinnamon-colored fingernails against the padded leather steering wheel, Maggie glanced around while she waited. From the look of it, not much of anything had changed in Ruby Falls.

On this fine September day, as they had every warm afternoon since anyone could remember, old men were playing dominos in the shade of the oak trees on the court-house lawn. Maggie recognized several of the silver-haired regulars—Ned Paxton, Oliver Jessup, the Toliver twins, Roy and Ray. Jeez Louise, there was even Moses Beasley. The old coot had to be pushing a hundred. The World War I veteran had been a fixture in the square all of Maggie's life.

A group of women poured out of the Elk Lodge onto the sidewalk just a few feet away from the car, chattering among themselves.

Ah, yes, another thing that remained constant, Maggie thought. Come hell or high water, the first and third Thurs-day afternoons of every month the Ladies Auxiliary met at the Lodge. Apparently the meeting had just ended.

Leading the pack was Edna Mae Taylor, Dorothy Purdue and Pauline Babcock, the three biggest gossips in town. The instant they spotted Maggie they came up short, gaping.

Immediately the others plowed into them from behind.

"What in the world? Goodness gracious, Dorothy, why'd you stop like th— Oh my stars! Isn't that—"

"Yes," Pauline snapped.

"That's her, all right."

"What's she doing here? She hasn't been back even once since she lit out of here seven years ago."

"I expect she's come to see her daddy. You know, what with him being so ill an' all."

"And about time, I'd say."

"*Humph.* I can't imagine that seeing the likes of her will be good for him." Pauline sniffed. "I heard he disowned her years ago."

"Oh, surely not. Lily would never let Jacob do that. She loves that girl somethin' fierce, you know."

"Well, all I know is Lily goes to New York to see her two or three times a year. Alone," Edna Mae added with a knowing look. "And Lucille was told by Inez, who got it on good authority, that Jacob hasn't so much as spoken to the girl on the telephone since she left."

"And who can blame him? She was a wild one. Used to drive poor Jacob crazy with her shenanigans. And after what she tried to do...well..."

"True. That was shameful. Still, blood is blood, and in times of crisis a man wants his family gathered around him."

"Yes, well, you'd think, under the circumstances, she'd at least have the decency to arrive quietly. But, oh, no. Not Maggie," Pauline huffed. "She had to make a spectacle of herself. Why just look at that car. And listen to that loud music. You mark my word—"

The traffic light turned green. Flashing the women a grin, Maggie reached over and cranked up the volume on the stereo. She punched the accelerator and squealed a right. "Love or Something Like It" blaring from the speakers in Kenny's whisky voice, the heavy throb of the base reverberating in the air like a giant heartbeat.

Nothing much distracted the domino players from their games, but the rumble of the Viper and the honky-tonk music grabbed their attention. Heads came up and swiveled in unison, following the sleek machine as it growled its way around three side of the square.

Maggie waggled her fingers in a flirtatious wave, then

winked, puckered her luscious red lips and blew them all a kiss.

At their slacked-jawed astonishment, she laughed and hung a right, speed-shifted into second and peeled rubber down Main on the south side of the square.

No, nothing had changed in Ruby Falls.

Before she'd gone a block, her laughter faded and she made a wry face at her own behavior. Lord, how easy it was to fall back into old patterns. In town five minutes, and already she'd baited the gossips. She hadn't resorted to that sort of thumb-your-nose-in-their-faces defense since she'd left here.

But then again, there had been no need.

Those few minutes in the square had distracted Maggie, but now, drawing close to home, the nervousness was back. Ever since that awful telephone call four days ago, she'd been wound as tight as an eight-day clock.

The call had come in the middle of the night while she had been on a photo shoot on an island off the coast of Greece. At her mother's first words she had bolted upright in the bed, her heart pounding.

''Maggie, you have to come home.''

''Momma? Is that you?'' All she'd heard was a sob, and she'd gripped the receiver tighter. ''Calm down, and tell me what's wrong.''

''Please, Maggie, you have to come home.''

''Oh, Momma, you know I'd like nothing better. But I can't. Nothing has changed.''

''Yes, it has,'' her mother had cried. ''You daddy is dying! Oh, God, Maggie, my Jacob is dying.''

The words had hit her like a fist to the stomach. ''Wh-what? But...but you told me just a few days ago that he was holding his own. That the tumor in his lung was shrinking. If I had known he was so ill I wouldn't have flown halfway around the world."

"I know, I know," Lily said in a chagrined voice. "I should have told you. But at the time Dr. Lockhart seemed so positive that another round of chemotherapy would halt the cancer, so I didn't see any point in alarming you needlessly. But it didn't work. Oh Maggie, that insidious disease is winning. It's going to take my Jacob from me."

Lily barely choked out the last, and Maggie fought back tears of her own as she listened to her mother's pitiful sobs. It was several seconds before the wrenching sounds turned to sniffs and Lily regained enough control to speak again.

"The doctors sent him home. There's nothing more they can do other than make him as comfortable as possible. They give him three or four months. Five at best."

"Oh, Momma." Maggie felt as though the ground had just dropped out from under her. Her father? Dying? No. No, it couldn't be. It was too soon. She needed more time!

"So you see, you have to come home."

"But…Daddy doesn't want me there."

"No! No, you're wrong! Believe me, when a man knows he hasn't much time left he sees things differently. Trust me, dear, your father wants you to come home."

"Did he…did Daddy actually say he wanted to see me?" She tightened her grip on the receiver, doing her best to clamp down on the hope swelling inside her.

"Well…maybe not in so many words—"

"Oh, Momma—"

"But he hinted at it," Lily insisted.

"Momma, please—"

"Maggie, I've been married to your daddy for almost twenty-nine years. I can read him like a book. He wants to ask, but you know his stiff-necked pride. He took a stance, and now he thinks he can't back down. But he needs to do this, sweetheart."

She waited a beat, then added, "So do you."

No fair, Maggie thought, tipping her head back to stare at the ceiling in an agony of doubt. No fair.

Lily's voice lowered, quavered with urgency. "This is the end of the line, Maggie. Your last chance to make peace with your father. If you don't you'll always regret it."

Sighing, Maggie closed her eyes and massaged her forehead with the fingertips of her free hand. "You make it tough to say no."

"Then don't. Come home, Maggie. I'm begging you. Please, *please* come home. Before it's too late."

The pathetic little catch in her mother's voice had been her undoing. That, and her own helpless yearning.

She had canceled all her bookings and caught the next flight off the island.

What choice did she have? Her father was dying, and he wanted to see her.

A mile past the city limits sign Maggie turned off the highway onto the black-topped road, and the knot of tension in her stomach tightened. No longer in the mood for music, she snapped off the CD player. After another mile she turned right onto a narrow lane. The Viper growled as she reduced speed. Gravel popped beneath the tires and bounced off the undercarriage, but her heart was knocking so hard and fast all she heard was its pulsing beat drumming in her ears. Bordering the lane on the left, the Malone home orchard flashed by, five hundred acres of mature peach, plum and pear trees marching in precise rows as far as the eye could see.

When she rounded the first curve, her family home came into view. Maggie stared, equal parts joy and nervous anticipation flooding her.

The large house sat far back from the lane on a two-acre patch of land dotted with towering oaks and pines and surrounded on three sides by the fruit orchard.

Heart pounding, Maggie turned into the drive and moments later brought the Viper to a halt in the circular section in front of the house.

For several minutes she sat motionless, still gripping the steering wheel, staring at the two-story, red-brick house. Her nerves thrummed like an oscillating engine. Tingles raced over her skin, making the fine hairs on her arm stand on end.

She was swamped with so many different emotions that she could barely breathe—grief and joy, regret and anticipation, sorrow and excitement, all tangled together.

All the doors and windows in the house stood open to take advantage of the unusually pleasant fall weather. Maggie eyed the screen door, expecting someone—either her mother or Ida Lou Neetles, their housekeeper—to appear at any moment, but no one came nor were there any sounds from within.

Automatically her gaze darted beyond the house in the direction of the cannery on the opposite side of the property, though it wasn't visible through the trees. These days, the Malone Cannery offered a full line of canned fruits and vegetables, but it was the smell of peaches stewing that she would always associate with home.

Home. Fixing her gaze on the house again, she drew a deep breath and reached for the door handle.

No one watching would ever imagine the turmoil going on inside her. She walked up the brick path and climbed the porch steps with her head high, her shoulders back, her hips swaying with sassy confidence. Maggie'd had years of experience at hiding her feelings. And one thing she'd learned since leaving home was how to project an image.

At the door she paused, not sure whether to ring the bell or just walk right in. Cupping her hands on either side of her eyes, she peered in through the screen down the long central hallway. There wasn't a soul in sight.

She hesitated, reluctant to call out or knock, in case her father was resting.

Oh, what the hell. This was her home, wasn't it? she thought, and opened the screen door and stepped inside.

She had barely taken a step when she heard a faint sound coming from her father's study. One of Maggie's eyebrows rose. Apparently he wasn't as sick as her mother had led her to believe if he felt well enough to work.

Her nerves began to jump. She had been longing for, praying for this meeting for seven years. Now that it was finally about to happen she was almost sick with nerves.

Pressing her fist against her fluttering stomach, she drew a deep breath and stepped to the study's open doorway…and froze.

"Who are you? And what the devil do you think you're doing?" she snapped.

The stranger rifling through her father's desk looked up. His rugged face remained impassive, but those silver-gray eyes pinned her.

Belatedly, Maggie recalled the numerous reports she'd heard on the evening news in New York about people who'd had the misfortune to stumble across a burglar. Immediately visions of murder and mayhem flashed through her head, and fear slithered down her spine.

For an instant she considered running, but it was too late. He would catch her before she made it out the front door. Besides, her knees were trembling so much she wasn't sure her legs would support her.

Left with no choice, she lifted her chin and stood her ground.

The man was big and tough-looking—at least six four. The rolled up sleeves of his shirt revealed muscular forearms dusted with dark hair, wide wrist and powerful hands. He had the kind of broad-shouldered impressive build that didn't come from working out in a yuppie gym three times a week.

Clearly she was no match for him.

But dammit, she was no wimp, either. Barefoot, she stood six feet tall and was in excellent physical condition. Maggie narrowed her eyes. *I may not win, but lay a hand on me, buster, and you'll damn well know you've been in a fight.*

She braced herself, but instead of rushing her, he straightened, crossed his arms over his chest and looked her up and down. "Well, well. If it isn't the prodigal daughter come home at last."

Silhouette invites you to come back to Whitehorn, Montana...

MONTANA MAVERICKS

WED IN WHITEHORN—
12 BRAND-NEW stories that capture living and loving beneath the Big Sky where legends live on and love lasts forever!

MM

June 2000—
Lisa Jackson *Lone Stallion's Lady* (#1)

July 2000—
Laurie Paige *Cheyenne Bride* (#2)

August 2000—
Jennifer Greene *You Belong to Me* (#3)

September 2000—
Victoria Pade *The Marriage Bargain* (#4)

And the adventure continues...

Available at your favorite retail outlet.

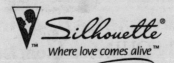

Silhouette®
Where love comes alive™

**Don't miss
an exciting opportunity
to save on the purchase of
Harlequin and Silhouette books!**

Buy any two Harlequin or
Silhouette books and save
$10.00 off future Harlequin
and Silhouette purchases

OR

buy any three
Harlequin or Silhouette books
and save **$20.00 off** future
Harlequin and Silhouette purchases.

**Watch for details
coming in October 2000!**

PHQ400

Silhouette®

SPECIAL EDITION®

COMING NEXT MONTH

#1345 THE M.D. SHE *HAD* TO MARRY—Christine Rimmer
Conveniently Yours
Lacey Bravo wasn't marrying a man just because she was in the
family way.... She was holding out for true love. And that meant
Dr. Logan Severance had to do more than propose. He had to prove he
was offering the real thing—his heart!

#1346 FATHER MOST WANTED—Marie Ferrarella
Being in the witness protection program meant not letting anyone get
too close. And that had been fine with Tyler Breckinridge—until his
three little girls led him to Brooke Carmichael, a woman whose
sweet temptations were breaking down his barriers and driving him
to distraction....

#1347 GRAY WOLF'S WOMAN—Peggy Webb
Lucas Gray Wolf wasn't about to let Mandy Belinda walk out of his
life. For she was carrying something that belonged to him—*his twins.*
But the red-hot passion this handsome loner felt for Mandy made him
want to claim more than his babies. He wanted to claim his woman!

#1348 FOR HIS LITTLE GIRL—Lucy Gordon
An unexpected turn of events had the beleaguered Pippa Davis
returning to Luke Danton—the man she'd loved but left behind. He
was the only one she'd trust to raise their daughter. Was his
undeniable connection to this beloved woman and child enough to
turn a bachelor into a devoted daddy?

#1349 A CHILD ON THE WAY—Janis Reams Hudson
Wilders of Wyatt County
Who was the delicate and pregnant beauty Jack Wilder rescued from
the blizzard? Lisa Hampton was a mystery to him—a mystery he
desperately wanted to solve. But would helping her recover the past
mean sacrificing his hope for their future?

#1350 AT THE HEART'S COMMAND—Patricia McLinn
A Place Called Home
With one sudden—*steamy*—kiss, Colonel John Griffin's pent-up
desire for Ellyn Sinclair came flooding back. His steely self-restraint
melted away whenever he was in Ellyn's irresistible presence. But
could a life-hardened Grif obey his heart's command?

CMN0800